Margo stood in the shrubbery peering through the Wakefields' living-room window.

Everything is perfect, she thought rapturously, devouring the details with hungry eyes. The glittering Christmas tree, the brightly wrapped gifts, the homemade breakfast, and best of all, the people. The sweet, lovely mother in her elegant satin bathrobe, distributing gifts and kisses; the tall, handsome father, smiling benevolently; the cherished twin daughters; the manly, protective older brother.

Lifting one hand, Margo brushed the windowpane with her fingertips. *My house. My family. Merry Christmas, everyone.* She smiled, wanting to laugh, to sing, to dance in the rain. *Next year it will be me!* Next year *she* would come down the stairs in her flannel nightgown; *she* would get kisses and hugs under the mistletoe; *she* would give and receive thoughtful, wonderful presents. She would be Elizabeth Wakefield.

SWEET VALLEY High®

Magna Edition

THE EVIL TWIN

Written by
Kate William

Created by
FRANCINE PASCAL

BANTAM BOOKS
NEW YORK · TORONTO · LONDON · SYDNEY · AUCKLAND

RL 6, age 12 and up

THE EVIL TWIN
A Bantam Book / December 1993

Sweet Valley High® is a registered trademark of Francine Pascal
Conceived by Francine Pascal
Produced by Daniel Weiss Associates, Inc.
33 West 17th Street
New York, NY 10011
Cover art by Bruce Emmett

ISBN: 0-553-29857-7

Published simultaneously in the United States and Canada

Bantam Books are published by Bantam Books, a division of Bantam Doubleday Dell Publishing Group, Inc. Its trademark, consisting of the words "Bantam Books" and the portrayal of a rooster, is Registered in U.S. Patent and Trademark Office and in other countries. Marca Registrada. Bantam Books, 1540 Broadway, New York, New York 10036.

PRINTED IN THE UNITED STATES OF AMERICA

OPM   0 9 8 7 6 5 4 3 2 1

To
Trinity Dawn Jensen

Chapter 1

Sixteen-year-old Elizabeth Wakefield stood in her bedroom in her robe and slippers on Wednesday morning, staring without enthusiasm at the contents of her closet. *It's the last day of school before Christmas vacation,* she reflected, examining a blouse and then a dress. Traditionally there were holiday parties in every class, and the entire Sweet Valley High student body dressed up for the occasion. *I should probably wear something nice. . . .*

Elizabeth sighed. She'd just as soon put on an old pair of khakis and a polo shirt; she didn't feel particularly festive. *How am I ever going to get into the holiday spirit?* she wondered.

Just then her eyes came to rest on one of her favorite outfits, a fancy tuxedo shirt with matching bow tie, trousers, and vest. A wry smile touched

1

her lips. Jessica had always loved this outfit, too—she'd borrowed it all the time in the old days. Elizabeth's mind traveled back to other mornings when her sister would bounce into her room to raid her closet. *That seems like so long ago. Well, it was long ago,* she reminded herself. *It was another lifetime. Before . . .*

A shadow clouded Elizabeth's blue-green eyes, and she pushed the tuxedo outfit aside with a sharp gesture. Those innocent days of sharing and giggling were long gone. Jessica was no longer truly her sister, no longer her best friend. Since the fatal night of the Jungle Prom, everything had changed.

Elizabeth turned away from the closet and sat down on the edge of her bed. She pressed the palms of her hands against her forehead, wishing she could squeeze the memories from her brain, but they were always there, just beneath the surface. *It started before the Jungle Prom,* Elizabeth recalled. *Jessica and I were supposed to be planning the dance together, but we couldn't agree on* anything—*except for the fact that we both wanted to be Prom Queen.* In retrospect, their rivalry for the queen's crown seemed ridiculous, but at the time, the competition between the two sisters had been in dead earnest. It wasn't until the last minute that Elizabeth had decided it was foolish to care so much about something so trivial. She remembered deciding to drop out of the Prom

2

Queen contest. But that was the last thing Elizabeth remembered about that night until after the accident.

The pain was still fresh; Elizabeth's eyes filled with tears. *Will it ever stop hurting?* she wondered. *And will I ever know what really happened?* No one knew how she and her sister's boyfriend, Sam Woodruff, had managed to get drunk that night. If their punch had been spiked, they hadn't realized it—they had left the prom to go for a drive without noticing their unsteadiness. The twins' Jeep had gone off the road and flipped over. Miraculously Elizabeth had survived the crash with minor injuries. But Sam wasn't so fortunate; he had died instantly.

Elizabeth's life had turned into a waking nightmare after the crash. Not only did she have to cope with almost unbearable sorrow and guilt, but she had been arrested for vehicular manslaughter. Because she'd blacked out from the liquor, she'd been unable to say anything in her own defense. On the verge of being convicted, Elizabeth had been saved when a young man came forward to confess that his own reckless driving had caused the accident, not Elizabeth's.

That was a turning point, Elizabeth mused. *After the trial I thought we could start putting the pieces back together.* Jessica had finally seemed ready to forgive her for the part she'd played in

Sam's death; they were so close to making up. And then . . .

Rising, Elizabeth crossed to her desk and pulled out a letter her boyfriend Todd had written to her during the trial—a letter in which he asked Elizabeth to forgive him for being cold and distant after the accident, for shunning rather than supporting her. Explaining that he'd been hurt and jealous at the thought that something had been going on between her and Sam, Todd had begged Elizabeth to give him a sign that she was ready to talk . . . and to forgive him.

As she skimmed the letter, Elizabeth's jaw tightened with anger. She pictured Todd hand-delivering the letter to her house, and then she pictured Jessica intercepting and hiding it as part of a cruel plot to steal Todd for herself.

Elizabeth grew furious all over again just thinking about it. *I felt so guilty—I felt so sorry for Jessica!* she thought. *And for all those horrible, painful weeks when I thought Todd had stopped loving me, Jessica was telling him I was the one who wanted nothing to do with* him. *We wasted so much time.*

But Elizabeth had discovered Jessica's treachery before it was too late. Since then Elizabeth and Todd had fallen more deeply in love than ever. *All's well that ends well,* she thought, returning Todd's letter to the drawer. All *hadn't* ended well between

4

her and Jessica, however; far from it.

Elizabeth slipped out of her robe and pulled a red V-neck top and black skirt from her closet. As she dressed, she listened to Jessica blow-drying her hair in the bathroom that connected their two bedrooms. For a moment Elizabeth's heart softened; she ached for all that had been lost, for the carefree, innocent days when she and Jessica were constantly in and out of each other's rooms, talking, laughing, bickering, sharing . . . just being sisters.

Will we ever be close again? Elizabeth wondered. It was hard to imagine, as bitter and estranged as they were now. Despite their personality differences, they'd always been completely in tune with each other. Lately, though, Elizabeth felt as if she were living with a total stranger who just *looked* like her identical twin. She couldn't begin to guess what Jessica was thinking and feeling.

Standing in the middle of her bedroom, Elizabeth looked around at her pretty furniture, her books and photographs and posters and stuffed animals. A strange premonition crept over her. *Things are going to get much worse before they get better,* Elizabeth thought, an unaccountable shiver racing up her spine.

Jessica unplugged the hair dryer and stuck it into the cabinet under the sink. She brushed out

5

her silky, shoulder-length hair, then shook her head to give her hair a more tousled look. She put on some lip gloss and a little mascara; she smoothed body lotion onto her suntanned arms and legs. Then she returned to her bedroom and began to dress.

She chose an outfit that was appropriate for the last day of school before Christmas vacation—a short, forest-green knit dress with long sleeves and a scooped neck—but she did it without really thinking. It seemed as if she did *everything* without thinking these days. *I might as well be a robot,* Jessica thought morosely as she contemplated her earring collection. *I'm just going through the motions. Get up, go to school, go to cheerleading practice, come home, eat dinner, go to bed. Nothing means anything anymore.*

At least she had a date to look forward to today. Her spirits lifted a little as she thought about James, the gorgeous dirt biker she'd fallen madly in love with after he won the Sam Woodruff Memorial Rally . . . Jessica's heart sank again. Sure, it was great going out with someone new—it boosted her ego to have a guy as sexy and intriguing as James paying so much attention to her. But she never would have organized the dirt-bike rally in the *first* place if Sam hadn't been killed in the tragic car crash the night of the Jungle Prom.

Tears welled up in Jessica's eyes and then

spilled over, streaking her mascara. She opened the top drawer of her dresser and removed the framed photograph she kept hidden under a tangle of socks and underwear. "I miss you so much," she whispered to Sam. "No one can ever take your place—not James, not anybody."

Lifting the picture to her lips, she kissed it lightly, then returned it to the drawer. Slowly but surely, she was getting over the pain of losing Sam. Organizing the dirt-bike rally had helped her come to terms with his death, and even though sometimes she still missed him so much it hurt, Jessica knew that one day her heart would heal. There was another wound, though, that cut even deeper, one that no one else could see. It tormented Jessica every moment of the day and night, waking or sleeping. Worse even than Sam's death was the terrible secret that stood between her and her sister. Jessica was the only person who knew the full truth about what had happened on prom night, and the knowledge was destroying her.

I wanted Elizabeth to make a fool of herself so people would vote for me for Prom Queen instead of her. For about the thousandth time Jessica recited the horrible confession in her mind. *I spiked her drink. I started it all.* Because of her malicious stunt, Elizabeth and Sam unknowingly got drunk and drove off in the Jeep.

And I let Liz take the rap for the accident,

Jessica thought. *If the guy in the other car hadn't come forward at the last minute, she would've been convicted of manslaughter and sent to a juvenile home even though it was all my fault, not hers. I would have let that happen to her. What kind of evil person am I?*

Jessica held back a sob. She wanted so desperately to tell Elizabeth the truth, to come clean, to absolve herself. Yet at the same time, she knew it was a truth that would make it impossible for them ever to be close again. If Elizabeth couldn't even forgive her for stealing Todd's letter . . .

Jessica crossed her room, preparing to head downstairs to breakfast. Halfway to the door she froze in her tracks, arrested by a sudden eerie sensation. It came and went in a flash, but the message was clear. *Trouble—there's more trouble for me and Liz. . . .*

Jessica tossed her hair back, shaking off the melancholy mood. *More* trouble? She had to laugh. *What on earth could be worse than what we've already suffered through?*

Steven Wakefield reached across the kitchen table for the pitcher of milk. "I can't believe I'm up this early," he remarked, stifling a yawn. "After pulling those all-nighters during finals week, I figured I'd sleep till noon every day of vacation!"

"Maybe you're getting used to living without

8

sleep," Elizabeth suggested as she spread some apricot jam on a piece of toast.

"Maybe." Steven dug into his cereal. "Or maybe I'll just have to take a nap this afternoon."

At that moment Jessica entered the kitchen. "Hi, hon," Mrs. Wakefield greeted her daughter.

"Morning, Jess," said Mr. Wakefield.

"Hi, everybody," Jessica mumbled, pulling out a chair and sitting down without looking at anyone.

Steven glanced from Jessica to Elizabeth and back again. Elizabeth didn't even look at her sister; Jessica, meanwhile, drained a glass of orange juice and started in on her cereal without another word. *I thought they'd be over this*, Steven reflected. *I thought I'd come home for Christmas vacation and everything would be back to normal around here. So much for* that *fantasy!*

At least his parents seemed to be in a cheerful mood. "It's been ages since we last went up to San Francisco, Ned," Alice Wakefield mused as she stirred milk into her tea. "I really can't wait! While you're in meetings, I can ride the cable cars and shop and maybe take in a museum or two."

"So it's all work and no play for me, eh?" Mr. Wakefield joked.

Mrs. Wakefield smiled, the dimple in her left cheek making her look more like the twins' older sister than their mother. "We can do some fun things in the evening, too," she promised her husband. "Go to the theater, the symphony . . ."

"What's this about San Francisco?" Steven interjected. "What meetings?"

"Don't you remember, Steven?" asked Mrs. Wakefield. Her blue-green eyes sparkled. "It's so thrilling! A major environmental-engineering firm is paying for both of us to fly to San Francisco a few days after Christmas. They're putting us up in the most elegant hotel in the city."

"Is this about that legal-consulting job you mentioned last time I was home, Dad?" Steven asked.

"To tell you the truth, I don't know for sure what it's about," Mr. Wakefield confessed. "I'm assuming it has something to do with the big antitrust suit they're involved in, but they haven't given many specifics. The letter I got included a complete itinerary, two plane tickets, and a hotel-confirmation number." He laughed. "They're sweeping me right off my feet. Usually there's more of a courtship involved—phone calls back and forth, negotiations over fees, that sort of thing." His brow furrowed. "It does seem a little odd, doesn't it? I've never even spoken with Michelle de Voice, my contact at Kotkin, Greiner, and Burns."

Mrs. Wakefield waved this consideration aside. "There was no need to. She'd already arranged every last detail, right down to a limo to meet us at

10

the airport. All we have to do is get our bodies on the plane!"

"I think it's a tribute to your legal reputation that the company's inviting you up with no preliminary dancing around, Dad," Steven commented. "Obviously they know you're the man for the job. Consulting projects are always kind of secretive, aren't they?"

"It'll be fun," Mrs. Wakefield declared. "San Francisco is one of my all-time favorite cities. The Golden Gate Bridge, Fisherman's Wharf, the cable cars, Chinatown . . ."

Mr. Wakefield grinned. "You're right. It has all the ingredients of an unforgettable trip. It's almost too good to be true!"

"Which reminds me," said Mrs. Wakefield, turning to Steven. "The girls don't need a baby-sitter, but we'd feel better if we knew you'd be home with them. You're planning on hanging around Sweet Valley this vacation, aren't you?"

Steven nodded. "You can count on me." He grinned at his sisters. "Just warning you, I run a tight ship. I expect to be able to bounce a quarter off your beds, and no male visitors without a chaperon present."

Elizabeth cracked a weak smile. Jessica shrugged. Steven sighed. He was happy for his parents, but it didn't look as if being home alone with the twins was going to be a barrel of laughs. For the entire meal Jessica and Elizabeth had been sitting right across from one another, pointedly ignoring each other. *And the worst thing,* Steven thought, *is that the rest of us are starting to get used to it.*

What happened to the old Liz and Jess? he wondered. The twins had been through a lot. . . . Had it changed their personalities forever?

Chapter 2

"I hate this Secret Santa candy-cane thing," Lila Fowler grumbled to Jessica and Amy Sutton as they found seats in the Sweet Valley High auditorium before the start of morning assembly. "How did such a dumb tradition get started, anyway? Every year I always get candy canes from total dorks."

"Maybe the dorks figure you'll be in the Christmas spirit and give them a chance," Amy reasoned.

"Dorks are dorks no matter what the season," Lila declared with a disdainful toss of her long, glossy brown hair. "Anyhow, it takes more than a cheap piece of candy to get *my* attention."

"I think it's a fun tradition," said Amy. "The way elves deliver the candy canes in the middle of class

13

and stuff—it's a great way to make sure we don't get any work done the day before vacation."

"Look at it this way, Li," Jessica suggested, slouching down in her seat. "All the proceeds from selling the candy canes go to the children's hospital, right? Being the object of so much unrequited adoration makes you a major-league philanthropist. They'll probably name a wing at the hospital after you."

Amy laughed. "Except the whole *hospital's* called Fowler Memorial already!"

Lila patted her mouth in a ladylike yawn. "Here comes ol' Chrome Dome. Wake me up when he's through talking."

The yawn was contagious. Jessica felt her eyelids drooping as Mr. Cooper, the bald principal of Sweet Valley High, reminded the students that even though there would be parties in most classes that day, they were expected to behave themselves as usual and not get too noisy. Then Ms. Dalton chatted for a minute or two about the next French Club outing. Just as Jessica started to nod off for real, she heard her sister's voice echo through the auditorium. She tensed, straightening in her chair.

"We all know *The Oracle's* the best high-school newspaper in Southern California," Elizabeth was saying cheerfully. "No, make that in the whole country!"

There was scattered applause from the audience. "With great columns like 'Personal Profiles'"—this remark was greeted with whistles and laughter—"you're probably wondering how we could make the paper better than it already is. Well," Elizabeth continued, "there's always room for innovation, and we know there's lots of untapped talent out there. So to kick off the new year, right after vacation the *Oracle* staff is holding a special meeting for people who think they might have an idea for a column or a cartoon strip or a feature article. Come bounce your ideas off us— you might end up on the front page!"

Jessica listened to her sister talk, a wistful half smile on her face. Elizabeth was really back in the swing of things these days, writing "Personal Profiles" and other stories for the newspaper, excelling in all her classes and extracurricular activities, dating Todd . . . *She always had it all together,* Jessica reflected. *The accident and the trial threw her off balance, but now she's on track again. Liz Wakefield, the golden girl who can do no wrong.* Jessica bit her lip. *And then there's me. . . .*

"So don't miss the meeting!" Elizabeth concluded, turning to leave the stage. Before she could step down, however, a tall, lanky elf in a bright red-and-green costume jumped up beside her. "Elizabeth Wakefield, I presume?" the elf bellowed.

Laughter erupted in the auditorium. "Santa

15

must be really desperate for help in the elf department if he's hired Winston," Lila said, rolling her eyes.

"Nice tights, Egbert!" somebody shouted.

Students laughed and cheered as the elf presented a blushing Elizabeth with a Secret Santa candy cane and note.

"I wonder who it's from," someone else called out.

Reading the note, Elizabeth smiled. When she stepped down from the stage right into Todd's arms, there was a roar of approval from the crowd. Jessica slumped in her seat again. *No one loves me that way,* she thought bitterly. *Not even James. And no one ever will again.*

"Are you going to sit here forever?"

Jessica blinked up at Lila, who was tugging on her arm. "C'mon, Jess, I want to get to math early and snag a seat in the back. I did *not* understand the homework—if Ms. Taylor calls on me, I'm dead."

Jessica trailed Amy and Lila out of the auditorium. They joined the flood of students heading to their first class of the day. "I didn't get the homework, either," Jessica mumbled. "But I really couldn't care less."

"You'll care if Ms. Taylor calls on you and you end up looking like a total idiot," Lila predicted.

Jessica waved a hand. "She never calls on me."

As soon as the bell rang, Ms. Taylor closed the classroom door and took up her usual post at the blackboard. "We're having a party, don't worry," she promised the class. "I've got doughnuts and Christmas cookies and other healthy stuff. First, though, let's go over last night's problem set. I don't want your brains to totally atrophy over vacation." She scanned the roomful of students. "Umm . . . Jessica. What did you come up with for problem number one?"

Lila snickered; Jessica gulped. "Uh—well . . ." She made a big show of thumbing through the pages of her spiral notebook. "Just a sec, I know it's in here somewhere. . . ."

Just then the door burst open. "Ho, ho, ho!" a male voice boomed.

A burly, broad-shouldered elf wearing red sweatpants and a green football jersey stomped into the room. The class laughed at the sight of Ken Matthews, Sweet Valley High's star quarterback, posing as one of Santa's helpers.

"Saved by the bell—I mean, the elf," Lila whispered to Jessica. "Boy, are you lucky!"

"Tell me about it," Jessica whispered back. "I wonder who the candy cane is for."

In answer to her question, Ken headed in Jessica's direction. "Ho, ho, ho," he chuckled again, pulling out a chair next to hers. "Jessica Wakefield, have you been a good girl this year?"

17

Jessica grimaced. The class laughed again.

"Well, I have a candy cane for you anyway," said Ken.

She shrugged. "OK. Hand it over."

"You know the routine, Jessica." Jessica couldn't help but laugh as Ken pulled her onto his lap. He winked at the class. "This is what I like about this job."

Jessica wagged a finger at him. "Just don't get fresh, Matthews."

Ken grinned. "I wouldn't dare. Now, tell Santa's helper what you want for Christmas."

"Well, let's see. . . ." Jessica tipped her head to one side, smiling slyly. "I'd like peace on earth . . ."

"Oh, you're such a saint," Lila said, rolling her eyes.

"And I'd like food for all the hungry people and no more pollution," Jessica continued. "And a red Mazda Miata and a new wardrobe."

Everyone laughed, including Ms. Taylor. Ken bounced Jessica on his knee. "Here's your candy cane, little girl. Ho, ho, ho, merry Christmas!"

Jessica made a dramatic show of unfolding the note that came with the candy cane. Her spirits soared; there was nothing she enjoyed more than being the center of attention. But as she read the message, her smile faded. The unsigned card read simply, "Happy Horrordays, Jessica."

"Who's it from?" Lila demanded.

"Let's see," said Ken, trying to snatch the note.

The whole class gazed at Jessica expectantly. She crumpled the note and hopped down from Ken's lap, forcing a smile. "It's from a secret admirer."

Ms. Taylor returned to the homework, mercifully forgetting that she'd called on Jessica right before Ken's interruption. Jessica stared at the candy cane lying on her desk. Happy Horrordays: What was that supposed to mean? Was it a reference to the car crash—to Sam's death? Who would write such a nasty thing?

Lila peered quizzically at Jessica. "You look pale," she whispered. "Are you all right?"

Jessica's fist tightened on the mysterious note. *Happy Horrordays* . . . Jessica shuddered involuntarily. Shoving the scrap of paper into her purse, she tossed the candy cane at Lila. "I'm fine. I just . . . don't like peppermint."

"That sounds like fun," Elizabeth remarked at lunchtime. Todd had just finished telling her about his family's plan to spend Christmas weekend skiing in the mountains. "I wish I could go with you. I have a feeling this isn't going to be the happiest holiday *my* family's ever had."

"We're not leaving until Saturday morning, so I'll be around for Christmas Eve dinner at your house," Todd reminded her. Leaning over, he

19

brushed her cheek with a light kiss. "It'll be fun, Liz, don't worry."

Elizabeth sighed. Fun? She didn't think so, although it was sweet of Todd to be so optimistic. Her family hadn't had fun together in ages. Even with Steven home, the atmosphere on Christmas Day was bound to be grim. *No wonder Mom and Dad are looking forward to their trip to San Francisco,* Elizabeth reflected glumly. *They probably can't wait to get away from their kids; they probably wish they'd never had us!*

"Elizabeth Wakefield, here you are!"

Elizabeth looked up at the sound of the husky, melodious female voice. Her preoccupied frown gave way to a broad grin; a particularly funky elf armed with a candy cane sauntered up to their table.

"Trust Dana to make even an elf costume look like this year's hottest fashion!" Elizabeth said laughingly to Todd.

Dana Larson, lead singer of the popular Sweet Valley High rock band The Droids, was wearing a bright-green minidress and red tights and gloves. She'd even tinted her short blond hair green and red for the occasion. "Ho, ho, ho," she sang to Elizabeth. "Here's another candy cane for you. You're really one of Santa's favorites this year! Save this for dessert, OK?"

Dana pranced off to deliver more candy canes.

Elizabeth tipped her head to one side, a smile still playing on her lips. "Who could this be from?" she wondered aloud. "I already got one from *you*, Todd."

Todd grinned. "If it's from a guy, I'm gonna be mighty jealous."

"It could be from Enid," Elizabeth guessed. Then she had a sudden, hopeful hunch. *Maybe it's from Jessica!* Maybe, in the spirit of Christmas, her sister wanted to make peace.

Eagerly, Elizabeth unfolded the note. But the message inside wasn't an expression of affection or an apology. It wasn't from a well-wisher.

The color drained from Elizabeth's face. Todd frowned. "What's the matter, Liz? What does it say?"

"It says, 'I'm dreaming of a red Christmas,'" Elizabeth read, her voice shaking slightly. "'Wreck the halls with bloody bodies.' It's not—it's not signed."

"What the—" Todd took the note from Elizabeth's trembling hand. After glancing at it briefly, he balled it up and tossed it toward a trash can. "It's just somebody's idea of a sick joke. Don't give it another thought."

Elizabeth nodded, but she couldn't get the frightening words out of her mind. *Wreck the halls with bloody bodies.* . . . An image of Sam's lifeless form being pulled from the wrecked Jeep flashed across Elizabeth's consciousness. "Who would do such a thing?" she asked Todd, her eyes wide with distress.

Todd shook his head. "I don't know, Liz. I just don't know."

I'm here, Margo thought jubilantly as she strolled down the empty halls of Sweet Valley High. *I'm finally here!*

She walked at a leisurely pace, savoring the feeling, familiarizing herself with every inch of the school where Elizabeth Wakefield spent so much of her time . . . where Margo would spend so much time when she became Elizabeth Wakefield.

It was all so beautiful: the airy, modern classrooms; the lush landscaped grounds and athletic fields; the energetic, talented teachers; the lively, attractive student body. Margo extended one slender arm to brush her fingers along a row of brightly painted lockers. *I belong here. I've earned this. At last . . .*

A thrill of excitement ran up Margo's spine, and her whole body felt charged with electricity. She'd worked so hard to reach this time and place! Now, in just a matter of days, she'd assume the identity she'd always dreamed of. She'd be a good, happy girl with a loving family, dozens of friends, and a handsome, devoted boyfriend—the brightest girl in the junior class, Sweet Valley High's most likely to succeed. *I'll be Elizabeth Wakefield, and Margo will cease to exist.*

A shadow darkened Margo's delicate features as she recalled the long, hard road she'd traveled for sixteen miserable years. Abandoned by the parents she'd never known, shuffled from one foster home to another, neglected or abused by foster parents and brothers . . .

Margo's fingers clenched into fists and her eyes glittered with rage. *They didn't break me, though,* she thought. *I beat them at their own game—I outsmarted them. I watched and waited for my opportunity, and then I took it.* What a magnificent escape she'd engineered, burning down her last foster family's home on Long Island! It was a shame that her young foster sister had had to die in the blaze, but it was a necessary sacrifice, part of Margo's plan to make sure her horrible foster parents were blamed for gross negligence and *two* deaths. Margo's body had been listed missing along with her little sister's.

Skillfully covering her tracks, she'd headed west to Ohio, where she was hired as an au pair by the Smith family of Cleveland. Margo had been more interested in Mrs. Smith's business as a jewelry dealer than in watching fat little Georgie Smith. Georgie was just a pain, although he *did* tell her where the key to his mother's safe was hidden. *For such a little kid, he had a big mouth,* Margo remembered, her lips twisting into a sneer. *I could never have trusted him to keep quiet about the jewelry. I took him for a "swim" at the lake just in the nick of time.*

With Georgie disposed of, she'd robbed the safe and split. That was when her luck really started to turn, when she knew for certain she was destined for big things, for a wonderful life, for a true transformation. She'd strangled that nosy old woman in the ladies' room of the Cleveland bus station and stolen her wallet and newspaper—the newspaper from Sweet Valley, California, with the picture of Elizabeth Wakefield in it.

Margo remembered her first glimpse of the beautiful face so much like her own. The photograph was a sign; it gave her a destination. Right then and there she'd bought a ticket to Los Angeles, and as the miles rolled away beneath the wheels of the bus, she'd devised a bold, brilliant plan. She hadn't wasted a minute since arriving in Sweet Valley a few weeks ago. Right away she'd plunged into the project of learning everything there was to know about Elizabeth Wakefield and her twin sister Jessica. She was paying James to spy on Jessica; she'd arranged to be hired by the company that catered the Fowler wedding; she watched the Wakefield house at all hours of the day and night. She'd studied the twins' voices and mannerisms—she knew who their friends were, what they liked to do after school and on weekends, what foods they liked, and what music.

I've already been Elizabeth once, Margo recalled with satisfaction. For her first brief impersonation, she'd walked right through the front door of the Wakefield home. And she'd fooled Mrs. Wakefield, Elizabeth's own mother!

I look the part; I am the part. Margo shifted her books to one arm and raised a hand to touch her hair—now as golden and silky as Elizabeth's. She'd bleached her dark hair; contact lenses shaded her gray eyes a clear, Pacific blue-green; she wore an outfit that could have come from Elizabeth Wakefield's closet. With a little more research, a little more practice . . .

Margo stopped at Elizabeth's locker. Everyone was in class; it was a good time to figure out the combination. Shadowing Elizabeth earlier, Margo had glimpsed the first two numbers. "Twenty-three, thirty-four," she mumbled as she spun the lock. *But what's the last number? I need to know this!* Margo was keeping notes on Elizabeth's schedule, the kids in her classes, her homework assignments. . . . She absolutely *had* to gain access to the locker.

Margo began to dial numbers at random, yanking on the locker handle each time. "C'mon, open," she muttered, her face growing purple with frustration. *I hate it when things slow me down. I hate it when things get in my way!* Grinding her teeth together, she tried a few more numbers, her temper rising, rising . . .

Suddenly, Margo was startled by a voice behind her. "Why aren't you in class, Elizabeth?" the woman inquired mildly. "Do you have a hall pass?"

The words were like a splash of ice water on her face; Margo regained her composure instantly. Pivoting slowly on her heel, she beamed a warm, sweet Elizabeth Wakefield smile. "No, I don't have a pass, Ms. Bellasario," Margo admitted, mentally patting herself on the back for recollecting the music teacher's name—it paid to study the photos on the faculty bulletin board. "Mr. Collins didn't bother writing one—I promised him I'd be super-fast getting this book." She waved one of the books she was carrying as evidence. "If it's a problem, I can get a pass for you."

Ms. Bellasario shook her head, smiling. "It's no problem, Elizabeth. I trust you."

Margo turned and hurried quickly down the hall, smothering a broad grin. "No problem, Elizabeth. I trust you. . . ." She liked the sound of that! *Elizabeth Wakefield has the world in the palm of her hand,* Margo gloated. *It will be fun being her!* Soon she'd get the respect she deserved; she'd have the opportunities she'd always been denied. Margo knew it *had* to be soon; Georgie Smith's older brother Josh was on her trail. She had given him the slip when he first confronted her in L.A., but recently she'd spotted him in Sweet Valley. She was pretty sure he'd recognized her despite the changes in her appearance. He wasn't smart, but he could get lucky—he could cross her path again by accident. *There's still so much to learn, but I have to hurry. I have to become Elizabeth so that Margo can disappear forever, without a trace.*

Margo smiled, thinking about the Secret Santa notes she'd sent to the Wakefield twins. This was going to be a special Christmas and New Year's for her; she couldn't resist spreading a little holiday cheer!

Chapter 3

Josh Smith stepped out of his room at the Dunes Motel on Wednesday afternoon and then paused, momentarily blinded by the bright Southern California sunshine. He shaded his eyes, blinking. Tall palm trees lined the sidewalk, their fronds waving in the mild breeze; beyond the grassy dunes, the blue-green Pacific Ocean glittered like a jewel. *California is sure a lot nicer than Cleveland in December!* Josh marveled. If only the beautiful scene weren't tainted by hidden evil. If only he were in Sweet Valley for a vacation instead of for revenge. *If only my baby brother were still alive.*

Josh strode toward the parking lot, his eyes keen with determination. Twenty minutes later he parked his rental car in front of a police station in the next county. *This is probably a wild-goose chase,* he told himself as he jogged up the steps to the entrance. What were the odds that Margo had anything to do with the recent hit-and-run murder he'd learned about from the Sweet Valley police? But Josh was so anxious to find Margo that he was willing to follow even the smallest lead. *She's a violent, calculating person,* Josh reflected grimly. *She's killed and robbed—she has no conscience. What's to stop her from killing again?*

The receptionist looked up as Josh crossed the lobby. "Can I help you?" she asked.

Josh nodded. "I'm a journalist with the *Sweet Valley News,*" he lied, "and I'm doing a story on unsolved crimes in the area. Would it be possible to talk to the officer who's investigating the hit-and-run accident that took place here a few weeks back?"

"That's Detective Vinograd. Let me see if she's free." The receptionist dialed an extension on her phone and spoke a few words, then nodded to Josh. "Down the hall, third door on the left," she instructed.

To Josh's relief the detective didn't question his falsified credentials. "It won't take long to fill you in," she said, tapping a pencil on her desk. "The victim came out of her home in a residential area and was crossing the street to her parked car when another car ran her down. The car that killed her was found abandoned a few blocks down the road."

"Were you able to trace the car's owner?" asked Josh.

The detective shook her head. "It was a rented car, and the person who hired it used a stolen driver's license as identification and paid in cash. It was a woman—a young woman. That's all we know for sure."

"Any fingerprints on the car?"

"Nope. Whoever she was, she knew what she was doing, and she was as cool as a cucumber. She didn't panic—before ditching the car, she wiped off the steering wheel and the door handles." Detective Vinograd shook her head again, mystified. "It certainly looks premeditated, but we're stumped on a motive. The victim was a young, single mother—she worked through a couple of temporary agencies, doing office work and catering. She was just an ordinary girl with no enemies. Why would someone want to run her down in cold blood?"

Josh had been taking notes on a legal pad in order to look more like a journalist. Now he froze, his pen clutched tightly in his fingers. *In cold blood . . .*

Margo, he thought, his own blood turning to ice in his veins. The hit-and-run killing sounded like her gruesome handiwork—Josh was sure she was in Sweet Valley, and up to her murderous old tricks. *She had to have a reason, though*, Josh thought. Margo was demonic, but her madness had a method to it. What did she stand to gain from that woman's death? Where was she now? Who would be next?

"Anything else I can help you with?" Detective Vinograd inquired, looking pointedly at her wrist-watch.

"Uh . . ." Jolted back to reality, Josh jumped to his feet. "I guess not. Thanks for your time." He headed for the door and then paused. He wasn't entirely satisfied; he still didn't possess a single clue as to Margo's whereabouts.

If I only knew why *she killed that woman*. Josh turned back. "Detective Vinograd, I think I'd like to talk to a few more people who knew the victim. Can you give me the phone numbers of any relatives or employers?"

Detective Vinograd pushed a manila folder across the desk toward Josh. "Help yourself. She didn't have any family in the area, but I spoke with some of her friends and people she'd worked with. I'm warning you, though, I came up empty-handed—I don't imagine you'll have any better luck."

"Probably not," Josh agreed as he scribbled down a few phone numbers. He pointed to one item on the list which had been crossed out.

"Valley Caterers in Big Mesa—what's the story here?"

"Right before her death she signed on for a catering job," the detective explained. "The folks at Valley Caterers were no help at all, though. She'd never worked for them before—they didn't know her personally."

Josh copied down the number anyway. Anything the dead woman had done in the days before her death was of interest to him. *I'll pay a visit to the caterers,* he decided as he left the police station. It wasn't much of a lead, but he had to pursue it. He had to track Margo down and see her brought to justice.

Sliding behind the wheel of his car, Josh sat for a moment without starting the engine. He thought of the long miles he'd traveled in search of his brother's murderer, how he'd started asking questions on his own when the Cleveland police didn't seem to be getting anywhere with the case. He'd finally cornered Margo in a diner in the L.A. train station—what a moment that had been!

What did the detective say—cool as a cucumber? What an understatement, Josh thought. Even with her back against the wall, Margo had managed to manipulate him, taking advantage of his nervousness and giving him the slip. Since then he'd covered the whole state of California looking for her, knowing she had to be there somewhere—

she'd come to the end of the continent, she couldn't get any farther west. Finally, he'd glimpsed a girl in Sweet Valley—blond, but undeniably Margo.

But just when I thought I was in control of the situation, things really got complicated, Josh remembered. He'd crashed a charity costume ball and had found not only Margo but two other girls who looked exactly like her! Margo had eluded him once again, but Josh felt in his bones that he'd run her to earth in Sweet Valley. There was a reason she'd chosen this town; the presence of her look-alikes, the Wakefield twins, couldn't be a coincidence.

Josh clenched his jaw tightly, struggling to rein in his emotions, but he couldn't stop the tears that rolled down his cheeks. *I'll get her—I'll get my revenge,* he thought grimly as he turned the car key in the ignition and the engine roared to life. *For Georgie's sake.*

Ten minutes before four o'clock on Wednesday afternoon, Margo approached the *Oracle* office on soundless feet. The door was ajar; Margo peeked inside and saw Elizabeth sitting at a desk with her back to the door, busily typing away on a computer. *Good,* Margo thought, continuing on down the hallway toward the library. Enid wasn't expecting Elizabeth until four—that gave Margo just enough time to whisk Enid off. "For some Christmas shopping and maybe an ice-cream cone," Margo murmured, mimicking Elizabeth's voice. She smiled to herself with satisfaction. That was *exactly* how Elizabeth had said it when Margo overheard the two girls talking earlier that afternoon. She had the impersonation down cold: the tone of voice, the tilt of the head, the smile. *And there's no time like the present to use it,* Margo figured as she pushed open the glass door to the Sweet Valley High library. *I might as well start getting in good with my new best friend!*

Just inside the library, however, she paused, at a loss. Enid had instructed Elizabeth to meet her "at my usual spot." But where was *that*?

She wandered around the library, casually scoping out every carrel and study table. *Well, I don't know where Enid likes to sit in the library, but I know everything else about her,* Margo thought. She chanted the pertinent facts in her mind. *Moved to Sweet Valley in eighth grade after her parents got divorced . . . became friends with Elizabeth in tenth grade . . . lives alone with her mom . . . a good student . . . dates Hugh Grayson from Big Mesa . . .*

"Hi, Liz," someone said in a soft voice.

Margo focused on the speaker. A slender, pretty girl with big blue eyes and tousled dark hair was sharing a study table with a handsome, broad-shouldered boy. *I know them, too,* Margo thought, her confidence growing by leaps and bounds. Pamela Robertson had recently transferred to Sweet Valley High from Big Mesa; she was dating Bruce Patman, the hunky star of the school tennis team *and* the richest boy in town.

Margo gave them a little wave in passing. "Hi, Pamela—hi, Bruce," she whispered. She resisted the urge to let her gaze linger on Bruce's athletic physique; Elizabeth Wakefield didn't make eyes at other people's boyfriends. *If I ever break up with Todd, though,* Margo speculated, licking her lips, *Bruce would be a mighty fine catch.*

Just ahead, in a corner carrel, Margo spotted a girl with curly, shoulder-length brown hair. *This is it,* she thought, hurrying forward. Her heartbeat remained steady; she was excited, but not nervous. Why be afraid of a mouse like Enid? It would be a breeze to win her over.

Stepping up behind Enid, Margo tapped her lightly on the shoulder. "Hi, Enid, ready to go?" she said in a low voice—in Elizabeth Wakefield's voice.

"You bet," Enid whispered in reply. She pushed her chair back and glanced up at Margo, smiling. "Let's get out of—"

The words died on Enid's lips; she froze, staring at Margo with wide green eyes. *Something's wrong,* Margo thought, her palms suddenly beginning to sweat. *Stay cool, stay calm.*

Standing up, Enid looked Margo straight in the eyes. "You're not Elizabeth," she declared after a long, pregnant pause.

Enid's words sliced into Margo like a knife. The blood drained from her face; she felt exposed and vulnerable. It was the first time she'd been challenged. How could this have happened?

Margo shifted her feet. "Wh—what are you talking about?" she asked, fighting to hold herself together. "Of course I'm Elizabeth!"

Enid shook her head in exasperation. "Jessica, what kind of silly game are you playing now? Whatever it is, I'm *not* playing along."

Grabbing her books, Enid stomped off in a huff. As soon as she was out of sight, Margo sank into a chair and closed her eyes, breathing hard. *Get a grip,* she ordered herself. *You're not off the hook until you're out of here.*

Margo forced herself to take a deep breath and slowly brought her emotions back under control. *It could have been worse,* she concluded after a few minutes. *Enid thought I was Jessica, after all—wrong twin, but at least she didn't suspect the truth.* Still, how annoying! It looked as if fooling loyal old Enid wasn't going to be so easy after all. Margo chewed on her lip, fretting. Then her expression brightened. *If I have to, I'll just kill her,* she decided. *She's not the kind of best friend I want, anyhow!*

At four o'clock Elizabeth turned off the computer she'd been working on and stuck her "Personal Profiles" folder in her book bag. She turned to leave the newspaper office just as Enid burst in. "The strangest thing just happened!" Enid breathlessly greeted Elizabeth.

"What?" asked Elizabeth.

"Jessica came to the library and pretended to be you," Enid informed her as they headed across the lobby toward the exit. "She came by my carrel and said, 'Let's go,' like she knew about our plans and everything. Isn't that bizarre?"

Elizabeth raised her eyebrows. "You're kidding!"

Enid shook her head. "It freaked me out for a second," she confessed. "Why would she do such a thing?"

"I honestly don't know," Elizabeth replied, baffled and angry. "I don't know why she does *any-thing* anymore!"

The two girls walked to the parking lot in thoughtful silence. A troubled frown shadowed Elizabeth's face. "It burns me up, these stunts she pulls," she said after a minute. "I don't trust her, not since the thing with Todd's letter. But I'm worried about her, too. I mean, she's always had a talent for getting into trouble, but there's usually been a reason for it. This is just . . . weird."

"I thought she was starting to get over Sam's death," Enid remarked as she unlocked the passenger door of her mother's blue hatchback for Elizabeth. "Now that she's dating that James guy, I thought maybe she was getting back to normal."

Back to normal . . . Elizabeth shook her head. "No. She's not back to normal," she said quietly. "Nothing's back to normal yet."

And as she climbed into the car, Elizabeth couldn't help wondering. Something had gone wrong inside of her sister since Sam's death. Would things *ever* be normal again?

"What can I get you?" the waitress at Kelly's Bar asked James, placing her hands on the table and leaning toward him flirtatiously.

James stubbed out his cigarette. *Man, I shouldn't be smoking these things,* he thought. "Uh, just a Coke," he told her, too distracted to flirt back.

"Cleaning up your act, huh?" she teased.

James shrugged. "Yeah, whatever," he mumbled.

With a sniff the waitress turned and flounced off. James slumped down in the booth and shook another cigarette out of the pack. As he struck a match, he noticed that his hand was shaking. *I can't believe it.* He almost laughed out loud. *I'm afraid of a sixteen-year-old girl!*

He lit the cigarette and this time just held it, not smoking. He'd pretty much kicked the habit since he'd been dating Jessica; he turned to it now only as a security blanket. He was waiting for Margo, and as much as he hated himself for the weakness, he was nervous.

The waitress slammed his drink down on the table without a word. James took a slug of the Coke and then a drag on the cigarette. Narrowing his eyes against the smoke, he looked around the dark, drab room. *I wish I'd never walked into this place,* he thought. If he hadn't been a regular at Kelly's, Margo wouldn't have gotten his name from the bartender. She would never have approached him about entering the Sam Woodruff Memorial Rally—she would never have offered him two thousand bucks to date Jessica Wakefield. Date her . . . and spy on her.

"I just want some information about her and her family," Margo had told him, fluttering those long dark eyelashes. "All you have to do is talk to her and then tell me everything she tells you. Ask a few questions, take a few pictures." James shuddered now as he remembered Margo's odd, humorless smile. "She's cute," Margo had added slyly. "She looks a lot like me."

It had sounded like an easy enough job to James, so he'd taken it. The money was really going to come in handy. Since then, though, Margo had gotten stranger and stranger. First James had discovered that the name she'd given him, Mandy, wasn't her real name. Then she'd bleached her hair blond and changed the color of her eyes and started to dress and talk differently. For some reason she wanted to look and act exactly like Jessica and her twin sister Elizabeth. *Why, though?* James wondered, draining the glass of Coke. *What's she up to?*

He didn't know for sure, but he was starting to suspect that Margo's interest in the Wakefield twins was malicious—maybe even deadly. She wouldn't permit him to ask any direct questions of her—that was part of their deal. But her veiled comments about her past gave him the distinct impression that she stopped at nothing to get what she wanted. And if anyone was foolish enough to get in her way . . .

As for him, he'd won the dirt-bike rally and struck up an acquaintance with Jessica Wakefield, and she'd fallen for him, just as she was supposed to. The only problem was . . .

James jumped, the burning cigarette slipping from his fingers. A girl had slipped noiselessly into the booth opposite him. She was young, blond, and beautiful; she looked exactly like the girl he dated these days—sweet, wholesome Jessica Wakefield. But this wasn't Jessica.

"Hi," Margo said, reaching across the table for the pack of cigarettes. Her hand brushed against his; James felt the hair on the back of his neck stand on end. "So what's new?" she asked briskly. "Got anything good for me?"

"Uh . . ." James retrieved the cigarette, stubbing it out. There was no point in beating around the bush. The sooner he got it over with, the sooner he could get out of there. "I want off your payroll, Margo," James announced.

Margo froze in the act of striking a match. "You *what*?" she repeated, her voice shrill with surprise.

"I'm not interested in the job anymore," James explained, looking down at the scarred tabletop. "Jessica Wakefield's a bore. I don't need the money that bad."

Margo lit the cigarette. Putting it to her lips, she sucked in a mouthful of smoke. Meanwhile she stared at James, her small, cold eyes seeming to drill right into his heart.

"You're not bored with her," she snarled after a long moment. "You've fallen in *love* with her, you pitiful fool!"

"That's not it," James protested, his face flushing.

"Don't lie to me!" she snapped. She tossed the cigarette into the ashtray and sat forward, gripping the edge of the table with both hands. "Did you say anything to her about me?"

41

James gaped at Margo. She panted like a cornered animal, her eyes wild. "No," he swore. "I haven't said anything to anybody about you."

Still tense and panting, Margo weighed his words. Finally she relaxed slightly, apparently concluding that he was telling the truth about this. "All right, James," she said, her voice low and even. "You can have what you want. You're off my payroll. You're just a bum, anyway—I got all I needed out of you."

Relief rushed over James. *I'm free,* he thought. *Jessica and I, our love—we're free.*

"But," Margo added, slamming the palm of her hand down on the table. James jumped. "If you betray me for Jessica—if you say another word to her, if you so much as *look* at her ever again, I'll kill you." James blanched and Margo smiled. "I'll kill you," she repeated in a harsh whisper. "But I'll make you suffer beforehand. I'll kill Jessica first."

James stared across the table at Margo. "You're bluffing," he said, his voice cracking.

The expression in Margo's crazed eyes was deadly serious. "I don't bluff."

What am I going to do? James thought desperately. There didn't seem to be any way out. How could he protect Jessica now without exposing her to greater danger? Both their lives hung in the balance; both of them were at the mercy of this monster.

42

"Who are you?" James whispered. "*What* are you?"

Margo stood up to leave. As she looked down at James, a subtle transformation came over her face. She smiled—*Jessica's* smile. "I'm exactly who I appear to be," she replied lightly.

Chapter 4

Alice Wakefield kicked off her pumps and curled up on the living-room sofa. On one side of her lay a paperback novel, on the other a stack of bills and her checkbook. She was home from work early for a change, her interior-design firm usually demanding longer hours—it was tempting to indulge. She looked longingly at the novel and then picked up the bills with a sigh.

As she tore out the first check, she heard the front door open. Someone stepped into the living room. "Hi, Liz," Mrs. Wakefield said, glancing up briefly at her daughter.

"Hi, Mom."

Mrs. Wakefield's gaze had dropped back to her checkbook; then she did a double take. Elizabeth walked toward her, an angelic smile on her face.

What's different about her? Mrs. Wakefield wondered, narrowing her eyes. Elizabeth, who was wearing jeans and a red V-neck T-shirt, looked perfectly happy and relaxed, and yet . . .

Mrs. Wakefield shook off the sensation as Elizabeth sat down next to her. "How was your day, honey?"

"Oh, just fine."

Elizabeth didn't volunteer any more information; she just sat quietly and stared at her mother with adoring eyes. Mrs. Wakefield shifted uncomfortably. "Liz, is anything the matter?"

"No, Mom," Elizabeth assured her, lowering her eyelashes and smiling again. "Everything is just perfect."

Leaning forward, Elizabeth gave her mother a quick, warm hug. As her daughter's arms wrapped around her, a strange chill penetrated Mrs. Wakefield's heart. She shuddered, momentarily overcome by a feeling of revulsion. Fortunately, Elizabeth didn't notice her reaction; humming cheerfully, she hopped to her feet and sauntered out to the hallway.

The feeling disappeared as quickly as it came, but Mrs. Wakefield was shocked to her very core. She stared after Elizabeth, her eyes wide with puzzlement and guilt. What had just taken place? Why would a hug from her daughter, whom she loved, stir such a feeling? *It was like being touched by a stranger,* Mrs. Wakefield reflected. The connection she usually shared with her daughters, the deep unspoken bond, had suddenly seemed to dissolve. Something was off; something was missing.

Mrs. Wakefield bit her lip, distressed. *What's happening to me? What's happening to all of us?* she wondered, tears springing to her eyes. Had the divisiveness in the family gone so tragically far that she was growing alienated from her own children?

She shuddered again, this time from recalling how close she'd come to a nervous breakdown during Elizabeth's trial. She'd protected herself from the horror by withdrawing; she'd turned her back on her family when they needed her most. The trial was over, but the pain lingered. Her daughters were seriously, perhaps permanently, estranged from one another. *I can't just detach myself from their problems again. I can't give up on them. If I do, we'll never be a real family again.*

Mrs. Wakefield pressed a hand to her throbbing forehead. *Maybe it's just as well Ned and I are going away for a few days,* she mused. *Maybe I need some time away from* . . . The thought dangled in her brain, incomplete. She stared blankly into space. Time away from what? From whom?

Margo walked up the staircase to the second floor of the Wakefield home, exulting in her success. She hugged herself, still tingling from her beautiful new mother's embrace. *Someone loves me at last!* she thought, stroking the banister possessively. *And this house, my house. It loves me, too. It wants me here, I can tell.* It felt so natural, just strolling in the front door and up to Elizabeth's bedroom. It felt so, *so* right.

Margo glanced warily over her shoulder as she pushed open the door to Elizabeth's room. She was pushing her luck a little; Elizabeth could return from her outing with Enid at any time. But Margo couldn't help herself. An excited laugh escaped her. She couldn't wait for her new life as Elizabeth Wakefield to begin!

Crossing the threshold, Margo sighed with pleasure as she surveyed the bright, airy bedroom. *Elizabeth has lovely taste,* she thought with approval. The walls and carpeting were a warm cream color; the furniture was glossy and new; everything was as neat as a pin. *She must enjoy coming home to this cozy little nest,* Margo imagined. Now, what would Elizabeth do if she'd just arrived home from school? Margo ran her fingers along the back of the soft, velvet-covered chaise near the window; would Elizabeth take a book from the shelf and curl up here to read? *Maybe she'd sit at her desk and type an essay for the newspaper,* Margo speculated, examining Elizabeth's collection of reference books. It was tempting to slip a piece of paper into the typewriter and play at being Elizabeth.

Not today, Margo reminded herself. Today she was there to snoop, to learn. In the future she wasn't just going to be impersonating Elizabeth; she was going to *become* Elizabeth. To be successful she needed to know every little detail about Elizabeth's life, every last secret of her heart.

Margo crossed purposefully to Elizabeth's desk and pulled open the bottom drawer. *Pens, pencils, an address book—that might be useful. And what's this?* Margo drew a small notebook from the back of the drawer. *Something for school?* She opened the notebook in the middle and skimmed a few lines of the neat handwriting. "I don't know what to do about the competition for Prom Queen. Jessica is set on winning the crown, but after all the work I've done, I think I deserve a shot at it, too, and everybody says . . ."

Margo nearly shrieked with delight as she realized what she held in her hands. Elizabeth's diary—what a discovery! Her fingers tightened around the precious book. "This is the key," she whispered. "It's all here, everything I need to know!"

Biting her lip, Margo glanced around the room. She had so much work to do: making notes on the contents of Elizabeth's closet and dresser drawers, going through her files, her books, and photo albums. But she couldn't resist the diary. Margo threw herself down on Elizabeth's comfortable bed—so different from the hard, small cots *she'd* had to sleep on as a foster child. Eagerly, she turned to the first page of the journal and started reading all about her new life.

Page by page Margo devoured the diary, internalizing every word, every emotion. "At this point I can't wait until the dance is over," Elizabeth wrote. "I almost don't care who wins the Prom Queen title, Jessica or me or somebody else altogether! Maybe once it's behind us, she and I can stop being so competitive and mad at each other."

Fat chance of that, Margo thought with an ironic smile. *I know what happens next!* She read faster. The handwriting grew uncharacteristically loopy and careless; Elizabeth was in despair. "I don't know how I can go on. Every morning, I wonder where I'll find the strength, the courage, to climb out of bed. How can I live with myself knowing I killed my sister's boyfriend? And tomorrow my trial starts. My God, I'm going to stand trial for manslaughter. . . ."

Pages and pages of agonized soul-searching, and then, finally, vindication. "I'm not guilty!" Elizabeth's relief seemed to pour from the book. "Someone else caused the accident—it wasn't my fault!" But Margo could see that Elizabeth continued to be haunted by remorse. "The outcome of the trial doesn't change the fact that Sam is dead.

Jessica doesn't eat, she doesn't go out, she doesn't talk to anyone. She still hasn't forgiven me—maybe she never will."

Hmm, Margo thought. *Nowadays Elizabeth is the one who's unforgiving. What caused that reversal?*

A few pages later she found out. The blue pen Elizabeth wrote with bit into the paper, almost ripping it in places; the journal seethed with anger. "I can't believe Jessica would do such a thing!! I can't believe she intercepted Todd's letter and hid it from me. She'd do anything to hurt me—she'd do anything to keep Todd and me apart so she can have him for herself." Margo clucked her tongue. *That Jessica. She's really a girl after my own heart!*

Then she caught herself. She wasn't supposed to be sympathizing with Jessica; she was on Elizabeth's side. Her heart was breaking over Todd, just as Elizabeth's had. *And now we're in love again.* Margo sighed as she read about Elizabeth and Todd's joyous reunion. *He's mine again, all mine,* she thought ecstatically. *And no one will come between us ever again.*

I should really be taking notes on this, Margo reflected. The journal was a treasure trove of personal observations about Elizabeth's friendships, family, schoolwork, *The Oracle*—it was all there. *Better yet, I should borrow it for a day and make a copy of the whole thing.*

As she turned to the journal's most recent entry, Margo suddenly realized she was squinting. Around her the room had grown dark. *God, what time is it?* she wondered, bringing her wrist close to her face and peering at her watch. *An hour— I've been lying here for an hour!* She'd stayed far too long.

Cursing her stupidity, Margo leapt to her feet. She flew across the darkened room to Elizabeth's desk and tossed the diary in a drawer at random. As she did so, she thought she heard footsteps in the hallway. Or was it just the sound of her own heart pounding? No, there it was again, coming closer. Someone was right outside the bedroom door!

Margo dived into the closet; there was no place else to hide. She pulled the louvered door shut in front of her just as the bedroom door swung open and a shadowy figure stepped into the room.

Sliding her hand along the wall, Elizabeth felt for the light switch and flipped it on. She closed the door behind her, a preoccupied expression on her face. *Mom's been acting so weird lately,* she thought, reflecting on the strange exchange they'd just had downstairs. *Talking about a conversation I don't remember us having, asking me why I changed my clothes . . .* Elizabeth looked down at her pink Oxford shirt. *I didn't change my clothes, and she hasn't seen me since breakfast anyway. What's the story?*

Elizabeth walked forward, preparing to toss her book bag onto her bed. Instead she stopped dead in her tracks. Instantly forgetting about her mother, she focused on her surroundings. *What the—?*

Elizabeth distinctly remembered leaving her bedroom as neat as a pin. But now . . . Her eyes darted around the room, taking in the signs of disorder. The papers on top of her desk were disarranged, and the top drawer jutted out, half-open; the bedspread was rumpled and the pillow dented. Someone's head had been resting there, and not too long ago. A chill ran down Elizabeth's spine. *Someone's been in here!*

Elizabeth put a hand to her throat, trying to ignore the frightened lump that had formed there. A creepy feeling made her whole body tingle. *Somebody's watching me.*

Silly, you're the only one here now, Elizabeth told herself. Striding to her desk, she yanked open the drawers one by one. Sure enough, though, the contents were jumbled—somebody *had* been there snooping through her things. But who? And why?

Then she noticed her journal. She always kept it in the bottom drawer, tucked far in the back; now it rested on top of a pile of letters and postcards in the top drawer. Someone had moved it.

It could only be one person. Elizabeth's jaw clenched angrily. She was no longer spooked; she was just plain *mad*. "Jessica," she exclaimed, breathless with outrage at the shamelessness of the violation. "How *dare* she, on top of everything else!"

Margo had left the louvered door open just a crack. Now, from the shadows of the closet, she peeked out at Elizabeth. Her heart pounded like a jackhammer; her position was incredibly perilous. Elizabeth didn't suspect an intruder; she thought Jessica was the one who'd been snooping around her room. But what if she opened the closet and discovered Margo crouching there?

Stronger than fear, however, was fascination. *She's so close,* Margo thought, electrified. *I can practically reach out and touch her.* Spellbound, she watched Elizabeth replace the diary in the bottom drawer and straighten the papers on top of the desk. Then, tossing back her hair, Elizabeth turned toward the closet. For a long moment Elizabeth stood as still as a statue, apparently lost in thought. Margo's eyes focused greedily on the other girl's slender neck, her bare, exposed throat. *It would be so easy,* Margo thought. Her palms itching, she fingered a silk scarf she'd picked up from the floor of the closet. *I could do it right here, right now. I*

*could just wrap this scarf around her neck and pull
it tight—it would only take a minute. No one
would hear, no one would know. Then I wouldn't
have to wait any longer. I could become Elizabeth
Wakefield right now!*

The prospect drove Margo to ecstasy. She
tensed, ready to spring forward. Then, with a mon-
umental effort, she restrained herself. *No,* Margo
thought, sinking back in the closet and letting the
scarf slip from her fingers. *No!* She squeezed her
eyes shut against the tempting vision of Elizabeth's
nearness and vulnerability. She'd almost let it carry
her away! But she couldn't afford to be be reckless.
What would she do with the body if she strangled
Elizabeth now?

And I'm not ready yet, Margo conceded
silently. Her failed encounter with Enid earlier
that afternoon was proof. She was an actress, after
all; she had to have every line and gesture down
cold before the curtain rose on opening night. She
had to be one hundred percent sure of her role
when she went on stage as Elizabeth Wakefield,
daughter of Ned and Alice, sister of Jessica and
Steven, friend of Enid, girlfriend of Todd, darling
of Sweet Valley, California. She couldn't afford a
single lapse—no one must ever, *ever* question her
identity.

Patience, Margo chastised herself. This was
only the dress rehearsal; she still needed practice.

Soon, though. Soon you'll get your chance.

Margo held her breath, waiting for Elizabeth to make her next move. To Margo's relief Elizabeth turned away from the closet and walked into the bathroom. As soon as the door closed behind Elizabeth, Margo darted silently from the closet and out into the hallway. She collapsed against the wall, expelling the pent-up air from her lungs in a loud sigh. Then she hurried down the stairs, careful not to make a sound.

On the second-to-last step she paused. Someone coughed nearby; Mrs. Wakefield was still in the living room. *I can't risk the front door,* Margo realized. *I guess that leaves the sliding glass door in the back of the house.*

Margo tiptoed toward the kitchen, hoping against hope that she wouldn't bump into anyone else, her fingertips brushing along the wall as she went. *Here's the closet . . . and another door. Where does this one lead?* As she eased it open. *The basement—of course!* Margo smiled in delight. Why hadn't she thought of that sooner?

She ducked through the door and ran down the cement stairs. It was hard to navigate in the dark, but she managed to grope her way across the cluttered basement toward a row of small, high windows. She could just reach them if she stood on tiptoe. *I need a stepladder,* she decided. *I'm sure a handyman like Ned Wakefield must have one of those!*

A minute later Margo was wriggling her way out of one of the windows. Stepping out into the shrubbery, she let the window swing shut behind her, careful to make sure it remained unlatched. Standing up, she brushed the dirt and cobwebs from her hands and started across the lawn, keeping close to the trees to avoid detection When she reached the street she turned to glance back at the Wakefields' house. With the windows glimmering like golden eyes in the night, it looked cozy, safe, and warm—a haven. Yes, the basement window had been a stroke of luck. How convenient to have a secret way in and out of the house! Feeling very self-satisfied, Margo turned away from the house. From now on she planned to spend *lots* of time there.

At ten o'clock that night, the telephone rang. Jessica wouldn't admit to herself that she'd been sitting close to the phone all evening praying for it to ring; such behavior was too pathetic for words. But when the phone finally *did* ring, she jumped to answer it.

"Hello?" she said hopefully.

"Jess, it's me," a husky voice mumbled.

"James, hi." Jessica's cheeks turned pink with pleasure and relief. "I was wondering when I'd hear from you! I thought—well, I thought we were going to do something together tonight."

James didn't respond right away. *Did I sound too desperate?* Jessica wondered anxiously. *Maybe I should cool it—independent guys like James don't go for girls who cling.* "It's not that big a deal," she hurried to assure him. "I—I had a bunch of homework to do anyhow."

"I thought Christmas vacation started tomorrow," James pointed out.

"Right. But I just got assigned this special, um . . . history project that's due at the beginning of January," Jessica fibbed. "So I was working on that. Anyway . . ."

Her voice trailed off and she waited for James to explain why he'd forgotten their date that night. *I'm sure he has a perfectly good reason,* Jessica rationalized. *He'll tell me what it is, and then I can stop worrying.*

"Well . . ." James cleared his throat. "Sorry about tonight. I meant to call you sooner to tell you I couldn't make it, but, um, something just came up."

"Oh." Jessica couldn't think of anything else to say.

"I'll call you tomorrow, OK?" James said. Now his tone was brisk, as if he couldn't wait to get off the line.

"Uh, sure." Jessica's shoulders slumped; she felt completely deflated. *Whatever happened to "How're you doing, how was your day, I miss you"?* she wondered. "See ya."

"So long."

Jessica held the phone for a moment after James hung up. "Something just came up"—she'd never heard such a lame excuse in her life! She replaced the receiver and started nibbling on her fingernails, running back over the brief conversation in her mind. Usually she and James gabbed for an hour or more. Tonight, though, he'd seemed awkward and distant. *He must've had something on his mind,* Jessica concluded. *But why wouldn't he talk to me about it?* A horrible possibility occurred to her, and her stomach promptly tied itself into an excruciating knot. *Maybe he couldn't talk to me about what's bothering him because* I'm *what's bothering him. Maybe nothing came up—maybe he just didn't feel like seeing me.*

Springing to her feet, Jessica began pacing around her bedroom. The purple walls seemed to close in on her; she kicked viciously at a pile of crumpled clothes on the floor. *But he can't be losing interest in me!* she thought. *Why, the last time we were together at the beach a couple of nights ago . . .* Jessica closed her eyes, remembering the way James had wrapped his strong arms around her and held her as if he'd never let her go. He'd never actually said he loved her, but when he kissed her, when he stroked her hair . . . *He does love me,* Jessica tried to convince herself. *He just has to love me.*

She undressed, adding her jeans and sweatshirt to the mess on the floor of her room. Pulling on the football jersey she liked to sleep in, Jessica crawled into bed and burrowed under the covers. For a few minutes she just lay curled up in a ball, feeling lonely and depressed. Then she tuned in to the sound of water running in the bathroom. Elizabeth was washing her face and brushing her teeth.

Once again Jessica found herself wishing desperately that she could confide in her sister the way she used to. *I could tell her about James,* Jessica thought wistfully. *She'd help me understand him—she'd make me feel better. We could talk about everything—we could just be sisters again.*

Suddenly, Jessica didn't think she could bear the loneliness for one more minute. *We can be sisters again, but somebody has to make the first move. It might as well be me,* Jessica decided. *I need to tell her the truth about prom night, and then we can take it from there.*

Jessica flung back the covers and jumped out of bed. There was no time like the present; why endure another sleepless night? *I'll go to Liz now, before I lose my nerve,* she decided. *I'll confess about the spiked punch, and then I'll tell her how sorry I am and how much I love her. And then . . .* Jessica crossed her fingers. *I'll just pray that she can begin to forgive me.*

Jessica tapped lightly on the bathroom door, then pushed it open. The bathroom was dark, but beyond it she could see that Elizabeth's bedroom light was still on. Jessica paused, one hand on Elizabeth's door. Taking a deep breath, she ventured quietly into her sister's room.

Elizabeth was standing in front of the mirror over her dresser, brushing her hair; Jessica cleared her throat. "Um, Liz, can we . . . can we please talk?" she asked. "I have something really important to tell you."

Elizabeth spun around, her hair flying. "What, that you snooped through my stuff and read my diary?" she cried, her eyes flashing with anger.

Jessica's eyebrows shot up. "Excuse me?"

"You couldn't find any letters from Todd to hide, so you figured you'd come up with some other way to make me miserable, is that it?" Elizabeth ranted on.

Jessica stared at her sister, baffled. "Liz, what are you talking about?" she protested. "I never read your—"

"I'm sick of your lies and your tricks," Elizabeth broke in coldly. "Just get out of my room."

Jessica stood frozen by confusion and misery, her eyes brimming with disappointed tears. "But, Liz," she whispered. "I didn't—I just wanted to—"

"I said, get *out*!" Elizabeth cried.

*　　　*　　　*

Elizabeth rolled over in bed, thrashing her arms restlessly. For a moment her eyelids fluttered as if she might wake up, and then she slipped back into a broken, dream-filled sleep.

I can't be asleep—I can't be dreaming. This is so real! She was standing before the mirror in her bedroom, brushing her hair. She pulled back a thick clump, fastening it with a jeweled hair clip. Then she put on the gold lavaliere necklace that her parents had given her for her sixteenth birthday. *I'm wearing a light-blue dress—I'm going to a party. No! It's the night of the Jungle Prom! I'm getting ready for the dance!*

The doorbell rang, and Elizabeth hurried from the bedroom, nearly colliding with her sister, who emerged from her own room at the same moment. Tension crackled between them as they went downstairs to join Todd. Todd and *Sam*. Sam! He wasn't dead! Elizabeth saw him as big as life—his curly blond hair, his twinkling blue eyes, that sheepish, endearing grin.

The boys were dressed up, and so handsome. They presented Elizabeth and Jessica with corsages, and the four of them posed for pictures in the living room. Then they all headed out into the night to go to the Jungle Prom.

Every detail is perfect, Elizabeth thought with satisfaction as she arrived at the gym. All those long hours of preparation had paid off. The decorations were beautiful, the kids were thrilled by their miniyearbook souvenirs, and the band, Island Sunsplash, was fantastic. She and Todd hit the dance floor, and they danced and danced. . . .

Until he was named Prom King and had to hustle onstage to take his throne. Elizabeth was so proud of him! But there was Sam, with no one to talk to or dance with because Jessica was off trying to drum up Prom Queen votes for herself. Elizabeth took a whirl with him. Sam was a great dancer. . . .

"How about a break?" Sam suggested. "I could use a drink." Elizabeth felt incredibly thirsty, too, so they returned to their table and drained a cup of punch. *The punch . . .*

Elizabeth came fully awake with a jolt, her eyes popping wide open. Her nightgown was drenched in sweat, and she was breathless as if from dancing. *What a dream!* she thought, shaking her head in amazement. It had been so vivid, she could practically taste the punch on her lips. *The punch—was there something about the punch?*

Suddenly Elizabeth shivered. She'd thrown off the covers in her sleep; now the breeze from the open window chilled her. Reaching for the bedspread, she pulled it up under her chin, but her teeth continued to chatter. *What a dream,* she thought again. She'd had other dreams about prom night—about the car crash and Sam's broken, bleeding body—and during the trial she'd been haunted by recurring dreams of a girl who looked just like her sister, but who had dark hair and a big butcher knife. But she'd never dreamed about the dance itself. Why was it coming back to her now?

There must be a reason I dreamed about the prom in such detail, Elizabeth mused. *Dreams are messages from your subconscious, right?* Part of the dream had to be significant, she thought, but *which* part?

Chapter 5

Another sunny day, Josh thought, rolling down the car window as he drove to Big Mesa on Thursday morning. How long could the flawless weather last? He glanced in the direction of the distant Pacific Ocean. While the sky overhead was a clear robin's-egg blue, a bank of gray clouds edged the far western horizon. *A storm is coming,* he guessed. He was almost glad. The postcard-perfect California sunshine was starting to grate on his nerves, seeming to make light of his misery.

Arriving in downtown Big Mesa, Josh parked the car in front of a small office with the name "Valley Caterers" painted in large, fanciful script on the plate-glass window. Before stepping out onto the sidewalk, he pulled a photograph from his jacket pocket. He stared down at the smudged, slightly crumpled image, his jaw tightening. He'd taken the picture himself just a few months ago, when Margo first came to his family as an au pair. In the photo Margo and her charge, Josh's little brother, Georgie, were standing in front of the family home in Ohio; Margo held Georgie's hand and smiled at the camera. "How could she do it?" Josh whispered to himself. He would never understand it, not as long as he lived.

"Can I help you?" the young woman at the reception desk asked cheerfully as Josh entered the office.

"I hope so," said Josh. "I'd like to talk to the person in charge of hiring."

"Ms. D'Angelo is the manager. Her desk is right around the corner. Come with me."

They found Ms. D'Angelo busily sorting through a stack of envelopes. She looked up with a smile as Josh approached her desk. "Hello. Are you interested in filling out a job application?" she inquired.

"Oh, no." Josh held out the photo of Margo and Georgie. "I was hoping . . . Can you tell me if you've ever seen the girl in this picture? By any chance did you interview or hire her?"

Ms. D'Angelo pushed her glasses up on her nose and studied the photo. After a long moment she shook her head. "No, I don't think so," she said. "I don't recognize her."

Josh had been holding his breath, his whole body tense with expectation. Now he sighed with disappointment, his chin dropping onto his chest.

"Well, just a minute. Caroline!" Ms. D'Angelo called after the retreating receptionist. "Let's ask her. Not everyone makes it back to my desk, after all!"

Caroline rejoined them, and Ms. D'Angelo passed the picture to her. "Has she been in here, do you recall?"

"No, I don't think so." Then Caroline squinted, peering more closely at the picture. "Wait—yes!" she declared. Josh's heart leapt to his throat. Caroline nodded emphatically. "The hair is different—she wears it pulled back—and she wears glasses now, too. But I would swear this is Margaret Wake, the girl we hired for the Fowler wedding. Remember?" she asked the manager.

Ms. D'Angelo's eyes brightened. "That's right!" she confirmed. "Margaret—now I recognize her. Yes, she came in and filled out an application, but at the time we didn't have any openings." She clucked her tongue sadly. "We ended up calling her at the last minute, after that poor young woman was killed by the hit-and-run driver."

My hunch was right! Josh thought, elated. *Fowler. That's Lila, who's friends with the Wakefield sisters. Of course: Wakefield, Wake. What an appropriate name for Margo to choose!* When she had

66

lived with his family, Margo had called herself Michelle, and now she was Margaret.

It was all becoming appallingly clear to him now. Margo wanted to be at the Fowlers' big party, so she killed that other woman in order to get her catering job. Was murderous violence Margo's answer to everything? Was no crime too heinous?

"Yes, that's Margaret, all right." Ms. D'Angelo returned the photograph to Josh. "We were just about to mail her paycheck." Shuffling through the envelopes on her desk, she waved one at Josh.

Eagerly, Josh leaned forward, trying to read the address on the envelope. It looked like Wentworth Avenue, but he couldn't see the number.

Suddenly he realized that both Caroline and Ms. D'Angelo were staring at him suspiciously. "What do you want with her, anyway?" Ms. D'Angelo asked, shoving the envelope back into the middle of the stack. "We don't give out information about our employees to strangers, you know."

Josh took a step backward. He'd gotten a good, solid lead on Margo's whereabouts. She was probably renting a room in an apartment or boarding-house of some kind, maybe even a motel. He'd just have to canvass the entire street.

"I don't need any information. Thanks," he muttered, turning to hurry from the building.

Sprinting to the curb, Josh jumped into his car and turned the key in the ignition. Tires squealing, he pulled into traffic and gunned the engine. *I've almost found her!* he thought, buoyed by his unexpected success. Margo was living somewhere on Wentworth Avenue in Sweet Valley . . . and Josh planned to get to her before the paycheck from Valley Caterers did.

Margo tossed her bikini onto the bed of her room in the guest house and slipped into a silk bathrobe, belting it snugly around her waist. After baking herself in the sun by the pool for a couple of hours, she felt deliciously warm. Extending an arm, she stroked her golden skin, pretending it was Todd touching her.

"How about dinner and a movie, Todd?" she said out loud, watching herself in the mirror as she spoke. She tilted her head and flashed her dimple. "How about dinner and a movie?" She added a laugh—a fond, lighthearted, knowing laugh, the kind of laughter she'd heard bubble up from Elizabeth when she was with Todd. Margo smiled at her reflection in the mirror. *That was perfect! I think I'm ready for him. Yes, I know I'm ready!*

Perching on the edge of the bed, Margo reached for the telephone. Her heart pounding, she dialed the phone number she'd memorized—

Todd's number. It was Thursday, December 23, a day she knew she would never forget as long as she lived. She was about to make her first date with her new boyfriend!

Todd answered after three rings. "Hello?"

Margo was so excited, she could hardly speak. Finally, she got the words out, and she was delighted by how much like Elizabeth she sounded. "Hi, Todd. It's me. What are you up to?"

"Hi, Liz! Not a lot. How about you?"

"Oh, I'm just hanging out," she replied. "What do you say we get together tonight? Dinner and a movie, maybe? There's an old black-and-white classic playing at the Plaza Theater—Dana says it's great."

"But I thought you were going Christmas caroling with Enid tonight."

Margo's lips curved in a sly smile. Todd was halfway right, of course. The real Elizabeth *would* be caroling with Enid that night; that was how the *future* Elizabeth, Margo, could make this daring move. "Enid canceled on me," Margo lied. "She's coming down with a cold." *And she'll be coming down with more than a cold soon, if I have anything to do with it!* "So how 'bout it?"

"Sure," Todd responded enthusiastically. "It sounds like fun. I'll pick you up around six, OK?"

"Uh . . ." Margo hesitated. The timing was going to be tricky—Elizabeth would be getting ready to meet Enid at the same time Todd arrived to pick up Margo for their date. *I'll wait outside for him,* she decided. *We'll just clear out of there fast.* "Six is fine," Margo agreed. "I'll see you then. And, Todd—" Her voice trembled with emotion. "I love you."

"I love you, too, Liz," he said, his own voice husky.

Margo hung up the phone and then hugged herself, an ear-to-ear grin on her face. No one had ever spoken to her in that tone of voice; no one had ever loved her. *At last!* she thought, delirious with happiness. At last she was going to have the things that Elizabeth Wakefield and kids like her took for granted: a loving family, a handsome and devoted boyfriend . . .

"A date," Margo said out loud, laughing triumphantly. "I have a date tonight." A date with Todd Wilkins, star of the varsity basketball team, the most popular boy at Sweet Valley High!

What on earth am I going to wear? she wondered, looking around the room at her skimpy wardrobe, much of which was lying crumpled and dirty on the floor. Since arriving in Sweet Valley, she'd purchased a few items of clothing and shoplifted some others; she'd also filched various accessories from the Wakefield twins' drawers. Margo wrinkled her nose. Nothing she owned was quite right for this very special occasion, though. Nothing was good enough for Todd.

"I want something new," she announced. "I want something unbelievably sexy." She laughed again, her eyes dancing with anticipation. *Todd thinks it's just dinner and a movie. Boy, is he in for a surprise!* In Margo's opinion she was taking over in the nick of time; Elizabeth's image definitely needed a bit of an overhaul. *She should take a page from twin sister Jessica's book,* Margo mused. Now, Jessica had real fashion sense. Jessica understood the advantages of high hemlines and low necklines—she wouldn't be caught *dead* wearing jeans and an Oxford shirt on a date. When Margo was in charge, Elizabeth would adopt a much hotter style . . . and tonight Todd Wilkins would be treated to a sneak preview.

Still high as a kite from the thrill of successfully making a date with Todd, Margo reached for the phone again. She wanted to go shopping . . . and who better to shop with than Lila Fowler? *Now, there's a choice best friend,* Margo thought as she dialed Lila's number. She'd observed that Elizabeth and Lila weren't exactly bosom buddies. That was going to have to change, too.

In the meantime I'll just have to pretend to be Jessica. No problem! James *had* been very useful to her for a while. Thanks to his spying and picture taking, Margo felt she knew Jessica even better than she knew Elizabeth.

Ten minutes later, having arranged to meet Lila at the Valley Mall, Margo stuffed a wad of cash into her handbag and swung out the door, whistling. *This must be the holiday spirit,* she exulted. Shopping at the mall, going out on the town with her gorgeous boyfriend—it was almost as if she'd begun her new life already. What a fabulous Christmas present to herself!

Lila pursed her lips as she contemplated her reflection in the dressing-room mirror at Bibi's, an exclusive boutique at the mall. "Maybe I should lose the scarf," she said to Jessica. "Don't you think it's a little . . . matronly?"

Jessica fingered the boldly patterned silk scarf that was looped loosely around Lila's neck. "Actually, I like it," she commented. "It's dressy—it's elegant. And then, see? You wear the dress with the scarf to the opera or whatever, but afterward . . ." Jessica unknotted the scarf and whipped it off with a dramatic flourish. "Voilà! Sexy, basic black for a night out in Paris."

Lila pivoted, admiring the way the short black jersey dress hugged her curves. "You're right," she agreed. "It works. I'll take it."

Running the scarf idly through her fingers, Jessica took a step back and gazed with pleasure at her friend. "You're really going to be the most beautiful girl in Paris, Li."

Lila grinned. "Well, that's a given, but it's nice of you to say so!"

"What a great way to spend Christmas," Jessica continued. "Jetting off to Paris with your parents . . ."

Lila turned her back so Jessica could unzip her. "It's a dream come true," she admitted. She reflected back on previous Christmases, before her mother came back into her life, when it was just she and her dad. Fowler Crest was always beautifully decorated for the holidays, and the staff would cook up a mouth-watering Christmas feast; George Fowler would shower his daughter with extravagant gifts—the fanciest toys and dolls when she was a little girl, breathtaking jewelry when she grew older. Still, those holiday celebrations had seemed hollow, contrived. *Dad's mind was always on business, not on me,* Lila recalled, surprised that she no longer felt bitter. *He'd be looking at his watch while I unwrapped my presents. The minute Christmas dinner was over, he'd disappear. Since Mom moved back from Europe, though, and they fell in love again and got married . . .*

"It's going to be different this year," Lila said out loud. "We're finally a *family*." She laughed wryly. "Believe it or not, Jess, that was all I ever wanted for Christmas—to be part of a family like yours. Is that corny or what?"

Jessica's lips twisted in a funny, hard-to-read smile. "No, it's not corny at all."

The two girls emerged from the dressing room, their arms laden with garments. "Now it's *your* turn," Lila declared generously after paying for her purchases. "Lytton and Brown's is having a holiday sale—want to check out their junior stuff?"

Jessica nodded. "Sure. Whatever you want to do, Li."

Diving into the mob of holiday shoppers, Lila led the way to the big department store at the east end of the mall. "Are you looking for anything in particular?" she asked Jessica as they flipped through the racks.

"Something to wear out tonight with T—with James," Jessica replied. "Something funky."

"Hmm . . ." Lila eyed a bright red miniskirt with a short, sailor-style jacket. "Cute. *Too* cute," she concluded, pushing it aside.

"What do you think about this?" Jessica held up a bronze silk tank top.

"Not your color," Lila said with an emphatic shake of her head. She narrowed her eyes, giving the tank top a closer look. "Actually, that's *my* color. Here, let me see that!"

Lila reached for the hanger, ready for a wrestling match. To her surprise Jessica handed it right over. "I can't believe you're giving up so easily!" Lila exclaimed.

"Why not?" responded Jessica. "You were right—it *will* look better on you."

Lila lifted her dark eyebrows. Since when was Jessica so thoughtful, so selfless? "You honestly think so?"

Jessica smiled. "Of course! There has to be at least one thing in this store that would suit me better than it would suit you, though. Help me find it, OK?"

Ten minutes later they agreed on a teal-blue dress with a deep, U-shaped neckline and a very short, flouncy skirt. "It'll knock James's socks off," Lila predicted as the clerk rang up the sale.

Jessica unzipped her purse, a secretive sparkle in her eyes. "It better!"

The saleswoman announced the total. Lila burst out laughing as Jessica pulled a wad of cash from her purse. "What did you do, Jess, rob a bank?" she joked.

Jessica's face turned scarlet. Peeling off a few bills, she quickly stuffed the rest back into her purse. "It's just, um . . . baby-sitting money I've been saving up for Christmas," she explained. She took her change from the clerk. "C'mon, let's get a cone at Casey's. My treat."

At Casey's Ice Cream Parlor, Lila picked Million Dollar Mocha, her signature flavor—two scoops in a dish. Jessica went for broke, ordering a hot-fudge sundae with whipped cream, nuts, and a cherry. As they dug into their ice cream, Lila contemplated her friend. *What's with Jess today?* she wondered. She was being so attentive and complimentary, asking Lila's opinion and hanging on her every pronouncement; she seemed so grateful just to have Lila's company. *Maybe she's feeling sentimental 'cause it's the holidays,* Lila surmised. *Or maybe it's me. Maybe I'm the one who's different.* Lila spooned up the last drop of ice cream. Now that her parents were back together, she was happy, relaxed, less self-centered. Wasn't it only natural that some of her new attitude would rub off on the people around her?

With a groan Jessica pushed back her empty ice-cream dish. "I can't believe I ate that. But, boy, was it good!"

"You may not be able to squeeze into that new dress now," Lila teased.

"So let's burn some calories." Jessica hopped to her feet, ready for action. "We still have to hit the whole west side of the mall!"

James sat on a bar stool at a seedy roadhouse in Moon Beach early Thursday evening, staring at the pay phone. *Just do it,* he told himself. *Quit putting it off.*

Instead of standing up, though, he gestured to the bartender. "Got any pretzels back there, Ted?"

Ted shoved a bowl of peanuts in James's direction. "Try these," he suggested. "So do you want a drink or not, bud?"

James shook his head. "Naw. I don't touch the stuff anymore." He laughed harshly. "I cleaned up my act. Didn't you notice I hadn't been coming around?"

Ted winked. "Man, so many bums hang around here, I can't keep track of all of you!"

Ted lumbered to the other end of the bar to wait on a customer. *A bum—that was me, all right,* James thought, grabbing a handful of salty peanuts. *I had nothing better to do with my time than hang around dumps like this. Then I met Jessica. . . .*

James tuned in to the country music ballad playing on the jukebox. A sardonic smile twisted his lips as he listened to the lyrics. Come to think of it, his life was a lot like the song, in which Mr. Always-in-Trouble meets a sweet, good-hearted girl and turns himself around. *Corny, but it's true. Being with Jessica changed me,* James reflected. *I started to think I could make something out of myself. I wanted to be a better person, for her sake.*

Yeah, that was the good part—meeting Jessica. The only problem was that he'd met Margo first.

James dropped his head into his hands. He felt drunk even though he wasn't; he felt like bursting into tears. "I love you, Jessica Wakefield," he whispered. "I never got a chance to tell you, but I really and truly do." He never got a chance . . . and now he never would. He *did* love her, and that was why he had to do what he was about to do.

Shoving back his bar stool, James got to his feet and staggered over to the pay phone. *Make it quick,* he counseled himself. *Don't give yourself a chance to chicken out.*

He jammed a hand in the pocket of his jeans and came up with some change. Sticking a coin in the pay phone, he punched in Jessica's number, more than half hoping she wouldn't be home.

She answered the phone right away, though, as if she'd been waiting for his call—which she probably had. "James, is that you?" she asked.

The sweet hopefulness in her voice made James feel sick. *Get it over with,* he commanded himself. "Yeah, it's me. I just wanted to let you know we won't be getting together tonight. We won't be seeing each other again."

He heard Jessica catch her breath on the other end of the line. "What do—what do you mean?" she stuttered, confused.

"I mean it's over. This is good-bye, Jessica."

"But, James . . . I don't understand." Jessica's voice grew shaky with tears. James bit his lip hard. "How can it be over? I thought we—I thought you—what did I do wrong?" she whispered.

"Nothing," he said gruffly. "It's nothing you did—don't take it personally. It's just not there for me, OK?"

Now Jessica was crying softly, and the sound almost broke James's heart. He pounded his left fist against the wall. *Hang up on her. Get it over with!* But he couldn't bring himself to do it. With his right hand he gripped the phone tighter. It was the last connection he would ever have with her—he couldn't break it yet.

"Can't I just see you?" Jessica pleaded. "Can't we talk this over in person? Please, James. Where are you? I'll come—"

A wave of longing washed over him. Maybe there *was* a way he could see her one more time, hold her one more time.

"No," he cut in. He had to stick to his guns. He couldn't ever see Jessica again without risking her life, and his own. He didn't have a choice; he had to cut off all contact with her and just pray Margo would leave them both alone. "Look, I said it's over," James repeated harshly as a tear slid down his unshaven jaw. "There's nothing to talk about. I—I never really cared about you. It was just a way to pass the time. Good-bye, Jessica."

Knowing he was on the verge of breaking down altogether, James slammed down the receiver. Closing his eyes, he rested his forehead against the pay phone, his last words echoing in his brain. *Good-bye, Jessica.*

Jessica sat cross-legged on her bed, the telephone receiver cradled against her chest. Sobs racked her slender body. "But *why*, James?" she whispered. "Why?" There was no answer, only the sound of the dial tone. James was gone.

Jessica hung up the phone, trading it for a handful of tissues. She pressed them against her face to sop up the tears that wouldn't stop flowing. *What did I do wrong?* There had to be an explanation. Something she said, something she did . . . *But he said he never really cared. Why? Why didn't he love me? Why doesn't anybody love me?*

Loneliness settled over Jessica like a heavy, smothering blanket. It was almost more than she could bear. Last night Elizabeth had made it clear she didn't want anything to do with Jessica—she was determined to go on hating her and blaming her even though she still didn't know the worst. And tonight, James . . .

It is *me*, Jessica thought, throwing herself down on the bed and burying her tearstained face in the pillow. *I'm horrible and unlovable. No one wants me. I don't belong here anymore, in this family, in this town. I might as well be . . .*

The thought was too terrible to contemplate. *But it's true*, Jessica concluded as she curled up in a tiny ball, wishing she could make herself disappear altogether. *I should've died in the crash, not Sam. No one would've missed me.* And then she wouldn't have had to live with the torture of knowing what she'd done to Elizabeth and Sam. She wouldn't have had to live with this loneliness.

Chapter 6

"So you didn't even tell me what you think of my new dress," Margo, in the guise of Elizabeth, said playfully to Todd.

They were sitting at an outdoor table at the Box Tree Café in downtown Sweet Valley, drinking iced tea and sharing a plate of appetizers. Thunder rumbled in the distance, but the storm was still a long way off; overhead the night sky was clear and shimmering with stars. The same breeze that ruffled Todd's dark hair raised goose bumps on Margo's bare arms. *He's so incredibly handsome,* she thought ecstatically. *And he's mine—all mine!*

"It's beautiful, Liz," Todd replied with a bemused smile. "You look fantastic. Maybe we shouldn't hide a dress like that in the dark at the movies—we could go to the Beach Disco instead."

Margo considered the proposal. Dancing might be fun. She imagined a slow song under the stars, her body pressed close against Todd's. It was a delicious prospect. Then again . . . "Let's stick with the movie idea," she said, lowering her lashes seductively. "I like that part about being together in the dark."

Under the table Todd brushed his foot against hers, sending a shiver up Margo's spine. It was all she could do to keep from pouncing on him right then and there. *Elizabeth is more demure than that,* Margo reminded herself. *Stay in character. Everything's going so well—don't blow it.* It was hard to contain herself, though; it was hard to act as if this were just another casual dinner date with her steady boyfriend Todd when in reality it was the most exciting night of her life. *The most exciting so far, that is,* Margo reflected. *Just wait until New Year's Eve!*

Their entrées arrived. Todd started eating, but Margo was too keyed up to be hungry. She poked at the pasta with her fork, chattering brightly about things she'd learned from reading Elizabeth's journal. "By the way, did I ever tell you about the last *Oracle* staff meeting?" she asked Todd, filling him in when he shook his head.

Telling the story made Margo wonder how Elizabeth could stand working with that bossy Penny Ayala. "You know, sometimes Penny really treats the rest of us like babies," she commented. "We can't do *anything* without asking her permission first."

Todd raised his eyebrows. "Well, she's the editor in chief, right? That's just her job."

"I suppose so." Margo bit back a laugh as an idea struck her. *If you ask me, Penny's been editor long enough—it's time someone else had a shot at the top. It's Elizabeth's turn! When I become Elizabeth, no more of this staff-writer stuff. I want power.*

Mentally, Margo flipped to the next page of the diary. "Remember talking about double-dating with Enid and Hugh to see a play in L.A.?" she asked Todd. "When do you want to go, and what do you think we should see?"

"Well, we could—"

"Oh, let's not see a boring old play," Margo interrupted. "How about going to a concert instead? We could hear . . ." She rattled off the names of a few heavy-metal bands.

This time Todd's eyebrows shot up so far, they almost disappeared into his scalp. "Since when do you like that kind of music?"

I almost forgot—Elizabeth's a bit of a fuddy-duddy that way. "Come on, Todd, I was just *kidding!*" Margo assured him with a high-pitched laugh. "I'd rather die than go to one of those concerts where the music is so loud you can't hear for a week afterward, and people trample all over each other. No, of course we should see a play, or maybe go to the symphony or the ballet."

Todd's smile was a shade uncertain. "Whatever you want, Liz. You and Enid can work it out and let me know."

With a smug smile Margo twirled some fettucine around her fork and lifted it to her lips. She'd never been on a date like this before—she was having such a good time! *The food, the conversation—everything's perfect,* she thought with satisfaction. *I bet Todd's not used to having this much fun with the* real *Elizabeth. He's just crazy about me—I can feel it!*

They skipped dessert so as not to be late for the movie. The lights in the Art Deco theater began dimming just as they hurried through the door. "Let's sit here," Margo whispered to Todd, propelling him into the back row and a pair of old-fashioned courting seats with no armrest between them.

As the black-and-white movie started, Margo snuggled close to Todd, squeezing his hand tightly. She waited for him to put his arm around her, but he was a little bit slow about making the first move. *No problem—I'll make it!* Margo thought, nuzzling his neck and then resting her head on his shoulder.

I'm really doing great, she decided with a happy sigh. Unlike Enid, Todd didn't seem suspicious in the least. *And why should he be?* Margo wondered. *I'm just like Elizabeth—I'm in love with him. That's all he needs to know, right?*

Margo gazed up at Todd's chiseled, masculine profile. Being with him like this was a dream come true. Yes, she was falling madly in love with Todd Wilkins, the cutest, most desirable boy in Sweet Valley. And the best thing was, she didn't have to win him over. She didn't have to agonize over him, wondering if he'd return her affection. As Elizabeth Wakefield, Margo didn't have to risk rejection ever again. Todd Wilkins was already hers.

"Don't take me home yet," Elizabeth begged Todd as they climbed into the BMW after the movie. "Let's go for a drive."

Todd started the engine. "Do you have anyplace specific in mind?"

She smiled at him, a meaningful look in her eyes. "How about Miller's Point?"

Miller's Point was at the top of a dead-end road, on a high bluff overlooking Sweet Valley. It was a popular parking spot, and Todd and Elizabeth had ended many a date by driving up there for a few minutes—or hours—of quiet time alone. Ordinarily Todd would have been very enthusiastic about Elizabeth's suggestion. Tonight, though . . .

He glanced sharply at Elizabeth. She leaned toward him, pressing herself against his arm. "Pretty please?" she murmured.

"Well . . . sure." Todd steered the BMW out of the parking lot, heading north toward Miller's Point. "That sounds nice."

Elizabeth chuckled low in her throat. "It'll be more than nice," she promised, placing a hand just above his knee and massaging the muscles in his thigh.

For some unaccountable reason Todd found himself recoiling from his girlfriend's touch. *She's really not herself tonight,* Todd thought, shifting uneasily in his seat. First she'd showed up in a short, flirty dress that looked like something Jessica would wear—not Liz's style at all, especially for a casual night at the movies. Then the nonstop chatter over dinner. *And she was all over me during the movie. I mean, not that I mind! But it's weird.*

They soon left the streetlights of downtown Sweet Valley behind and started climbing a narrow, tree-shadowed road. Reaching Miller's Point, Todd coasted up to the guardrail and killed the engine.

"Good, we're the only car up here," Elizabeth exclaimed, wrapping her arms around Todd's neck and kissing him passionately.

All at once something clicked in Todd's brain. Elizabeth was affectionate, but not *this* affectionate. She never threw herself at him like this . . . but recently someone else had.

The dress! Todd thought, pulling back from her with a start. It was more Jessica's style because it *was* Jessica's dress. That was what this strange behavior reminded him of: the desperate way Jessica kept after him when they were dating briefly during Elizabeth's trial. The girl in his arms was *Jessica*, not Elizabeth!

Todd suppressed an urge to leap from the car and sprint for the main road. *No, it can't be,* he told himself. *You're losing your mind. Just calm down.*

He couldn't help shrugging away from her, though. "Where are you going?" Elizabeth—or Jessica—murmured, trying to pull him close again. "We're finally alone. How about a little hug?"

"I just thought maybe we could talk," Todd said lamely. "I want to hear about your plans for vacation. What are you going to do while I'm away skiing?"

Elizabeth laughed. "Do we really need to go over that now?" She put her face close to his, brushing his lips with her own. "Isn't this"—she kissed him softly—"more interesting?"

It was, without a doubt, and yet Todd still felt spooked. As he returned Elizabeth's warm, eager kisses, he grew more and more uncomfortable . . . and more and more convinced he was actually kissing Jessica. *But why?* he wondered, his head swimming. If Jessica wanted to see him, why would she masquerade as Elizabeth? Why would she do something this far out and . . . twisted? What kind of trouble was she trying to stir up now?

I've got to get out of here, Todd thought, feeling guilty even though he hadn't done anything wrong. *In case it is Jessica—in case I'm kissing my girl-friend's sister instead of my girlfriend!* Todd put both hands against Elizabeth's shoulders and gave her a little push. "I'm sorry, Liz, but I really have to be getting home. I have to get up early in the morning to . . ."

"To what?" she asked, her forehead wrinkling with displeasure.

"To finish my Christmas shopping."

"Well—" Elizabeth laughed. "OK. As long as you're shopping for *me*," she teased.

With an ill-disguised sigh of relief, Todd started the engine. Shifting to reverse, he hit the gas, gravel flying. On the road again, he relaxed some-what, but he kept his foot heavy on the gas pedal, and they reached Calico Drive in record time.

By the time he pulled up in front of the Wake-fields', however, Todd was having second thoughts about his second thoughts. Shifting into neutral and letting the engine idle, he glanced at Elizabeth, who was gazing out the window, her expression soft and pensive. Suddenly she looked and felt familiar to him again. Was it Jessica pretending to be Eliza-beth, or was he with the real Elizabeth after all?

Maybe I've been imagining things, Todd thought, his emotions doing another flip-flop. *Maybe she's just got something on her mind, and that's why she's acting strangely. She was pretty upset about that anonymous note yesterday.* "Penny for your thoughts, Liz," Todd said.

Elizabeth turned to him with a radiant smile. "I was just thinking how lucky I am to be going out with a guy like you," she replied. "And how perfectly, blissfully happy."

Todd smiled back, crookedly. "I feel lucky, too. Uh, you should probably be getting inside—it's late." He unbuckled his seat belt. "C'mon, I'll walk you to the door."

"No," Elizabeth said quickly. "Don't bother. I'll just run in." Bending forward, she gave him a fast kiss, meanwhile reaching for the door handle. "Good night, Todd. I love you."

Todd raised his eyebrows. One minute she was all over him; the next, she couldn't wait to get out of the car. "See you tomorrow night," he said.

"Tomorrow night?" she echoed as she stepped out onto the curb.

"Christmas Eve dinner—your mom invited me over, remember?"

"Of course!" Elizabeth blew him a kiss. "So long."

Todd watched her for a moment as she hurried toward the house. Then he shifted the BMW into first gear, shaking his head. *What a weird night,* he thought wryly.

As he pulled away from the curb, he glanced once more at the house. He blinked, surprised. Was he seeing things, or had Elizabeth just darted around the side of the house toward the backyard? Why would she do that instead of entering through the front door or the garage?

But now the yard was empty, bathed in peaceful moonlight. Todd shook his head again. "You're ready for the nuthouse, Wilkins," he muttered to himself as he roared off down the street.

At the end of Elizabeth's street he turned right, heading for his own home on Country Club Drive. Already the evening with Elizabeth—or Jessica— was starting to take on the fuzzy unreality of a dream. *What should I say to Liz next time I see her?* Todd wondered, scratching his head. *Or should I even say anything at all?* If that *was* actually Jessica and not Elizabeth, then Elizabeth would be furious. She'd be livid! Todd really didn't want to stir up more trouble between the two sisters; Elizabeth was still steaming about the stolen letter, and he knew her whole family was suffering because of it.

But if all the trauma she's been through is turning Jessica into some kind of psycho . . . A shiver ran through Todd's body, making his hair stand on end. What kind of sick stunt might she try next?

"Good night, Mom—night, Dad," Elizabeth called to her parents. She smiled as she padded down the hall to her bedroom. She was so hoarse from caroling, she barely recognized her own voice. *I should call Todd and pretend to be a secret admirer,* she thought mischievously, *and make him guess my identity!*

It was kind of late for a phone call, though; she always liked to hear Todd's voice before she went to sleep, but she didn't want to wake up his parents. Stepping into the bathroom to wash her face and brush her teeth, Elizabeth listened for sounds from her sister's bedroom. All was quiet; Jessica must have gone to bed early. *I wonder what's going on with her and James,* Elizabeth mused as she patted her face dry with a towel. *I thought they had a date, but Mom and Dad said she didn't leave her room all night.*

Back in her bedroom Elizabeth flicked off the light and pulled back the covers. She was about to climb into bed when she heard an engine being revved on the street outside. *That's funny. . . .* Elizabeth didn't know much about cars, but she was pretty sure she recognized that particular rumble: It sounded just like Todd's car.

Elizabeth went to the window and pushed back the curtain, staring out into the night. As she peered up the street, she glimpsed a car speeding away. In the blink of an eye, it left the pool of light cast by a streetlamp and faded into the shadows. Still, Elizabeth could have sworn it was a black BMW.

She let the curtain fall, shaking her head. *It couldn't have been Todd,* she told herself. It just didn't make any sense. What would he be doing cruising down her street at this hour?

Elizabeth got into bed and pulled the covers up to her chin. How silly, to miss Todd so much that she imagined hearing his car on her street. She closed her eyes, and the melodies of Christmas carols started chasing through her sleepy brain. It really had been a fun evening, going from door to door in Enid's neighborhood singing carols and being plied at each house with plates of Christmas cookies or mugs of steaming hot chocolate. *Deck the halls . . .* Wreck the halls!

Elizabeth's eyes flew open, her cheerful mood dissolving. She had to get that song out of her head before she fell asleep, or nightmares would be sure to follow.

Chapter 7

"I probably don't need to take so much stuff," Lila said to Jessica on Friday morning. "I mean, we're only going for a couple of days, after all. But Paris is Paris. I can't risk not having the right outfit for every occasion!" She sat on the largest of her three overstuffed suitcases, trying to squish it down enough so it could be zipped. "Help me here, would you, Jess?"

Obediently, Jessica knelt next to the suitcase. Lila bore down on it with all her weight, and Jessica yanked the zipper. "Got it," Jessica grunted.

"Thanks." Lila stood up and placed her hands on her hips, surveying her luggage with satisfaction. "That just leaves my cosmetics case. I'm almost ready!"

She beamed at Jessica, expecting to see her

friend beaming right back at her. Instead, Jessica sat down cross-legged on Lila's bed, her chin on her fist and a hangdog look on her face. *Something's bugging her,* Lila speculated. Ordinarily Jessica would be very interested in the process of sorting through clothing and accessories with an eye toward what would go over on the sidewalks of Paris. This morning, though, she seemed thoroughly down in the dumps, a complete turnaround from her bubbly mood the previous afternoon when they went shopping.

"What's the problem?" Lila asked, trying to kid Jessica out of her gloom. "Didn't James like your new dress?"

To her surprise Jessica burst into tears. "Jessica, what's the matter?" Lila exclaimed, scurrying to her friend's side.

"We b-broke up." Jessica sobbed into her hands. "Last night. He called and told me he didn't want to see me again."

Lila put an arm around Jessica's shoulders. "Just like that? Over the *phone*?" she asked incredulously.

Jessica nodded, wiping her eyes on her shirtsleeve. "Can you believe it?"

Lila shook her head, her eyes flashing with indignation. "What a heartless, cowardly jerk! What did he say? What was his reason?"

"He didn't even *have* a reason," Jessica wailed.

"He just had enough of me, that's all. He never really cared about me—he was just looking for something to do."

Lila handed her a tissue. "Why didn't you tell me sooner?"

Jessica blew her nose loudly. "It's too depressing. I haven't even told my family about it. I didn't want to ruin your trip to P-P-Paris. . . ."

Jessica started bawling again. Lila enfolded her in a big hug. "Oh, Jess, I hate to leave you like this! With Amy going away, too, to that sportscasters' convention with her mom." *And she can't exactly lean on Elizabeth's shoulder,* Lila thought. "But you'll be OK," she said with soothing certainty. "He was just a dumb guy—there are lots more out there who are nicer and cuter and smarter. Don't let it get you down."

"You're right." Jessica pushed Lila away. Tossing back her hair, she attempted a brave smile. "I feel better already, just from spilling my guts. I'll be fine, really. So don't worry about me, OK?"

Lila gave Jessica's shoulder a supportive squeeze. "OK." Hopping to her feet, she crossed to the bathroom and began throwing makeup and toiletries into her cosmetics case. "Just promise you won't return that cute new dress, all right?" she called back over her shoulder. "Save it for your first date with Mr. Right, whoever he turns out to be."

Jessica blew her nose again, her voice muffled

by the tissue. "What cute new dress?"

"The teal-blue one from—Shoot, where's my mousse?" Lila grabbed a handful of cotton balls from a glass jar on the vanity and tossed them in the case. *Maybe I should drop the dress subject,* she reflected. *It'll just remind her of James.* "Never mind," she hollered.

She returned to the bedroom, lugging the cosmetics case. *"Voilà. Je suis . . ."* She snapped her fingers. "What's the word for 'ready'?"

Jessica rolled her eyes. "If Ms. Dalton could hear you now."

"I'm sure my French will improve a thousand percent while I'm away," Lila predicted. "I'll be teacher's pet, just you wait."

"Lila!" a voice called from the hallway. The bedroom door opened and Grace Fowler peeked in. "Honey, the car is here to take us to the airport. Anytime you're ready, I'll send someone up for your bags."

Lila gestured at her luggage. "I'm all set!"

Mrs. Fowler smiled. "Good. We'll see you in a few days, Jessica—merry Christmas."

Jessica smiled feebly. "Merry Christmas, Mrs. Fowler."

Lila slipped on the cropped black jacket that went with her red-and-black traveling dress. "So how do I look?" she asked Jessica, twirling.

"Great," Jessica said glumly.

Lila slung her purse over her shoulder. *I'm on my way to Paris!* she thought, thrilled from her head to her toes. It was her favorite city in the whole world, and she'd be traveling with her favorite people: her mother and father, who'd gotten married again and were totally in love. What could be better?

Jessica walked Lila downstairs to the front door. "Have a fun trip, Li," she said morosely.

Lila's exuberant mood faltered. Jessica was going to have an absolutely rotten Christmas—it just wasn't fair. "I'll be thinking about you," Lila promised.

The two girls hugged good-bye. As she pressed her face briefly against Jessica's, a strange foreboding filled Lila's heart; she had a sudden unaccountable intuition that her friend's troubles went deeper than a broken romance. *There's danger,* Lila sensed. *Something could happen while I'm away. I may never see her again.*

Her arms tightening around Jessica, Lila pushed the odd premonition from her mind. "Take care," she whispered.

"I really enjoy the sunset service on Christmas Eve," Mr. Wakefield declared as he struck a match to light the candles on the dining-room table. "The carols, the readings." He started singing cheerfully. "Deck the halls with boughs of holly . . ."

Elizabeth almost dropped the salad bowl she was carrying. "How about putting on a CD, Dad?" she suggested quickly. "Everybody likes that Bing Crosby one." *And it doesn't have "Deck the Halls" on it!* she added silently to herself.

Elizabeth had enough on her mind without thinking about the anonymous Secret Santa note. Right before Todd had arrived for dinner, Elizabeth had joined her mother in the kitchen to see if she could help get the meal together. "You were already a big help this afternoon," Mrs. Wakefield had replied. "Dusting and vacuuming the whole house."

"Not me, Mom. I was at Olivia's all afternoon," Elizabeth had reminded her mother. But Mrs. Wakefield had insisted. "Who else was sneaking just-baked Christmas cookies from the rack while they were cooling?" she'd teased her daughter. "Honey, I *saw* you."

It must've been Jessica, Elizabeth had thought, dropping the subject. *Mom's just confused. The holidays are always so hectic.* A slip like that didn't have to mean her mother was going off the deep end. But Elizabeth was still unsettled by the conversation.

Shaking off her preoccupation, Elizabeth turned to watch as Steven walked around the table, filling everyone's glass with sparkling cider. "It looks beautiful, doesn't it?" he said to his sister.

Elizabeth nodded. Draped in a cranberry-red cloth accented with crisp white linen napkins and sparkling with silver and crystal, the table *did* look exquisite. Elizabeth had arranged the centerpiece of evergreen boughs herself. The whole house was bright with holiday decorations, just as in previous years. *Yes, it all looks beautiful,* Elizabeth thought. *But that doesn't change the fact that—*

"Dinner's ready," Mrs. Wakefield called from the kitchen. "Will someone help me carry the food in?"

Elizabeth, Todd, Jessica, and Steven all crowded into the kitchen. A minute later the table was laden with platters and bowls. "Wow, this looks delicious, Mrs. Wakefield," Todd said as he took a seat across from Elizabeth and next to Jessica.

Mrs. Wakefield gave him a bright smile. "I like to go all out on occasions like this," she explained. "It's really special for us all to be together on Christmas Eve."

"Hear, hear," Steven said, raising his glass. "Happy holidays, everybody."

Elizabeth thought she saw Jessica flinch, and she had a hard time smiling herself. "Happy holidays," she echoed, lifting her glass. Jessica's lips also formed the words, but no sound came out.

There was an awkward pause. "Well," Mr. Wakefield said with forced cheerfulness, "let's dig in."

A silence fell over the table as everyone began eating. Outside there was a sudden crash of thun-

100

der. Elizabeth jumped, dropping her fork with a clatter. "I—I guess that storm that's been threatening is finally here," she said lamely.

"Yep, we're going to have a Southern California version of a white Christmas," Todd quipped with false heartiness. "A *wet* Christmas."

Lightning flickered; Elizabeth braced herself for another thunderous boom. Meanwhile Steven struggled to keep the conversation flowing. "This is the best lamb I've ever tasted, Mom," he raved. "Is it a new recipe?"

"No, it's the same old way I always fix it."

"I guess I just appreciate your great cooking more now that I'm trying to cook for myself up at school," Steven explained.

"We really should get out the video camera," Mr. Wakefield interjected, "and get a shot of this feast before it's completely devoured. Son?"

Obediently, Steven trotted off to find the camcorder. Returning, he aimed it at his family and Todd. "It's Christmas Eve and Todd's over for dinner," Steven narrated into the microphone. "Mom whipped up an amazing feast, as usual." He zoomed in on the leg of lamb. "OK, everybody, smile for Santa!"

Elizabeth stretched her mouth in a fake smile; Jessica did the same, with even less success. Even Todd looked distinctly uncomfortable, Elizabeth observed. *What a terrific moment for the Wake-*

101

field family, she thought ironically, waving the camera away as Steven pointed it in her direction. *I'm sure glad we caught it on film!*

Steven turned the camera on Mrs. Wakefield. "Here's the provider of our bountiful feast—my mom, Alice Wakefield. Happy Christmas Eve, Mom!"

With a queasy, anxious feeling in the pit of her stomach, Elizabeth watched as her mother smiled brightly for the camera. *Mom looks OK,* Elizabeth observed. *She's acting like everything's normal. So where did that bizarre stuff about cleaning the house and stealing cookies come from?*

Another burst of thunder shattered the night. Elizabeth's fingers inadvertently tightened on the dinner roll she was buttering, crushing it. *Well, if Mom's a little out of it tonight, she's not the only one,* Elizabeth thought. For some reason, she was so jittery, she could barely hold her fork.

Steven was still gamely trying to keep the conversation alive. "So, guys," he said, putting the camera aside and addressing his sisters and Todd. "What did everybody do last night to celebrate the start of vacation?"

"Enid and I went—" Elizabeth began.

"Liz and I went—" Todd said simultaneously.

They both bit off their sentences and stared across the table at one another in surprise. "What were you about to say?" Elizabeth asked, puzzled.

"I went caroling with Enid last night."

"Umm . . ." Todd shot a glance at Jessica, who continued to eat her dinner in a methodical fashion, seeming oblivious to what was going on around her. "I was just going to say we were talking about seeing that movie at the Plaza," Todd mumbled. "If you hadn't already made plans with Enid."

Elizabeth wrinkled her forehead. "What movie at the Plaza? What are you *talking* about?"

Todd shrugged, darting another look at Jessica, who lifted a forkful of salad to her mouth, her expression a total blank. "I meant to say . . . I guess I was just *thinking* about seeing the movie," he answered lamely. "I was going to mention it to you, but I must've forgotten."

Elizabeth shook her head. She had absolutely no idea what Todd was talking about. *He's getting as bad as Mom!* she thought. *Thinking he talked to me about something when I know for a fact he never did.*

Todd dug into his meal, clearly hoping someone else would pick up the slack in the conversation. Elizabeth gazed thoughtfully at her boyfriend's averted face.

Suddenly, out of the corner of her eye, she glimpsed something at the dining-room window . . . a pale blur against the black of the stormy night. She turned her head quickly, but it was gone. A shiver sped up Elizabeth's spine. Was she imagin-

103

ing things, or had there been a face looking in at them through the rain-streaked panes of the picture window just an instant before?

It was a feeling that had been bothering her a lot lately, a skin-crawling sensation that someone was watching her, and that if she could turn quickly enough, she would catch him—or her, or them—in the act. *I can't stand it any longer.* Abruptly Elizabeth jumped to her feet. Striding to the window, she yanked the drapes closed.

Back at the table Steven had turned to Jessica. "What about you, Jess? Did you do anything fun last night?"

"No," Jessica said flatly. "I didn't do anything. I didn't go anywhere."

Todd twisted in his chair to stare at Jessica. Elizabeth, meanwhile, stared at Todd. *Why does he keep looking at her?* she wondered. *Where is all this tension coming from?*

Suddenly Elizabeth found herself wondering. She and Todd were back together; their relationship was stronger than ever. Todd's little fling with Jessica was a thing of the past, and he was just as angry about the stolen letter as Elizabeth was . . . or was he? Elizabeth took a sip from her glass of sparkling cider; her hand shook, and she spilled some on the tablecloth. Could Jessica still be interested in Todd? Could *Todd* still be interested in Jessica?

Elizabeth suddenly remembered the car she'd seen on the road late the night before. Did Todd and Jessica have some kind of secret rendezvous? *Don't be ridiculous,* she lectured herself. *Jessica said she didn't go out, and Mom and Dad said the same thing. She's in love with this James guy now.* Still, something funny was going on here. The twisted Secret Santa message she received a few days earlier sprang to Elizabeth's mind. Could *Jessica* have sent it? *No, she could never be that mean,* Elizabeth tried to convince herself. *She could never be that sick.*

A thunderous boom shook the night; the lights flickered. Elizabeth jumped again. Across the table Jessica didn't even blink; she continued to sit like a statue, apparently devoid of all emotion. Elizabeth shuddered. Her identical twin seemed like a stranger these days. She pictured Jessica snooping around her room, going through her drawers and reading her diary—she recalled Enid's strange tale about Jessica's impersonation in the library. *She's worse than a stranger,* Elizabeth had to acknowledge. *She's turned into my enemy.*

The meal continued to the strains of Christmas music wafting from the stereo speakers. To Elizabeth the whole scene was a horrible sham. *And this is supposed to be the happiest night of the year,* she thought, bitter and uneasy. *So much for peace on earth, good will toward men!*

A thunderstorm raged outside, but the house was quiet. *Not a creature is stirring,* Jessica mused ironically as she roamed around the empty rooms. *Everyone else is snug in their beds. So how come I can't sleep?*

She wandered into the shadowy living room and flicked the switch on the wall. The Christmas-tree lights blinked on, twinkling magically in the darkness. Jessica curled up in an armchair and gazed at the tree, her mind traveling back to memories of previous Christmas Eves. A sad, wistful smile softened Jessica's face as she remembered how, when she and her sister were little girls, they would sit by the window in their pj's, waiting for Santa, imagining they heard sleigh bells. . . .

Jessica's eyes flickered to the window, and her body tensed, listening. Had she just heard something outside—a scratching against the window-pane?

Crossing over to the living-room window, Jessica peered out into the stormy night. *It was just a tree branch scraping against the glass,* she decided. She shuddered, however, as if feeling a cold draft. Hurrying into the hallway, she checked the front door, making sure it was bolted. Then she darted into the kitchen; good, the sliding glass door to the patio was also latched. On her way back to the stairs, Jessica tried the basement door, which was usually kept locked. To her surprise it opened right up. She pressed the button to lock it, but it just popped up again. *The lock's broken,* she realized with dismay. *I'd better remember to tell Dad to fix it.*

At that moment a bolt of lightning illuminated the pitch-black hallway. Shivering, Jessica hurried toward the stairs, eager to retreat to the security of the second floor, where her family all lay sleeping. Suddenly, she wanted comfort—she wanted to tiptoe into Elizabeth's room the way she used to before the Jungle Prom.

I can't go through Christmas feeling this way, Jessica thought as she mounted the staircase. *Bottling up all my emotions and walking around like a robot. I'm on the verge of a total meltdown.* If she could only talk to Elizabeth about how much she was hurting, about what had happened with James, about the feelings of uselessness and doom that weighed her down. *What did that anonymous card say again? It summed everything up perfectly: "Happy Horrordays."*

In her bedroom Jessica changed into her sleepwear, but she hesitated before climbing into bed. Maybe, in the spirit of Christmas, Elizabeth would be willing to give her another chance. *I'll try again,* Jessica resolved, noiselessly pulling open the bathroom door. *I'll confess my horrible secret and Liz will forgive me and then we'll wait up for Santa together like in the old days.*

Spurred by hope, Jessica tiptoed through the bathroom and eased open Elizabeth's door. The room was dark, but Jessica saw that, like herself, Elizabeth was restless and still awake; she sat on the edge of her bed by the window, watching the storm.

Silent on her bare feet, Jessica approached the bed. Before Jessica could speak, Elizabeth turned her head as if somehow sensing her sister's presence. Obviously startled by the vision of Jessica's ghostly figure, Elizabeth shrieked at the top of her lungs.

"What are you *doing*, sneaking around my room like some kind of ax murderer?" Elizabeth demanded, pressing a hand against her heart.

Elizabeth's screech had started Jessica's own heart pounding madly. She lost her train of thought completely. Not that it mattered; clearly, Elizabeth wasn't in any mood for sisterly confidences. "I thought, with the storm, you might be scared and want some company," Jessica began lamely.

Elizabeth flung out her arm, pointing to the door. "You thought wrong," she snapped. "Please just leave me alone, OK?"

Ducking her head, Jessica shuffled back into her own bedroom. Outside there was a crash of thunder. It sounded to Jessica like some evil spirit laughing at her failure to break through the wall that separated her from her sister.

⁎ ⁎ ⁎

At long last Elizabeth slipped into a restless, troubled sleep. Immediately she began to dream. She was at the prom again; again Todd was named Prom King, and she clapped until the palms of her hands stung. Then she asked Sam to dance. . . .

They were having a blast—Sam really knew some fancy footwork, and his jokes kept Elizabeth laughing. Nevertheless, Elizabeth had time to notice something out of the corner of her eye. . . .

She'd last seen Jessica working the crowd and trying to drum up last-minute Prom Queen votes, so Elizabeth was surprised to glimpse Jessica wasting precious time talking to a stranger, a boy who definitely wasn't a Sweet Valley High student. *One of the Big Mesa crowd looking to stir up trouble,* Elizabeth surmised as Sam twirled her in a dizzy circle. What could Jessica possibly have to say to him?

Sam twirled her, and twirled her. *Stop,* Elizabeth wanted to tell him. *I need to be still—I need to think!* But he didn't stop. Elizabeth kept twirling, growing dizzier and dizzier.

Elizabeth's eyes snapped open, and she stared up at her bedroom ceiling. She realized she wasn't dancing in crazy circles at the Jungle Prom—she was in her own bed, lying perfectly still. It was a relief, and yet it was also frustrating. *I blacked out about a lot of things, but maybe my brain knows what happened that night and is trying to tell me,* she guessed. *If only I didn't always wake up before all the puzzle pieces come together.*

She rolled over onto her side, punching her pillow. Through the window she could see tree branches tossing wildly in the wind; enormous raindrops splattered against the glass. Instead of being blanketed by the usual cozy warmth of Christmas Eve, Elizabeth felt as if she were alone in a tiny boat tossing on a stormy sea. She lay awake for hours, until the first light of a gray, sunless dawn chased the ominous shadows from her room.

Chapter 8

Josh sat on the edge of the sagging mattress in his motel room on Christmas morning, staring at the garish wallpaper. The pattern seemed to swim before his eyes; for a moment he almost felt as if he were going to faint. *I need to eat something,* he thought, glancing at the jar of peanut butter and loaf of bread on the dresser. He didn't get up and make a sandwich, though. His money was running out, so he was skipping meals as often as he could manage; the food had to last him for a couple of days. *Because I'm here for the duration,* Josh reminded himself. He wasn't leaving Sweet Valley, California, until Margo was behind bars.

Will I ever find her? Where is she? In the forty-eight hours since he'd spoken with the women at Valley Caterers, Josh's confidence level had plummeted; once more he was in the depths of despair. He'd hiked the whole length of Wentworth Avenue, a street in the less affluent part of Sweet Valley, knocking on doors and ringing bells. No one was sheltering Margo or had even seen anybody who fit her description in either of her two guises, as a dark-haired girl with glasses or a Wakefield twin look-alike.

Starting Monday, I'll get back on the street, Josh decided tiredly. *I'll check out the post office and mailing-supply stores, see if she's rented a PO box. I'll stop in at some more temporary employment agencies—maybe even some nanny services.* It was a horrible thought, but a definite possibility that Margo could be living with another unsuspecting family like his own, using an assumed name as she had with his family, entrusted with the care of innocent little children. . . .

Gritting his teeth, Josh reached for the telephone on the bedside table. He wasn't looking forward to this call, but he had to make it; it was Christmas Day, after all.

He reversed the charges to save money. "Tell her it's her son, Josh," he instructed the operator.

His mother answered the phone and accepted the charges. "Hi, Mom," Josh said with false heartiness. "Merry Christmas."

"Josh, honey?" The voice was quavery and uncertain.

112

"Mom?" Josh said. "How are you doing?"

By way of an answer his mother began crying softly. Josh's own eyes brimmed with tears. "Please, Mom," he whispered hoarsely. "Don't do this."

"I just can't bear it," Mrs. Smith sobbed. "I keep thinking of last year, and the year before that, when we were all together as a family for Christmas. And now . . . and now Georgie is gone forever. . . ."

Josh bit his lip, hard. He refused to break down; he refused to give in to the sorrow and despair that threatened to drown him as Georgie had drowned. "I know how much you miss him, Mom," he said, his voice cracking with suppressed emotion. "I miss him, too. There's not a minute of the day that I don't think about him. But we've got to try to look forward instead of back."

"I can't. The other day I found myself in the toy store, and I just had to buy something for Georgie for Christmas. I couldn't bear to think of him with nothing to play with."

His mother started crying again, and Josh could tell she wasn't going to be able to stop. He couldn't take it any longer; her pain made his own pain a thousand times worse. "Good-bye, Mom," Josh whispered. "I love you. I'll stay in touch."

He hung up the phone and dropped his head in his hands, missing his little brother so badly, he ached. *Oh, Georgie,* Josh thought, choking back a sob. *Why did you have to die?*

Josh threw himself down on the squeaky motel bed. For a long while he just lay there, staring at the ceiling but seeing nothing. All he could feel was the unbearable pain of losing Georgie. Then slowly his eyes focused again. Swinging his legs over the side of the bed, he rose and crossed to the dresser to make a peanut-butter sandwich.

I won't give up, he vowed, tearing hungrily into the sandwich with his teeth. *I have a reason to go on living, to go on fighting, to go on searching.* A red-hot fire burned in Josh's weary eyes; his shoulders straightened. Georgie was his reason; Margo was his reason. He couldn't bring his little brother back, but he could get the girl who killed him. And he would.

"Merry Christmas, kids!" Mrs. Wakefield called cheerfully. "Wait, wait, don't come down the stairs yet. Let me get a picture of this."

Jessica scowled; Steven saw Elizabeth roll her eyes. "Really, Mom, do we have to do this?" he grumbled. "We're not babies anymore."

"It's the traditional Christmas-morning photo," Mrs. Wakefield cajoled. "C'mon, kids. Say cheese!"

Steven was tempted to say something else, and he had a hunch his sisters were, too. But they all held their tongues and smiled obediently, standing in a row on the stairs in their robes and slippers.

114

"That was just adorable," Mrs. Wakefield gushed, putting her thirty-five-millimeter camera down on the hall table and picking up the video camera. "Now let's get an action shot of you seeing the presents under the tree. One, two, three . . . we're rolling!"

Like tin soldiers Steven and the twins marched into the living room and uttered mechanical oohs and ahs over the piles of attractively wrapped packages. "There's way too much stuff here," Steven declared, trying his best to be jovial. "You went overboard again, Mom."

"Don't look at me," she joked. "Santa brought it all!"

Just then Mr. Wakefield entered the living room, a steaming plate in each hand. "Who's ready for a Ned Wakefield special Christmas breakfast?" he asked with a grin. "Scrambled eggs, sausage links, cinnamon rolls, and hot chocolate's on the way. Come and get it!"

Steven accepted a plate and sat down on the couch to eat. He couldn't help feeling sorry for his parents; they were trying so hard to pretend that nothing was the matter. *It's a farce, though,* Steven thought as he took a bite of his eggs. They were all going through the motions, just as they had during the Christmas Eve dinner the night before, but it was a hollow performance. Nobody was fooling anybody else.

Poor Mom is getting the worst of this, Steven decided as his mother selected some packages from under the tree, one for each child. Her overcheerful behavior reminded him of Elizabeth's trial, when Mrs. Wakefield had dealt with her distress by simply not admitting that anything out of the ordinary was taking place. His mother turned to him with a glowing smile, but Steven knew that under the surface she was worried and unsure.

"Who wants to go first?" she asked.

"Steven always does because he's the oldest," Elizabeth replied.

"OK, Steven, here's a present for you from—" His mother read the tag. "From Liz."

Steven put on a big show of unwrapping the package, tying the ribbon around his head bandanna-style and closing his eyes when he ripped off the paper. "Wow, this is great!" he exclaimed, displaying the hardcover novel for everyone to see. "I've been wanting to read this, Liz. Thanks a lot."

"Now it's your turn." Mrs. Wakefield handed a small box to Elizabeth.

Elizabeth took the present, peeking at the gift tag. Steven saw her jaw tighten. "This is from Jessica," Elizabeth announced, her tone formal. She unwrapped it in a businesslike manner, showing everyone the store name printed on the box. "It's from Blue Parrot Crafts. I wonder what it could be." She methodically removed the box top and said flatly, "Earrings. These are very pretty, Jessica."

Jessica shrugged. "When I saw them, I thought of you right away," she said, her voice equally expressionless.

Steven clapped his hands together. "OK, Jess. You're up. What have you got?"

The stilted, joyless exchange of gifts continued with Jessica unwrapping a present from "Santa." Steven glanced at the pile of packages still under the tree and stifled a groan. *At this rate it's going to take us all morning to finish!* He wasn't sure how long he could go on smiling this goofy, fake grin; his face already felt as if it were about to crack.

As he gazed toward the Christmas tree, something caught Steven's eye—a shadow passing rapidly in front of the window. He squinted, wondering what it could have been. *Just the weather,* he figured, watching the rain pelt against the glass. The storm didn't show any signs of abating; the sky was as low and gray as the mood in the house. Steven slumped down in his seat, not even bothering to fake interest in the new blouse Jessica was holding up. *Ho, ho, ho,* he thought glumly.

Margo stood in the shrubbery peering through the Wakefields' living-room window. She'd forgotten to wear a jacket, and the driving rain had soaked her to the skin, but she didn't feel the cold—she was warmed, electrified by the spell-binding scene within.

Everything is perfect, she thought rapturously, devouring the details with hungry eyes. The glittering tree, the brightly wrapped gifts, the homemade breakfast, and best of all, the people. The sweet, lovely mother in her elegant satin bathrobe, distributing gifts and kisses; the tall, handsome father, smiling benevolently; the cherished twin daughters; the manly, protective older brother.

Just then Steven glanced toward the window. Margo threw herself down into the bushes, pressing her body against the side of the house. She waited for a minute that seemed like an eternity, counting out each second in her brain, and then cautiously raised her head again. She knew she should probably go back to her guest house, but she couldn't tear herself away from Christmas morning at the Wakefields'—not yet.

Lifting one hand, Margo brushed the windowpane with her fingertips. *My house. My family. Merry Christmas, everyone.* She smiled, wanting to laugh, to sing, to dance in the rain. *Next year it will be me!* Next year *she* would come down the stairs in her flannel nightgown; *she* would be served a special breakfast by her loving father; *she* would get kisses and hugs under the mistletoe; *she* would give and receive thoughtful, wonderful presents. She would be Elizabeth Wakefield in just one week.

Chapter 9

"Let's just go over the checklist one more time," Mrs. Wakefield said on Tuesday afternoon as the whole family gathered in the kitchen. "Here's the plumber's phone number, and the electrician's, and if there's a fire, God forbid, dial nine-one-one and get out of the house. Now, I've told the Beckwiths and the Egberts that we're going out of town, and if you need anything, you can call them. Remember, no parties and no—"

Mr. Wakefield grabbed his wife's arm and propelled her toward the door. "They've heard the speech a hundred times," he told her. "Do you want to miss our plane to San Francisco?"

"We're already running late," Steven chimed in, looking at his watch. "C'mon, Mom. Let's go. I don't want to have to speed on these wet roads."

Still, Mrs. Wakefield continued to hang back, her eyes moving from Elizabeth's face to Jessica's and back again. "I know there are some other things I need to tell you," she said worriedly.

"Mom, you'll only be gone a few days," Elizabeth reminded her. "We'll be fine!"

"We might die of boredom—that's the worst that could happen," Jessica contributed morosely.

Elizabeth glanced at her sister. Amy and Lila were still out of town, and Jessica was moping big time. *Come to think of it, James hasn't called or stopped by in ages, either,* Elizabeth realized suddenly. *I wonder what's going on.*

"Well, you have our number at the hotel," Mrs. Wakefield said, "and we'll call you as soon as we get there."

"Go on." Smiling, Elizabeth made a shooing gesture. "Have a good time!"

Mrs. Wakefield bit her lip, her gaze still fixed on her daughters. Suddenly she hurried back to give them each one last hug.

"I'll miss you," Mrs. Wakefield murmured to Elizabeth.

Elizabeth kissed her mother's cheek; to her surprise it was wet with tears. "I'll miss you, too, Mom. Don't worry about us, OK?"

Wiping her eyes, Mrs. Wakefield ducked

through the door, followed by Mr. Wakefield and Steven with the luggage. Elizabeth waved after them. "So long. Good luck, Dad!"

The door slammed. Elizabeth turned and saw that Jessica had already disappeared. She sighed, suddenly overwhelmed by loneliness. Jessica wasn't the only one who'd been moping lately. *Thank goodness Todd comes back today!* Elizabeth thought. He'd promised to stop by her house first thing, and she couldn't wait. So far this Christmas vacation was living up—or rather, down—to all her gloomy expectations.

James stepped through the door of his house early Tuesday evening, scuffing his muddy boots on the welcome mat and shaking rainwater from his tangled light-brown hair. Another storm was coming through the area, and it had just started to drizzle. He briefly considered grabbing a bite to eat and heading back out to a bar somewhere, then nixed the idea. It was a good night for sticking close to home; the wind was howling and the roads were slick. *I'll order a pizza,* he decided. *See what's on cable.*

He crossed to the bedroom, shrugging out of his leather jacket and stripping off his T-shirt. As he searched through his drawers for a clean shirt, he noticed a piece of folded paper lying on top of the bureau. He froze, his heart thumping painfully. It was a note . . . another note.

James stared at the piece of paper for a long moment, feelings of fear and anger surging inside him. Without even reading it he knew that the note would be unsigned, but he also knew beyond a shadow of a doubt who'd written it.

It was the third note Margo had left for him since their last, fateful meeting at Kelly's almost a week ago—the third note accusing him of double-dealing even though he'd broken up with Jessica and was steering clear of her the way Margo had commanded him to—the third note informing him that Margo was watching him, that Margo was just waiting for him to slip up . . . that Margo was going to get him.

A shudder of revulsion ran through James's body as he thought of Margo in his room, invading his house so freely. *She's insane,* he thought, amazed by how bold she was—and how evil. *She's really and truly insane.*

Grabbing the note, James crumpled it without reading it and hurled it into the wastebasket. The gesture made him feel a little bit better—a very little bit. The note was out of sight, but Margo was still out there somewhere, watching and waiting.

James strode over to the window to shut the blinds. He wished he could just laugh off the notes, chalk it up to a girlish prank. But there was absolutely nothing girlish or playful about Margo. He had no hard evidence that she'd committed any crimes or that she *intended* to commit any; still, instinct told him that she was more than capable of making good on her murderous threats.

And I'm a threat to her, James realized. *Even though I don't know what she's trying to pull off in Sweet Valley, I know too much. I know her—I know she's a lunatic.*

James looked around the room, viewing it with dispassionate eyes. It wasn't a home anymore; he wasn't safe there, and he never would be again. Three notes, three death threats. One of these days Margo was going to come for him, not with a letter but with a gun or a knife. *But I won't be here when she does,* James determined. *It's time to get out of town.*

He tried to see the situation in a positive light. Leaving town wasn't that big a deal, really. He was young and mobile; he didn't have any ties or responsibilities in Sweet Valley. In fact, before he met Margo and agreed to spy on Jessica, he'd been thinking about taking off for greener pastures.

Jessica . . . James frowned, the memory of her face bringing tears to his eyes. Who was he trying to kid? He *did* have ties and responsibilities in Sweet Valley, and he couldn't leave town without facing up to them. He couldn't leave town without warning Jessica about the danger she was in.

James flung himself down on the bed, lying on his back with his head pillowed in his arms. *If only I knew exactly what that danger is, when it's going to strike,* he thought. And what about Margo's vow to harm them both if James tried to see Jessica again? *Maybe it's a no-win situation. Things don't look good for Jessica either way, so what's the point of trying to be a hero? I might as well just split and save my own skin, right?*

He considered this possibility, but only for a second. It was the route the old James would have taken—the James who made the deal with Margo. But the person he was now, the guy who'd fallen in love with Jessica Wakefield and who genuinely cared about her safety, couldn't turn his back. He had to take action.

I've got to tell her what she's up against, James decided. *That way, at least she'll have a fighting chance against Margo. She can be on her guard.* Having made up his mind, he reached for the phone, ready to call Jessica and risk one last rendezvous. All at once his somber expression brightened. *Maybe I can talk her into coming with me!* James thought, his spirits lifting. They could run away together—they could be happy and safe somewhere far from Sweet Valley . . . far from Margo.

124

Quickly, James dialed Jessica's phone number. "Jess, it's me, James," he announced when she answered the phone.

There was a moment of shocked silence. "James?" Jessica finally said in disbelief.

"I have to see you," he told her, his voice vibrating with urgency. "Can you meet me in an hour or so? Meet me at . . ." He drummed his fingers on the nightstand, considering. They needed someplace private, out of the way. Afterward they could head straight up the coast highway. "At the marina—the old pier at the end," he told her. "Seven o'clock, OK?"

Jessica hesitated. "The—the marina?"

"Please, Jess, it's important," James begged. "Incredibly important. I can't explain over the phone, but your life—" *Your life may depend on it*, he was about to say, but he didn't want to scare her off. "Just come." His voice cracked. "Please."

"OK," Jessica whispered at last. "I'll meet you on the pier at seven."

The instant he hung up the phone, James began tearing around his room, rummaging through his closet and emptying drawers. Things he thought he could live without he tossed aside; everything else he stuffed into his army-surplus duffel bag. Once he headed out to meet Jessica in an hour, he wasn't coming back.

* * *

Jessica replaced the telephone receiver and put her shaking hands up to her face. Her cheeks were red and hot; she had a hunch her pulse was off the charts. *James finally called me!*

She'd just about given up hope that she'd ever hear from him again. The break had seemed pretty complete; he'd made it clear he didn't want to see her anymore, and she had too much pride to go after him and demand an explanation of his behavior.

He's had second thoughts, though, Jessica realized, hope blossoming in her heart again. *He wants to see me!*

But was that all there was to it? Jessica considered the phone call, her brow knit in a puzzled frown. James had sounded so peculiar, almost frantic. *Something's wrong,* she sensed. *Something's going on that he didn't want to talk about over the phone.* Jessica folded her arms, suddenly feeling chilly in her thin T-shirt. James's request that she meet him at the marina was mysterious . . . but also incredibly thrilling. *I'll be with him in an hour,* she thought. She still didn't understand what she'd done wrong; now she could find out and make it up to him. This was their chance to start over.

Outside there was a loud crack of thunder. Jessica jumped. As she stood in her bedroom listening to the sound of raindrops splattering against the windows, she started to wish she'd invited

James over. She didn't exactly relish the idea of venturing out on a messy night like this. She had no choice, though. For all she knew, James was in some kind of trouble. He needed her—she had to go to him. A little bad weather couldn't keep her away.

I wish someone else were home, Jessica thought. But she was alone in the house; Elizabeth was at Todd's, and Steven had taken their parents to the airport in the Jeep. Lightning flashed, and there was another thunderous boom. In the distance Jessica heard a crash, as if a tree had fallen. Her bedroom light flickered and went out, leaving her in darkness.

A power line must have been knocked down, Jessica realized, distressed. Her heart racing, she fumbled her way blindly toward her bedroom door. Ever since Jungle Prom night and Sam's death, she'd hated the dark.

Her hand fell on the coolness of the doorknob. *Mom keeps a flashlight and some candles in the kitchen,* Jessica remembered as she launched into the hallway, feeling her way cautiously through the pitch-black nothingness before her. Then she felt something in the nothingness. Right outside her bedroom door Jessica crashed into something solid. A *body*. Raw, primitive terror washed over her like a tidal wave. Opening her mouth, she screamed at the top of her lungs.

*   *   *

At that instant the lights blinked back on. "Oh, Liz, it's *you!*" Jessica gasped. She clutched her sister's arms, laughing hysterically. "Sorry for yelling right in your face, but you scared me half to *death*. For a second there I thought you were some kind of . . . Where did you come from, anyway? I thought you were over at Todd's!"

Margo smiled to herself as she gave Jessica a quick, reassuring hug. Not too long or too warm; she was supposed to be Elizabeth, and Elizabeth was still mad at Jessica, after all. "I just got back," she answered. "Where are *you* off to in such a hurry?"

"I was going to hunt up a flashlight, but now . . ." Jessica put a hand to her gold necklace, toying with it distractedly. "I'm going out in an hour or so."

"Hmm." Margo shrugged carelessly, the way she imagined Elizabeth would at a moment like this. "Well, see you."

"See you," Jessica echoed as she stepped back into her bedroom.

Margo returned to Elizabeth's room, a smug, cruel smile creasing her face, and looked at the telephone she'd held pressed to her ear just a few minutes before as she'd eavesdropped on Jessica's conversation with James. *I knew he'd call her! I knew he'd betray me as soon as he got the chance.* Margo's fingers curled into angry fists. *He won't get*

128

away with it, though, she vowed silently. *I'll make him pay.*

In the meantime she knew she should bolt down to the basement and get out of the house; Elizabeth could return from Todd's at any moment. But something she'd just seen Jessica do—an unconscious, perfectly natural gesture—had put an idea into Margo's head.

Hurrying to Elizabeth's dresser, Margo opened the jewelry box that rested on top. Would it be in there, or was Elizabeth wearing it? She rummaged through the jewelry and then let out a cry of triumph. She'd found it!

Margo seized the object of her search, holding it up against the light so she could admire it: a gold lavaliere necklace exactly like the one Jessica was wearing. *Now it's mine,* Margo thought, smiling at herself in the mirror as she fastened it around her neck. She shivered with delight. With the cool gold against her skin, she could almost *feel* it—she was becoming more like Elizabeth Wakefield with every passing minute.

She turned away from the mirror with a reluctant sigh. She really didn't want to head back out into the cold, wet night; she didn't want to leave this cozy, comfortable bedroom. The room and everything in it already felt as if it belonged to her. But she couldn't linger. It was just too risky.

In just a few nights I'll sleep for the first time in this bed, Margo consoled herself as she drifted past the bed toward the hallway. In the meantime there was still important work to be done.

Chapter 10

Josh hit the windshield-wiper switch on the dashboard of his rental car and tapped the brakes. *The rain's really coming down now,* he observed as he coasted up to a red light at an unfamiliar intersection about a mile from downtown Sweet Valley. *I guess I might as well turn in for the night.* There was really no point in continuing to drive aimlessly around Sweet Valley, just hoping he'd stumble across Margo. Since Christmas he'd come down with the flu; he was nearly delirious from weakness and fatigue. *I'll try again tomorrow,* he thought, struggling to remain alert. *Maybe if I can get a good night's sleep for a change, I'll be able to come up with some kind of strategy. A good night's sleep . . .*

Suddenly weariness hit Josh like a brick. He slumped forward, dropping his head onto his arms, which were draped across the steering wheel. *I'll just close my eyes for a second, until the light changes.*

The sound of a car honking behind him jolted Josh upright again. Slapping his face to wake himself up, he stepped on the gas and proceeded through the intersection. As he did, he glanced up at the road sign. He was crossing Westwood Avenue, a street he hadn't been down before. Westwood Avenue . . .

All at once something clicked in Josh's feverish brain. Westwood Avenue . . . *Wentworth* Avenue. The two names looked a lot alike. *Maybe I misread Margo's address on the envelope at Valley Caterers,* Josh thought. Maybe it said *Westwood*, not Wentworth!

Josh slammed on the brakes. The car behind him honked again, coming perilously close to rear-ending him, but Josh didn't care. Tires squealing, he pulled a U-turn and sped back to the intersection.

Once there he faced a choice: left or right? Randomly, Josh turned right, heading toward town. He had no idea what he was looking for; most likely he'd have to come back the next day when it was light. Just to be on her street, though . . . A shot of adrenaline started Josh's blood pumping; he felt more alive than he had in weeks. *I'm getting close,* he sensed, staring eagerly at the houses as he drove slowly past.

Then he saw it: a renovated three-story Victorian with a small, neatly painted sign by the mailbox. The name on the mailbox was Palmer, and the sign said simply, Guests. Josh's eyes glittered with hope. *It could be—it could be!*

Parking the car, he jumped out and hurried through the rain to the house, cautiously eyeing the windows to see if anyone—if Margo—was looking out at him. Making it to the porch undetected, he paused by the front door and peered at the handwritten directory someone had taped up by the bell. With a trembling finger he traced the names. P. Alden, M. Chaitovitz, E. Thorne, M. Wake. "M. Wake," Josh breathed, his heart skipping a beat. "Margaret Wake . . . Margo. She's here."

Next to each resident's name, a room number was noted; Margo was in room 12. *Number twelve,* Josh thought, placing a hand on the doorknob. *I'm so close now—*

He tried the knob, expecting to find it locked. To his surprise it turned noiselessly, and the heavy front door swung open.

Exhilarated, Josh stepped into the guest house. The foyer was dimly lit and empty. So far, so good—no one would question his right to be there. He'd be able to walk right up to Margo's door and confront her, corner her. "I've almost got her, Georgie," Josh whispered. "I'm going to go for it, little buddy."

With slow, purposeful steps, Josh climbed the wide carpeted staircase to the second floor. Room 10, room 11, room 12 . . . He stopped before Margo's door. Closing his eyes, he said a silent prayer. Then he took a deep breath and gently tried the doorknob.

The room was locked. Bending forward, Josh put an ear to the door. *Quiet—dead quiet. She must be out,* he guessed. This was even better than finding her at home. He'd jimmy the lock; it was a perfect chance to investigate.

His hands shaking with excitement, Josh fumbled in his trouser pockets for an object suitable for lock picking. The small blade of his Swiss Army knife worked beautifully. After jiggling it in the lock for just a few seconds, he heard a muffled click, and the knob turned in his hand.

Josh gave the door a light shove, and it swung inward. The room was dark. Reaching along the wall, he flipped on the overhead light and then froze in shock.

Oh my God, he thought, fighting down a wave of nausea. *Oh my God.* Instantly Josh knew beyond a shadow of a doubt that he'd found her. And he also knew, beyond a shadow of a doubt, that she was as evil as he'd thought she was—perhaps even more so.

The room was like a direct glimpse into Margo's diseased, rotten soul. Her fresh-skinned, beautiful face was a mask; this was the *real* Margo. Slowly, Josh ventured forward, his stomach heaving as the rank odor assailed his nostrils. The room was a filthy mess. Dirty, rumpled clothes were piled everywhere. As Josh walked, he kicked aside half-eaten bags of chips and donuts and greasy paper plates holding the moldy remnants of fast-food meals. More appalling than the garbage, though, more frightening even than the assortment of knives carelessly scattered on the desktop, was the bizarre way in which Margo had decorated her temporary home. *My God, look at the walls,* he thought.

Josh turned on his heel and faced the wall to his left. It was plastered with glossy color photographs, some regular-sized and others enlarged. *The Wakefield sisters, Jessica and Elizabeth!* Josh recognized. *And their house . . . and that man and woman must be their parents.*

Margo hadn't only been collecting pictures, however. Also tacked to the wall were issues of the Sweet Valley High newspaper and countless narrow-ruled sheets of scribbled notes: class schedules, lists of names and addresses, and what looked like handwriting exercises. Most telling of all, however, was the message Margo had left on the mirror. Josh stood before the glass, seeing not the reflection of his own horrified face but the three words scrawled there in blood-red lipstick: "I am Elizabeth."

Josh stared at the words, paralyzed by the terrible realization. Finally, all the pieces were coming together. He knew exactly what Margo intended to do, exactly how wicked and depraved she really was. God help poor, innocent Elizabeth Wakefield.

No, Josh determined. *I won't let her hurt Elizabeth like she hurt Georgie and who knows how many others. It's time for this to stop.*

His hands clenched into fists as he anticipated how he would seize Margo when she returned to her room and haul her into the police station. He'd waited long enough for this moment—this time he wouldn't waste his opportunity. This very room contained all the evidence he needed to prove that Margo was a homicidal maniac.

Tonight was the night. He'd wait for her, right there. Margo had come to the end of her murderous road.

Margo checked her watch as she trotted up the steps of the guest house. Six thirty—she had only half an hour to dress in a Jessica-style outfit and hurry to the marina. *Less than half an hour,* she corrected herself. Because of course she had to arrive before the real Jessica did. She had to deal with James.

Inside, Margo took the stairs to the second floor two at a time. She dashed to her room, number 12, and then pulled up short, her hand just inches from the doorknob. *Someone's been here,* she realized, taking in the state of the lock with a single practiced glance. She stared at the telltale scratches, her mind running in circles like a hamster on a treadmill. *Someone's been here, but who? When? Why?*

Just then she heard a rustling sound on the other side of the door. Someone had indeed been there—and that someone was still in her room!

Bending over, Margo put her eye to the damaged keyhole and peeked through. She recognized Josh Smith immediately. Emotions surged up in her, boiling like a storm-tossed sea: fear that he'd come so close to apprehending her, fury and indignation at this violation of her jealously guarded privacy. *How dare he?* she raged silently. *How* dare *he?*

Straightening up again, Margo stood tapping her foot for a moment, unsure of what to do next. She felt cornered and helpless. Josh had seen it all; he was probably just waiting to jump on her and take her to the police, if he hadn't called them already.

Slipping a hand into her purse, she felt the handle of the small knife she kept handy. *I could burst in on him and stab him,* she thought. But no, Josh was probably armed himself, and if he wasn't, he could just grab any one of the knives she'd left on the desk—all of which were much bigger than the one she carried.

I'll just . . . I'll just have to leave, Margo realized, biting her lip. *I'll hide somewhere and hope I get a chance to clean out the room before he comes back with the cops. If not, I'll just lay low for a while and look for another chance, another way. . . .*

The thought of having to postpone her dream of becoming Elizabeth Wakefield brought hot tears of disappointment to Margo's eyes. She wanted to sob, to howl. And then . . . her anger dissipated like a Pacific mist on a sunny morning. All at once she was in command of herself again—and in command of the situation. *I should have more faith,* she berated herself. As always a brilliant idea had come to her just in the nick of time.

So Josh Smith wants to follow me, does he? He wants a piece of the action? Margo wanted to laugh out loud. *How stupid he is,* she thought with a disdainful sneer, *to imagine he could beat me at my own game!*

Stepping a few paces down the hall, Margo positioned herself right at the top of the stairs. "I just stopped by to drop off the rent check," she announced loudly to the empty hallway. "I'm heading over to the marina to meet a friend at seven." She paused, allowing time for an imaginary reply, then continued. "Thanks, Mrs. Palmer. I *will* have a good night."

Margo raced down the stairs and out the door. She noticed a green car parked alongside the curb

138

right in front of the house—Josh's car, she guessed. Her own vehicle was across the street, pointing in the opposite direction.

In the blink of an eye, Margo had unlocked the driver's-side door and slithered behind the wheel of her car. She slouched low in the seat so that she couldn't be seen from the sidewalk and trained her eyes on the Palmers' guest house. Sure enough, a minute later Josh, wearing a denim jacket and baseball cap, came sneaking out of the house. Margo smiled to herself as he jumped into his car and raced off. "Thank you, Josh," she said. "You'll fit into my plans just *perfectly*."

"The good thing about being in the mountains," Todd told Elizabeth as he pulled the BMW out of his family's garage, "is that we got snow the whole time instead of rain."

"Lucky you." Elizabeth rubbed her hands together. "It *feels* cold enough to snow here, though. It's just so damp and raw."

Todd turned up the car's heat. "That any better?"

Elizabeth nodded. "Much. Tell you what, though, do you mind stopping at my house on the way to the restaurant so I can grab a heavier sweater?"

"No problem." Steering with his left hand, Todd slipped his right arm behind Elizabeth's shoulders. "I wish I'd had you to cuddle with in my

139

snowbound mountain cabin. I would've kept you nice and warm."

Elizabeth nestled against Todd—as much as the bucket seats and shoulder belts would allow. "Sounds cozy," she murmured, stretching to give him a kiss on the cheek.

Todd slowed at a stop sign before turning onto Calico Drive. They could feel the wind buffeting the small car. "Wow, it's vicious out there!" Todd exclaimed.

Elizabeth gazed out at the storm-tossed trees. It made her teeth chatter just to think about how cold that wind was. "I'll be glad to get to Guido's," she remarked. "This is no night to be outside."

Todd pulled into the driveway at her house, and Elizabeth braced herself for the short sprint to the front door. It was just a few yards; still, the wind seemed to slice right through to her bones. With Todd behind her Elizabeth burst into the house, stomping her wet shoes on the mat in the front hall. She was about to head straight upstairs when she heard a clatter coming from the kitchen. Someone was throwing things around and muttering. *Jessica's having a fit about something*, Elizabeth surmised, going to the kitchen to check it out.

She found her sister frantically rifling through cupboards and drawers. Pot holders and place mats flew through the air; utensils of all kinds cluttered the countertops.

140

"I'm looking for the keys to Mom's and Dad's cars," Jessica explained without even looking up. She slammed shut one drawer and yanked open another. "I thought they said they were going to leave them in the dish-towel drawer. Or was it in the candy dish on top of the microwave? Oh, I've looked everywhere!" Jessica moaned.

Elizabeth shrugged. "Oh, well, they'll turn up," she said, turning to leave.

"Liz, Todd, hold on. You guys have got to give me a ride," Jessica begged. "Steven took the Jeep to the airport because it's the only car big enough for Mom and Dad's luggage."

Elizabeth pivoted to face her sister again. "What's the emergency?" she asked, more than a trace of annoyance in her voice.

Jessica blinked at Elizabeth, staring at her as if she'd suddenly sprouted horns. "Wait a minute, Liz. Didn't you come in—weren't you wearing . . . ?" Jessica shook her head. "Never mind, I must be going nuts," she muttered. "This is the thing—I need to meet James at the marina, but I don't have any transportation. Can you drop me off there?"

"Well . . ." Elizabeth folded her arms across her chest, scowling. She really didn't feel like doing Jessica any favors. *When was the last time Jessica went out of her way for* me? she reflected. No, in Elizabeth's opinion Jessica deserved to be left to stew in her own juices. She could walk to the marina if she wanted to get there so badly. On the other hand, though, Jessica did seem genuinely desperate and rattled. Elizabeth glanced at Todd. He lifted his shoulders. "Oh, all right," Elizabeth told Jessica. "I *suppose* we can drop you off. We're heading in that direction anyway."

A minute later the three of them piled into Todd's BMW and started off. They hadn't gone a hundred yards before Jessica leaned forward from the backseat and tapped Todd on the shoulder. "Can't you drive any faster?" she demanded. "I'm already late and this is really important!"

"Sorry, Jess, this is the best I can do," Todd snapped. "The roads are pretty slick. If it's OK with you, I'd rather not end up in a ditch."

Elizabeth flinched, remembering her fatal accident with the Jeep. *Why are we even out on a night like this?* she wondered, wishing they'd all just stayed home. They were approaching downtown Sweet Valley; just ahead of them a traffic light turned from green to yellow. "Go for it!" Jessica yelled.

Todd applied the brakes, rolling to a stop just as the light turned red. Elizabeth thought Jessica was going to explode. "Oh, God," Jessica muttered, glancing anxiously at the illuminated clock on the dashboard. "I can't explain it, but I just have this terrible feeling. . . ."

Wind rocked the car; lightning flickered on the

horizon. "We'll get there," Todd assured Jessica. "Keep your shirt on!"

The red light seemed to last forever; finally, it changed to green. The BMW surged forward. "Please hurry," Elizabeth heard Jessica whisper in the backseat.

A few blocks farther along, they got stuck at another red light. This time Elizabeth really thought Jessica would jump out of her skin, or maybe jump out of the car so she could *run* the rest of the way to the marina. Elizabeth listened to Jessica mumbling to herself in the backseat with increasing alarm. *What's going on?* Elizabeth wondered, suddenly realizing her own palms were damp with sweat, as if a portion of her sister's distress had transmitted itself to her. Why was Jessica even meeting James at the marina on a terrible night like this, and why was she in such a nervous, frazzled state? What kind of rendezvous were they heading for?

Chapter 11

The engine of his dirt bike rumbling in low gear, James rode cautiously along the rain-slick board-walk, heading for the old pier at the far end of the Sweet Valley marina. At such a slow pace the bike wobbled; it was unwieldy, weighted down with all his possessions. When he reached the last pier, James parked the bike and walked the rest of the way.

There were no boats moored along the old pier, which extended far out over the water and was wider and longer than the other piers at the marina. At the end were some wooden benches and a snack bar; on sunny days people came there to fish and feed the gulls. Tonight, though, the pier was as dark and deserted as the rest of the marina.

James turned up the collar of his leather

jacket and narrowed his eyes against the drizzle, pacing restlessly. He checked his watch in an agony of suspense. It was seven o'clock on the dot, and still no sign of Jessica. *Will she show or won't she?* he wondered, slapping his arms against his sides to keep warm. Maybe she'd regretted her promise to meet him. After all, he'd treated her pretty callously—he'd really hurt her. *I wouldn't blame her if she didn't show,* James thought. *But I hope she does. God, I hope she does.*

Reaching the end of the pier, James leaned gingerly against the decrepit wooden railing and glanced downward. Angry waves crashed against the dark, jagged rocks; the storm that was poised to sweep through the area had already stirred things up out at sea.

James turned away from the railing . . . and there she was, hurrying down the pier in his direction, a slim figure with pale hair covered by a baseball cap, her chin tucked down into the collar of her denim jacket. "Jessica!" James cried, his heart almost bursting with joy.

She ran into his arms and he held her tightly, his whole body rocked by the powerful relief he felt at finally holding her again. "I've missed you so much!" he murmured, kissing her cheeks, her forehead, her hair. "Oh, Jessica, if you knew what I've been going through . . ."

"Oh, James," she whispered, burying her face against his chest.

"I never meant to hurt you," James swore, locking his arms around her shoulders. "I broke things off because I had to. You see . . ." James hesitated, but only for an instant. He knew he had to give Jessica the whole story—he couldn't hold anything back if he wanted her to understand how dire the situation was.

"You see, there's this girl, Margo, who looks exactly like you," James began. "I know it sounds crazy, but it's true. And she's plotting something, something wicked, and somehow it involves you and your sister. She—" James clenched his jaw and forced himself to continue. "She hired me to go out with you, Jessica, because she wanted information about you and your family. You've got to believe me, I would never have done it if I'd known what she was really like. But I didn't know her—I didn't know *you* at that point. It was just an easy way to make a buck. It was never just a job, though, Jess. I fell in love with you—how could I help it? And I told her I wouldn't take her money anymore—I wouldn't spy for her anymore. That's when she threatened to kill me, and kill you, too."

Jessica was quiet, obviously overwhelmed by the strangeness of his story. James held her closer, hoping she could feel how much he loved her.

146

"Your life is in serious danger, Jessica," he concluded, his voice low with urgency. "That's why I called you tonight. You have to come away with me. I'll protect you—we'll be happy together, I swear. Say you'll come. Please. I can't stay in Sweet Valley, and I won't leave without you."

James waited for Jessica to respond. She held him tightly, but she didn't speak. Pulling back slightly, he tried to see her expression, to gauge her reaction to his story and his proposal. "I know it sounds totally insane. And I know I haven't played the noblest part," he said humbly. "But I'm only thinking of you now, Jessica. I love you, and—"

James tipped Jessica's face to his and then froze, the words dying on his lips. He looked down into Jessica's face . . . but it *wasn't* Jessica's face. His blood ran cold and his arms dropped limply to his sides. The body, the clothes, the hair, even the necklace, all belonged to Jessica. But the expression on that lovely face was monstrous. James was staring straight into the eyes of a killer. "Margo," he whispered, horrified.

"Hello, James," she whispered, smiling.

James stood like a statue, paralyzed with fear. Before he could move away from her, Margo placed both her hands against his chest and shoved him with all her might.

James toppled, knocked off balance. He felt his

boot heel skid on the wet pier; stumbling, he realized too late how close to the edge they'd been standing. Margo pushed him again, and James crashed with all his weight against the railing. For a second he thought it would hold him; then his body broke through the rotten wood. He shouted, scrambling for a foothold or handhold, but it was too late. There was nothing to hold on to but air. With a terrified scream James plunged over the edge of the pier and plummeted to the treacherous rocks below.

Before Todd could even kill the engine in the parking lot of the marina, Jessica was out of the car and running down the boardwalk to the far pier. "Slow down!" she heard Elizabeth calling after her. "You'll slip and fall!" But Jessica didn't care about her own safety. The psychic message had been coming to her, loud and clear, the whole time they were driving to the marina. James was in danger, Jessica was sure of it. He was in danger, and she had to get to him before—

Reaching the old pier, Jessica paused momentarily. She heard Elizabeth and Todd's feet pounding on the dock behind her . . . and she heard other sounds ahead of her in the dark at the far end of the pier. Someone was there!

More than one person, Jessica realized, dashing forward. Despite the rain and gloom, she could see a blur of bodies scuffling. James was in some kind of fight! And then she saw the taller figure topple. The leather jacket—the shaggy brown hair . . . A scream ripped from Jessica's throat. "No!"

She was too late. James had fallen over the edge, and Jessica knew what lay far below: vicious, deadly rocks. "James!" she cried, faltering. "James, no!"

Panting from the exertion, Todd and Elizabeth sprinted up. "What's going on?" Elizabeth cried.

In the gloom at the edge of the pier where James had been standing only a moment before, a shadowy figure was visible—a man in a denim jacket and baseball cap. Jessica pointed to him. "Get him!" she screamed to Todd as she collapsed into Elizabeth's arms.

The man whirled, preparing to run. Spurred by Jessica's words, Todd sprang forward to block his escape. "Get him," Jessica repeated, tears mingling with the rain on her face. She clung to Elizabeth, half fainting. "He killed James!"

Her eyes wide with terror and confusion, Elizabeth watched anxiously as Todd tackled the man in the baseball cap, their bodies hitting the pier with a thud.

That man killed James? Elizabeth thought, hugging Jessica. *But who is he? How could this have happened?*

One thing was for sure: The man was dangerous, and Todd might need help. Her arms still around her sister, Elizabeth stumbled toward the end of the pier.

Todd and the stranger were wrestling, rolling over and over, terrifyingly near the edge of the pier and the shattered railing. After a tense minute, to Elizabeth's immense relief, Todd got the upper hand. Flipping his opponent onto his stomach, Todd yanked the man's arms behind his back and held him pinned.

The man continued to struggle, his body writhing on the wet planks of the pier. "You've got the wrong person!" he shouted, trying to twist out of Todd's grasp. "It wasn't me—I didn't do it. It was Margo! She killed my brother and now she's killed this boy, and who knows how many others will die before—"

Suddenly the man spotted Elizabeth and Jessica. His wild eyes grew even wilder. "Them!" he panted. "She looks just like those two girls, your friends. She's a psycho, I tell you, and she's getting away! You have to let me go after her!"

Jessica had been wobbling, as if about to pass out. Now her eyes fluttered, her body slumping heavily against Elizabeth. Elizabeth lowered her sister's unconscious form to the ground, holding

150

Jessica on her lap like a baby. She turned her head away, wishing she could block out the murderer's crazed eyes, his wild, senseless words. But glancing over the edge of the pier, Elizabeth encountered an even more horrifying sight: James's lifeless, broken body lying sprawled on the rocks below.

For an instant Elizabeth feared that she, too, would faint. She bent her head, a wave of weakness washing over her. Out of the corner of her eye, she saw Todd jab his knee into the small of the killer's back; Todd now had the man in an unbreakable hold.

Suddenly, Elizabeth realized she was crying. *How did we get into the middle of this nightmare?* she wondered as she rocked her sister's trembling body in the cold, relentless rain.

Margo lingered for a moment, viewing the scene from behind the snack-bar shack. *Looks like Todd has things under control,* she observed with satisfaction. *My hero!*

Margo waited until Elizabeth's attention was directed toward Todd and Josh, then emerged from the shelter of the shack and darted up the pier. *There's a pay phone at the other end of the marina,* she recalled, suppressing a cold-blooded cackle as she caught sight of James's dirt bike, parked and waiting. On a whim she grabbed his duffel bag—

there could be something valuable inside. *And James won't be needing it anymore. . . .*

Reaching the pay phone, Margo dialed the police emergency number. "I'd like to report a crime. A murder," she declared, quickly rattling off the basic facts. "A man pushed another man off the old pier down at the Sweet Valley marina. Some eyewitnesses caught the killer, but they need help. Please hurry!"

Margo hung up the phone before they could ask her name. She wished she could go back down to the old pier and feast her eyes on the delicious sight of Todd restraining Josh, of Elizabeth comforting Jessica, of James's conveniently dead body.

It went even better than I planned! she exulted, her cheeks glowing pink with triumph. James and Josh had played right into her hands, and Todd showing up to apprehend the "criminal" was an unexpected but perfect final touch. *I really love it when everything comes together like this! I'm just so, so good.*

Too bad your foot slipped, James, Margo thought nonchalantly as she sauntered back to her car. *We had a good partnership going there for a while. But you'd played your part. I didn't need you anymore.*

Tearing off her baseball cap, Margo shook out her hair and tipped her face to the rain, smiling as a bolt of lightning shattered the night sky. James had played his part . . . and now she was ready to play hers. The rain ran down Margo's face and soaked through her clothes, and she reveled in the icy, stinging, cleansing sensation. *I've learned my lines, and it's almost show time,* she thought. *It's almost New Year's Eve. Soon I'll be a Wakefield!*

Chapter 12

"That's the kind of flight that makes me never want to get on an airplane again," Mrs. Wakefield declared as she and her husband disembarked at the San Francisco airport on Tuesday night. "I really don't know how the pilot pulled off that landing— the fog is as thick as pea soup!"

"It was a bumpy one, all right," Mr. Wakefield agreed, taking his wife's arm as they zigzagged through the crowd on their way to the baggage-claim area. "But we made it safe and sound. In half an hour we'll be relaxing in our hotel room." He winked at his wife. "I'd be up for ordering room service. How 'bout you?"

She smiled. "You're on."

While Mr. Wakefield waited for their two small suitcases to come around on the luggage carousel, Mrs. Wakefield looked around for their limousine driver. There were a dozen or so drivers from various livery services standing near the glass exit doors, each displaying a sign printed with a customer's name. *Kaplan, Lee, Stevenson, Higgins . . . hmm, no Wakefield,* Mrs. Wakefield noted.

Her husband joined her, a suitcase in each hand. "I don't see our driver," Mrs. Wakefield told him, her expression anxious.

Mr. Wakefield wasn't concerned. "He's probably waiting for us outside where there's less of a crowd. C'mon."

They hurried out to the sidewalk, where a number of limousines and shuttle vans were lined up by the curb. "You wait here," Mr. Wakefield said, placing the suitcases by his wife's feet. "I'll just check with these guys and see which car is ours."

Mrs. Wakefield watched her husband approach each limousine in turn, her anxiety mounting. She could hear snatches of the brief conversations, and it wasn't encouraging. ". . . name is Wakefield . . . expecting a car . . . Kotkin, Greiner, and Burns . . . the Fairmont Hotel . . . ?" Mr. Wakefield gave the same speech every time, and the reply was always the same: a shake of the head, a shrug of the shoulders.

Shaking his own head in puzzlement, Ned

Wakefield returned to his wife's side. "No luck, honey. Ms. de Voice said there'd be someone here to meet us, and we're right on time. . . ." He checked his watch. "If our car isn't here by now, it's not coming. There must have been a mix-up about which flight we would be on," he concluded.

It was a logical explanation. Still, for some reason Alice Wakefield didn't find it entirely satisfying. "I suppose you're right."

Mr. Wakefield put an arm around her shoulders and gave her a quick squeeze. "It's just a little mix-up—nothing to be upset about," he reiterated. "We'll hop in a taxi and be at the Fairmont in no time."

There was a long line at the cab stand, however, and it was another half hour before they were finally on their way into San Francisco. Mrs. Wakefield stared out the window of the taxi, her hands clasped tightly in her lap. A steady rain had begun to fall, turning the black city streets into glistening mirrors. *It's no big deal,* she reasoned silently with herself. *Just a little mix-up, like Ned said.* Nevertheless, she couldn't shake the gnawing sense of anxiety that had stolen into her heart. It wasn't just the missing limousine that troubled her, either. *Jessica . . . Elizabeth . . .* Mrs. Wakefield glanced at her husband's handsome profile. His expression was unconcerned, peaceful. *I've never been able to explain my mother's intuition to him. He doesn't believe in it; he thinks it's just my imagination. But something's wrong.* Mrs. Wakefield could feel it, deep in her bones. Something was wrong at home. Something was wrong with her girls.

Mrs. Wakefield thought back to their parting earlier that afternoon. Why had her eyes flooded with tears as she hugged them? Why had she felt as if she were saying good-bye to them for a long, long time instead of just for a few days? *Where did that feeling come from?* Mrs. Wakefield wondered as the cab rounded a corner and pulled up in front of the elegant Fairmont Hotel. Where did any of the strange, troubling feelings she'd had lately about her daughters come from?

Mr. Wakefield paid the cabdriver and once again hoisted the two suitcases. "Gorgeous, isn't it?" he remarked as they entered the ornate hotel lobby. "I have a hunch this will more than make up for the misunderstanding at the airport."

They stepped up to the reservations desk. "We'd like to check in to our room," Mr. Wakefield stated. "Our name is Wakefield."

The clerk typed rapidly on her computer keyboard, her eyes on the screen. "I'm sorry," she said a moment later, "but I don't see a reservation for Wakefield. Could it be under another name?"

"Hmm." Mr. Wakefield's brow furrowed. "Well,

you might try de Voice. Ms. de Voice of Kotkin, Greiner, and Burns made the reservation for us."

The clerk studied the computer screen, frowning. "I'm afraid there's nothing under de Voice or Kotkin, Greiner, and Burns, either." She lifted her shoulders regretfully. "I'm sorry, Mr. Wakefield."

"Now, this is definitely odd," Mr. Wakefield admitted, turning to his wife. "Supposedly Ms. de Voice took care of all these arrangements, but so far nothing's happening the way she promised in her letter. No car, no room . . ." He faced the clerk again, reaching for his wallet. "Well, since we're here, we'd like to take a room. Let me give you my credit card."

The desk clerk smiled apologetically. "I wish I could help you, Mr. and Mrs. Wakefield, but this is the busiest week of the year, and we don't have a single room available."

Mrs. Wakefield bit her lip. "We're not stranded yet," her husband consoled her. "There are plenty of other hotels in the city."

"That's right," the clerk chimed in. "Why don't you try the Royal Palm Court on the next street? It's very nice. Here, let me call ahead for you and make sure they have a room."

Five minutes later Mr. and Mrs. Wakefield were trooping down the block in the rain with their suitcases. Mr. Wakefield whistled through his teeth as if nothing were the matter. But Mrs. Wakefield couldn't hide the fact that she was upset. She was getting a strange feeling about this whole trip.

Why didn't we just stay home in Sweet Valley? she wondered, walking more briskly. All she could think about was checking into their room at the Royal Palm and phoning home to make sure her kids were all right.

Todd stood at the door of the Sweet Valley police station watching Steven drive off in the rain with Elizabeth and Jessica. As soon as the sisters finished giving their statements to the police, their older brother had hustled them into the car. "The girls are in shock," an officer had told Steven. "They need to get warmed up and they need *sleep*. Get them home and give them a cup of hot chocolate, and then put them straight to bed."

Now Todd was alone at the station. It was his turn to give a statement about what happened at the marina. Officer Reyes smiled at him as they sat down across from one another at a conference table. "You could probably use a cup of something hot yourself," she commented. "Should I have someone bring in a pot of coffee?"

Todd shook his head. "No, thanks. I guess I'd just like to get this over with."

"You bet. All you need to do, Todd, is tell us in

your own words what happened tonight." She nodded toward the other end of the table where a police stenographer sat, her fingers poised over the keyboard of a portable computer. "Chris will type it up as you say it, and then we'll have you read over the printout and sign it to make it official. Let's start with how you came to be at the marina in the first place."

Todd explained about Jessica's date with James. "It seemed like a funny place to be meeting on such a crummy night," he said, "but I didn't really think about it. I figured it was her business. She did seem worried, though, as if she knew something bad was going to happen." Todd frowned. "But she couldn't have known that some crazed maniac would come out of nowhere and push James off the pier, could she?"

"Let's stick with the facts for now," Officer Reyes advised. "Tell us what you *saw* when you arrived at the pier."

"OK." Todd took a deep breath, making an effort to sift through the chaos of images and emotions tumbling around in his frazzled brain. "We parked the car at the marina and Jessica ran ahead, looking for James. Liz and I were pretty much right behind her. Then, just when she got to the old pier at the end, she stopped in her tracks and started screaming, screaming that someone—that guy—had killed her boyfriend, James."

"Did you actually witness the murder?" Officer Reyes prompted.

Todd closed his eyes, forcing himself to return, mentally, to that fateful moment at the marina. "No," he said after a moment. "It was rainy, and dark. I saw . . . something . . . people, I mean. More than one person, in the distance. And I saw James go over the edge. But I didn't see the actual push as clearly as Jessica did. It had to be that guy, though. There was a fight of some kind, and somebody shoved James through that rotten railing. That guy—"

Officer Reyes provided the name. "Smith. He says his name is Josh Smith."

"James ended up dead on the rocks below, and that guy Smith was the only person left standing." Todd looked down at his knuckles, which were scraped raw from the struggle to subdue Josh Smith. "There's no doubt in my mind," he declared hoarsely. "He did it."

Officer Reyes glanced at the stenographer and then back at Todd. "Thanks, Todd. That'll do it for now. Why don't you take a seat outside? We'll be right with you."

Todd returned to the waiting area, slumping down in one of the uncomfortable plastic chairs. His clothes were still damp, and his entire body was starting to stiffen up. In general, basketball kept him in good shape, but he definitely wasn't accustomed to down-and-dirty fistfights with homicidal maniacs. *I'll be sore tomorrow,* he anticipated. A shudder ran through him, and suddenly he had to fight back tears. He'd be sore tomorrow, but James was *dead.* Not just beaten up, but dead and gone, forever. Just like Sam.

Suddenly a door burst open, breaking Todd's morbid train of thought. Josh Smith appeared, handcuffed and flanked by two burly police officers.

Todd stared curiously, getting his first good look at James's killer. The young man's head was down; he was pale, unshaven, and almost painfully thin. *Where'd he get the strength to put up such a fight?* Todd wondered, recalling their vigorous wrestling match. *I guess maybe craziness makes up for muscle power.*

Just then Josh Smith looked up . . . and looked right at Todd. Recognition glinted in Smith's bloodshot eyes. "You!" he shouted, trying to lunge in Todd's direction. "You've got to listen to me! Those two blond girls, your friends—they're in great danger!"

The officers gave Smith a rough shove, hurrying him along. "Shut up and keep moving!" one of them snapped.

But the prisoner continued his maniacal, bloodcurdling outburst. "It's Elizabeth she's after—she looks just like Elizabeth and she'll stop at nothing,"

Smith ranted. "Nothing, I tell you! She's still out there. . . ."

One heavy door slammed behind Smith and the two officers, and then another, but Todd was still shaking. "What a psycho," he muttered to himself, thinking maybe it was time to take Officer Reyes up on her offer of a hot cup of coffee. "Poor James was really in the wrong place at the wrong time, crossing paths with a nut like that."

Todd couldn't help being disconcerted by the maniac's words. *Who is that guy?* he wondered, staring at the door through which Josh Smith had disappeared. *And how did he know Elizabeth's name?*

Even though he thought Smith's story was hogwash, the hair on the back of Todd's neck stood on end as he remembered the bizarre words. *"She looks just like Elizabeth and she'll stop at nothing. She's still out there."*

What a night! Margo thought as she snuck into the hallway from the Wakefields' basement. *I am just exhausted. I wish Steven would tuck me into bed!*

She smiled at the thought. Steven was such a hunk, she had to keep reminding herself that he was going to be her *brother*. She'd have to keep her hands off him!

He's the best brother in the world, too, Margo

reflected as she settled on the living-room couch and wrapped an afghan around her legs. Right now he was driving through the rain to a twenty-four-hour pharmacy to buy some aspirin for Elizabeth, who was coming down with a cold and had a splitting headache. Elizabeth, meanwhile, was upstairs with Jessica, who as far as Margo could tell was still in hysterics over the "accident" at the marina. *Poor Jessica,* Margo reflected idly. *Did she really* care *for that low-life bum James? What a little fool!*

When the phone by her elbow rang, Margo picked it up quickly and calmly. She'd been expecting this call.

"Liz?" a worried voice inquired. "Is that you?"

"Hi, Mom," Margo said brightly. "How *are* you? How was your flight to San Francisco?"

"Well, not too good," Mrs. Wakefield replied. "The flight was hair-raising, our limo didn't show up at the airport, and the hotel didn't have a reservation for us." She gave a brittle laugh. "But other than that, it's been fine!"

"Oh, dear," Margo commiserated. "Where are you calling from, then?"

"Our new hotel, the Royal Palm Court. Do you have something to write on? I'll give you the phone number so you'll know how to get in touch with us."

"Just a sec, let me get a pen," Margo said. She

placed the receiver against her chest, silently counting to ten. "OK, Mom. Shoot."

Mrs. Wakefield recited the phone number and then sighed audibly. "I feel so much better now," she exclaimed. "Just hearing your voice. For some reason I've been worried. But everything's all right at home? You're OK?"

"Of course, Mom," Margo assured her. "We're fine! Don't worry about a thing. Just have a good time, OK?"

"OK, hon. Call us, though, if anything comes up."

"Sure, Mom. I love you. 'Bye."

Margo hung up the phone, incredibly pleased with herself. It had been very important that she be there to intercept that call. She didn't want Mr. and Mrs. Wakefield learning about James's death—they would certainly come rushing home to be with their traumatized children. And Margo needed them out of the way until after she'd enacted her transformation.

They haven't figured out yet that the whole thing is a hoax, Margo thought, delighted with her cleverness. *That plan's working out perfectly, too!* Mr. and Mrs. Wakefield—Margo's own, dear parents—were off in San Francisco, and Margo was now the only person who knew how to get in touch with them; Elizabeth, Jessica, and Steven wouldn't be able to sound the alarm.

"Perfect, perfect, perfect," Margo sang softly to

herself. "Yes, I've thought of absolutely everything!"

The phone rang again, and Margo grabbed it fast. In case it was Mrs. Wakefield calling back, she didn't want to risk one of the twins answering it upstairs. "Hello?"

"Liz?"

"Todd!" Margo cried. "Are you still at the station? Are you all right?"

"I'm home now," Todd told her. "And I'm fine. I could sure stand a long, hot shower, though. But I wanted to call you first."

"I'm glad you did," she breathed, her spine tingling deliciously at the tenderness in Todd's voice. "So did anything interesting happen after we left?"

"Actually . . ." Todd filled her in on his conversation with Officer Reyes and then described the murderer's strange warning. "I know he's a nut, but it got to me anyway," Todd confessed. "I can't help feeling worried, Liz—worried for you."

"You don't need to be," Margo told him, gratified by his concern, loving the feeling of being loved. "That guy is just some lunatic, a complete psycho. He's behind bars now—he can't hurt us, or anyone, again."

"You're right," Todd conceded. "I'm just glad I was there, on the pier. What if—" His voice cracked. "What if he'd gotten you and Jess?"

"I'm glad you were there, too," Margo whispered. "You were so brave."

"I'll always be there to protect you—I promise. I love you, Liz."

Margo smiled. Life as Elizabeth Wakefield was going to be so sweet; she'd have her very own personal knight in shining armor! "I love you, too, Todd," Margo purred.

Chapter 13

Elizabeth sat on a chair next to Jessica's bed, clasping her sister's hand. At long last Jessica seemed to be dozing off. Her swollen eyelids drooped; slowly the lines of her blotchy, tear-streaked face relaxed; the hand that Elizabeth held in her own grew limp. Bending forward, Elizabeth listened for a moment to Jessica's breathing. It was slow and even. *Good,* Elizabeth thought, gently disengaging her fingers from Jessica's. *I hope she sleeps through the night. It would be the best thing for her.* She tiptoed into the bathroom, easing the door shut quietly behind her. Fatigue and stress battled inside her; she was still keyed up, but she also felt on the verge of collapsing. *What a night,* she thought, stifling a sneeze.

Steven had left a bottle of aspirin on the counter

for her. As she swallowed two tablets with a glass of water, Elizabeth found herself thinking back over the night's mysterious, and deadly, events. *Why was Jessica meeting James at the marina at night, anyway?* Elizabeth pondered the question as she headed into her bedroom. Why had Jessica been so upset on the way there—was it just because she hadn't seen James in a while and things weren't going so well between them? Did James know the guy who pushed him, or was he just unlucky, a random victim? And what about the person the killer tried to hang the blame on, Margo? Did she even exist?

At her dresser Elizabeth opened her jewelry box to put away her earrings. Her head was spinning, but not so much that she didn't notice right away that her gold lavaliere necklace was missing. *That's funny,* she mused. *I haven't worn it in a couple of days. I wonder where I could have left it.* With a sigh she turned away, too tired to search for the necklace now. Shrugging off her bathrobe, she crawled into bed.

For a few minutes she lay there, her sleepy eyes fixed on the telephone on her nightstand. *Todd said he'd call from the police station,* she recalled fuzzily. *Mom and Dad might call, too. Although they could have called already—with the extension in Jessica's room unplugged, I wouldn't have heard the phone.*

Elizabeth's eyelids started to flutter, and her body grew heavier and heavier. She wanted to stay up for Todd's call, but she couldn't fight her exhaustion any longer. Reaching up, she switched off the light. The darkness closed around her like a grave. *What kind of horrible dreams will I have tonight?* Elizabeth wondered fearfully as she drifted off to sleep.

Although her eyes were closed and she was sound asleep, Jessica's lips moved in a voiceless cry, and she tossed on her bed as if she were trying to run. In her dream she had returned to the pier. "What did you want to tell me?" she shouted desperately in her dream. "James, wait!" But once again she'd arrived too late. James didn't answer her question; he didn't even hear it. He was already toppling to his death.

As if Jessica's unconscious mind knew that the horror and the pain were too much for her to bear, the scene in her dream shifted abruptly. She found herself in a new setting, in a new frame of mind; all thoughts of James had disappeared. There was a wide emerald-green lawn, and in the distance, a sandy beach and the shimmer of blue water. *I know this place*, Jessica thought in her dream. *It's Secca Lake. I've always loved it here.* The sun was warm overhead, and the grass was silky and cool under her bare feet. It was summer.

170

Jessica wandered happily toward the water. In her dream it didn't strike her as strange that the scenery contained elements from other places she knew and loved: the Beach Disco's dance floor, the pool house at Fowler Crest.

As she stepped onto the sand, Jessica looked around, expecting to see Lila or one of her other friends. Instead, she saw Elizabeth, running toward her from the other end of the beach. A smile of welcome lit up Jessica's face. *Elizabeth's coming to see me,* she thought, her own footsteps quickening. *We're going to be friends again.*

But as Elizabeth drew nearer, Jessica's smile wavered. The girl coming toward her . . . she was Elizabeth, and yet she wasn't. Even though the weather was warm, she was wearing a funny blue ski cap, and while she had Elizabeth's features, there was something odd, almost threatening, about her expression. Her blue-green eyes were stony and cold.

In her dream Jessica froze. "Elizabeth?" she said, uncertain.

The girl continued to advance, one hand held behind her back and the other extended to Jessica. *Should I run and embrace her, or run away from her?* Jessica wondered, torn by conflicting impulses. She did neither; she just stood, paralyzed, while the girl came closer . . . closer . . .

Suddenly, with the hand that was visible, the

girl reached up and whipped off her ski hat. To Jessica's astonishment long black hair tumbled to the girl's shoulders. Jessica gasped. "You're not—!"

Before she could finish her sentence, the girl brought forward her hidden hand, revealing a huge butcher knife. Jessica stared at the knife, her heart in her throat. Now that she wanted to run, she found that she couldn't; all at once she was no longer on the beach, but in some kind of small room, with her back firmly against a wall. There was no way out. "Don't do it," Jessica whispered.

But the girl had no mercy. Smiling cruelly, she raised the gleaming knife and lunged forward, the blade aimed straight at Jessica's heart.

"No!" Jessica screamed. "No! No! No!"

It took a few seconds for Jessica to realize that she'd woken up—that she'd screamed out loud. She sat up in bed, tears streaming down her face, her throat aching from the scream. She'd never felt terror like this in her life—never. And though the dream had ended with the scream that awoke her, the horror of it, the danger, still seemed to surround her, palpable in the darkness.

Sobbing, Jessica leapt from her bed and ran blindly across her room and through the bathroom toward Elizabeth's room.

"I'm thirsty, aren't you?" Elizabeth said to Sam

in her dream. "Let's take a break from dancing and get something to drink."

The dance floor was packed with rowdy Jungle Prom–goers, and it was like swimming against a riptide to get back to the table where she had stowed her purse and Sam had dumped his tuxedo jacket. Finally, though, they were almost there.

She was having a good time chatting with Sam; she wasn't really paying attention to what was going on around her. But now, in her dream, Elizabeth forced herself to focus. *Look*, she commanded herself. *Look. What do you see?*

It was no use. There were too many people in the way. *No, wait a minute,* Elizabeth thought. *There!* Through the crush of bodies she glimpsed a slender arm reaching out to touch one of the punch cups she and Sam had left on their table. Someone darted away; Elizabeth saw only the swirl of a skirt, and then the person—the girl—was gone. Elizabeth shook her head, not sure whether to believe the fuzzy evidence of her own eyes.

What did it matter, anyway? Why should she care? They reached the table, and with a careless shrug Elizabeth toasted Sam with her punch cup and put it to her lips. Then she remembered. *The punch—had someone spiked it?*

I'm almost there, Elizabeth realized, adrenaline coursing through her veins. *I'm getting closer to something, to finally understanding what hap-*

pened to me that night! I'm on the verge—

Suddenly Elizabeth was staring into blackness. The brightly lit school gymnasium, Sam and the other students, the band and the decorations, had all disappeared, and she was alone in deep, silent dark. Or was she?

What woke me up? Elizabeth wondered, befuddled. And then, in front of her staring eyes, a ghostly apparition loomed over her bed—a pale face with a gaping black hole for a mouth, and two pale arms reaching out to grab her.

Covering her eyes with her hands, Elizabeth screamed at the top of her lungs.

After leaving Elizabeth's aspirin in the twins' bathroom, Steven stood in the kitchen, took two slices of whole-wheat bread from the bag, and tossed them onto a plate on the kitchen counter. Unscrewing the lid from a jar of mustard, he dipped in his knife, coating the bread thickly. A couple pieces of ham, a couple pieces of Swiss . . .

Slapping the sandwich together, Steven raised it to his mouth and took a big bite. He wasn't even hungry; he was eating only because he had to do *something*. It was late, but he knew there was no way he'd be able to fall asleep for hours.

My sister's boyfriend got murdered, he thought in disbelief, chewing hard. *Man, this is crazy. This is sick. James—that poor kid. And poor Jess! I can't believe this happened the minute Mom and Dad left town. Thank God I was here, anyway.*

He took another hefty bite of ham and cheese, his brow furrowing as he thought about the call he'd just placed to the number his parents had left. He wanted them to know what had happened—he knew his mother at least would want to come right home. But to his consternation the Fairmont Hotel had informed him that no one by the name of Wakefield was staying there.

I don't get it, Steven mused, his eyes straying to the rain-streaked window over the sink. *If their plans changed, why didn't they call? Geez, Mom nearly had a conniption before they left, going over the phone numbers a million times,* Steven remembered. And now they were staying someplace else, and they didn't even call to tell their kids about the switch? They were usually so conscientious about that sort of thing—it just didn't fit.

Steven picked up his plate, preparing to make short work of the second half of his sandwich just as he had the first. At that instant the silence of the night was broken by a bloodcurdling scream.

Steven dropped the plate, and it shattered into a million pieces on the floor. *That came from up-stairs!* he realized, the shock sending his heartbeat into a mad gallop. One of his sisters was in trouble!

Steven launched forward like a sprinter from the starting blocks. As he raced from the kitchen, another scream echoed through the dark house. *What on earth is happening?* Steven wondered as he tore up the stairs three at a time. A hundred horrible images flashed through his brain. *The killer,* he thought irrationally. *He murdered James and now he's come for my sisters, too!*

Reaching Jessica's bedroom, Steven yanked open the door. He saw her bed, the rumpled covers . . . empty! Panting with terror at the thought of what he might find there, he dashed on to Elizabeth's room.

And there they were, both his sisters, kneeling on Elizabeth's bed, sobbing and hugging each other tightly. "What's wrong?" Steven cried, rushing to their sides. "Jess, Liz, what happened? Tell me. Tell me!"

Margo slipped out of the den, where she'd hidden when Steven had returned from the store, and crept up the stairs toward the sounds of sobs and murmured voices. *All this drama,* she thought, licking her lips. She had to see it, she had to share it. It was hers, after all—her creation.

Elizabeth's bedroom door was ajar. Crouching in the dark hallway, Margo peered into the room, now brightened by a bedside lamp.

It was like a scene from a movie, her own private movie. Steven sat on the edge of the bed with his arms wrapped around both his sisters, murmur-

176

ing comforting words. "It's all right, I'm here," he said in the deep, manly voice that always sent a thrill up Margo's spine. "Ssh. Ssh. It's all right. Just take a deep breath, Liz, and tell me what happened. I heard a scream—two screams. What scared you?"

"It was J-Jessica," Elizabeth stuttered. "I was asleep, and all of a sudden she was standing over my bed. She scared me half to death and I screamed, but I think she screamed first."

Jessica was still crying, her face pressed against Steven's shoulder. "What was it, Jess?" he asked. "Did you have a bad dream?"

"I did—it was horrible. . . . Oh, Steven!" Violent tremors shook Jessica's shoulders. "I saw—I saw—"

Jessica was trying to speak, but she was crying so hard, she could make only incoherent animallike sounds. Steven pulled her closer. "OK. Give yourself a minute," he advised her. "Just relax, Jess. I'm here. We're both here with you."

And I'm here, too, Margo thought, smiling. She felt both tender and scornful toward the twins, her future sister and her future self. What jumpy, sensitive things! *They were upset by what they witnessed at the marina tonight*, she guessed. *Really, they've been so sheltered, it's almost unbelievable!* Well, soon there wouldn't be a need for any more violence. Just one more death, and then peace. Contentment. Safety. Love.

Margo's smile grew misty. Before pulling back from the door, she took one last, lingering look at the scene in the bedroom. Steven was stroking Jessica's hair with a firm but gentle hand; his other arm remained tightly wrapped about Elizabeth's shoulders. They looked like a statue: three figures carved from the same piece of marble, entwined and inseparable—an emblem of perfect family love.

Soon it will be me, Margo thought as she stole away down the stairs and into the basement. *I'll be part of that little family.* She contemplated James and Josh, the two thorns in her side, now both out of the way, disposed of in a masterful fashion. The road ahead was clear; she could see its end. *Soon,* she thought. *Soon!*

With the light on and with Steven nearby, Elizabeth gradually grew calm. Finally even Jessica caught her breath enough to speak. "What *happened*?" Steven asked one more time. "What set you two off?"

"I ran into Elizabeth's room because I had a nightmare and I was scared," Jessica whimpered, clinging to her brother and sister. "It was so horrible. Oh, Liz . . ."

"What was it about?" Elizabeth prompted gently, cradling Jessica much as she had earlier that evening. "You'll feel better if you tell us about it."

"It was—it was about *you*," Jessica said, sniffling.

Elizabeth raised her eyebrows in surprise. "A nightmare about me?"

"It was you, only it wasn't you," Jessica tried to explain. "It just looked like you, but it was really someone else. I was on the shore at Secca Lake, and you—she—came running toward me. You had on this funny blue hat, like a ski cap."

Steven snorted. "Sounds scary, all right," he kidded her.

Elizabeth didn't smile. To her the odd details of Jessica's dream were anything but amusing. *It can't be the same,* she thought, astonished and terrified. "Go on," she pressed her sister. "What happened next?"

"Then you—she—" Jessica burst into tears again, hiding her face against Steven's chest.

Steven met Elizabeth's eyes over Jessica's bent head, his expression puzzled. "Whatever it was, it must've really been awful. But you woke up," Steven reminded Jessica. "You're OK. You're safe."

"I know what it was," Elizabeth whispered.

Now Steven really looked mystified. "What?" he said. Even Jessica lifted her head at this comment.

Elizabeth stared straight into her sister's eyes. "I know what happened next in your dream," she said quietly. "The girl pulled off her hat and she had dark hair instead of blond. And she was carrying a knife—a big butcher knife."

Jessica's mouth dropped open. "Yes," she said.

"How did you know?"

"I've had the same dream," Elizabeth told her. "Night after night for the past month or so. The same exact dream."

The twins gaped at each other, their eyes wide with shock and terror. The dream seemed twice as frightening now that they'd both experienced it. *What does it mean?* Elizabeth wondered. She and Jessica had always possessed a special twins' intuition, and in spite of their recent estrangement, that intuition was still in effect. But what was it trying to tell them? An uncontrollable trembling seized Elizabeth's body. Could the dream be some kind of omen—a deadly prophecy?

"Ohmigod, Liz, this is so freaky," Jessica cried, pressing her hand against her mouth. "Do you think—what if—"

Steven could see that his sister was on the verge of another hysterical outburst. "Let's all take a deep breath and count to ten," he recommended, gently grasping Jessica's shoulder and giving her a little shake. "C'mon, help me out here. One, two, three, four . . ."

Obediently, Jessica drew in a deep, ragged breath, and Elizabeth did the same. "Good," Steven praised them. "Now, let's get calm and try to stay calm, OK?"

Steven knew it was easier said than done, though. He wasn't about to admit it to his sisters, because they were looking to him to be the Rock of Gibraltar, but the account of the strange, coincidental dreams had shaken him up, too. *Freaky isn't the word,* he thought, jumping to his feet and pacing restlessly around the room.

Despite the confident, competent big-brother act he was putting on, Steven felt helpless. Murders, dreams . . . his sisters seemed to be threatened from every direction, from the outside *and* the inside. *If only Mom and Dad were home,* Steven found himself wishing for about the hundredth time that night. Somehow, even though he knew all the doors and windows were tightly locked, the big, dark house around them didn't feel like much protection.

Crossing to the window, Steven peered out into the dark drizzle, just as a car that had been parked across the street flicked on its headlights and pulled away from the curb. Steven gulped. The driver had long blond hair—from the back, she almost looked like one of the twins.

You're seeing things, Steven lectured himself, turning his back to the window. Obviously all this talk of dreams was starting to get to him! *If only Mom and Dad were home,* he thought. *If only the sun would rise so this weird, awful night would be over.*

Chapter 14

"It was thoughtful of Kotkin, Greiner, and Burns to schedule my first meeting for late in the morning so we'd have time for sight-seeing. But it's not the best day for it," Ned Wakefield admitted.

He and Mrs. Wakefield walked along Fisherman's Wharf on Wednesday morning, huddling close together under an umbrella. The fog was so dense it felt like rain, and Alice Wakefield pressed close to her husband's side, chilled to the bone despite her scarf, gloves, and wool-lined trench coat. "That's the understatement of the decade." She pointed into the fog, laughing wryly. "I know the Golden Gate Bridge is out there somewhere! I'll just have to pretend."

Turning, they headed back the way they'd come. "Let's warm up with a cup of coffee at

Ghirardelli Square and then take the cable car back to the business district," Mr. Wakefield suggested. "It won't hurt to show up a few minutes early."

The cup of steaming almond-scented coffee brought some color back to Mrs. Wakefield's cheeks. But as she and her husband squeezed into seats on the trolley, she still felt cold. With a cheerful clang of its bell, the cable car started forward, heading up a steep hill. Mrs. Wakefield stared at the quaint, pastel-painted houses without really seeing them. Instead, in her mind's eye, she saw her daughters' faces. Sweet, pretty, familiar faces, but so hard to comprehend sometimes! They'd been acting so strangely lately, she reflected, so distant and unpredictable. Blowing hot and cold toward each other, and toward her and Mr. Wakefield and Steven, alternately needy and withdrawn . . .

The cable car continued to climb up and up. *Have I been any better, though?* Mrs. Wakefield asked herself. *My emotions are about as steady as a Ping-Pong ball lately!* There were moments when she wanted to push her daughters away, and other times when her maternal instincts were as ferocious as a lion's.

A troubled frown creased Mrs. Wakefield's smooth forehead as she remembered the wave of protectiveness that had washed over her as she hugged her daughters good-bye. It didn't matter that everything had been fine when she checked in last night—she should have heeded her instinct; she should have stayed home. As the cable car crested the hill and swept down the breathtaking drop on the other side, Mrs. Wakefield was overcome by an inexplicable sense of dread and powerlessness. She closed her eyes, bracing herself against the back of the seat. *I shouldn't have left them. I should have stayed home.*

Mr. and Mrs. Wakefield hopped off the trolley half a block from the modern glass high rise where the offices of Kotkin, Greiner, and Burns were located. Despite the disappointments of the previous night, Mr. Wakefield's mood was upbeat. "I'm looking forward to meeting these folks," he told his wife as they crossed the airy, plant-filled lobby to the bank of elevators. "It'll be great to finally satisfy my curiosity about this consulting job."

Trying to dismiss her glum musings, Mrs. Wakefield smiled encouragingly at her husband. "I'm sure they're looking forward to meeting you, too."

The elevator soared upward, depositing them on the seventeenth floor. "Here we are," Mr. Wakefield said, ushering Mrs. Wakefield through the door into the elegant offices of Kotkin, Greiner, and Burns.

Their feet sinking soundlessly into plush carpet-

184

ing, they approached the reception desk. A young woman in a peacock-blue dress greeted them with a warm smile. "Can I help you?" she asked Mr. Wakefield.

"I'm Ned Wakefield from Sweet Valley," he announced, returning her smile. "I have an eleven o'clock appointment with Michelle de Voice."

The receptionist's smile faltered. "I'm sorry, with whom?"

"Michelle de Voice," Ned repeated. "In the legal department. I'm here about a consulting project."

The receptionist flipped through the appointment calendar on her desk, shaking her head, and a sickening feeling of déjà vu settled in Mrs. Wakefield's stomach. *It's just like last night at the hotel!* she thought.

"I'm sorry, but there's no meeting scheduled for you, Mr. Wakefield, at eleven or at any other time today. In fact, no one by the name of de Voice is employed here. Is it possible you could have gotten the date wrong, and the name, too, perhaps?" the receptionist suggested politely.

Mrs. Wakefield could see that her flustered husband was having a hard time holding on to his temper. "No, it's not possible," he declared, his face reddening. "I am absolutely certain that I was invited by Michelle de Voice to attend a meeting at eleven A.M. on Wednesday, December twenty-ninth."

"Well, I don't have any record of—"

"Then there must be some mistake. Is there someone else from the legal department or management that I could speak with?"

The receptionist mustered another halfhearted smile. "I wish there were, but unfortunately most of the senior management are still out of the office on holiday vacations." Her eyes brightened. "I'll tell you what—can you come back tomorrow? The head of the legal department will be in, and I'm sure he can help us straighten this out."

Mr. Wakefield let out a frustrated sigh. "It doesn't look as if we have a choice. Yes, we'll come back tomorrow. Thank you," he added gruffly.

Turning, he strode briskly from the office, Mrs. Wakefield hurrying after him. "Ned, *what* is going on?" she exclaimed when they were alone in the elevator.

"I don't know any more than you do," he responded, raking a hand through his hair. "How can the company's receptionist know nothing about Ms. de Voice and this meeting? It's just preposterous."

On the sidewalk outside the office building, they paused, at a loss for what to do next. Mrs. Wakefield could no longer keep her apprehensions to herself. "Ned, there's something very strange going on here. I think we should try to catch the next plane back to Sweet Valley."

"What, write the whole thing off?" Mr. Wakefield exclaimed.

"Something's wrong, here and at home," Mrs. Wakefield insisted. "I—I just have this *feeling*."

Mr. Wakefield took her hand and squeezed it. "You spoke with Liz last night, and she said everything was fine," he reminded her. "As for this meeting, I'll admit things could be getting off to a better start. But now that I've had a minute to cool off a little, I'm not so worried. I'm sure everything will get straightened out if we stick around one more day."

Mrs. Wakefield hesitated. "I still think . . . the kids . . ."

"They have our number at the Royal Palm," Mr. Wakefield said soothingly. "If any kind of problem comes up, they'll call us."

"Well . . . I suppose you're right," Mrs. Wakefield agreed at last. "And since we've come all this way—"

"We might as well make the best of the situation," Mr. Wakefield concluded. "That's the spirit, sweetheart. We can still do all the fun things we planned: tour a museum, make dinner reservations someplace special, go to the theater."

Putting up the umbrella, Mr. Wakefield held it over Mrs. Wakefield's head, and they strolled in the fine gray mist toward the fashionable shopping district. *Ned's right,* Mrs. Wakefield tried to convince herself. *Steven's with the girls, and they're all old enough to take care of themselves. I'm silly to let my imagination run away with me.*

But no matter how much she reasoned with herself, her vague sense of dread persisted. *Because reason has nothing to do with it,* Mrs. Wakefield realized. *Logical or not, I just have a feeling.*

Somewhere far away Lila heard a doorbell ring, followed by the sound of muffled voices. "Umm," she murmured, rolling over in bed with a luxurious yawn. "Ooh, what a great dream I was having. . . ." She pulled the covers over her head so she could drift back to sleep, and back into the arms of Jean-Claude, the handsome young Frenchman of her dream.

Just then there was a knock on her bedroom door. "Whoever you are, go away," Lila grumbled sleepily.

The door creaked open. Lila opened an eye. Jessica was peeking in at her. "What are *you* doing over here at the crack of dawn?" Lila wanted to know. "You usually sleep later than I do on vacation!"

Jessica laughed merrily. "It's not the crack of dawn—it's almost noon!"

"It feels like the middle of the night to me," Lila complained. "Haven't you ever heard of jet lag?"

"I know I should have waited," Jessica admitted, bouncing across the room to perch on the edge of Lila's bed, "but I just couldn't wait to hear about your trip to Paris! What did you do? What did you see?"

It looked like Jean-Claude would have to wait. With a disgruntled sigh Lila sat up in bed, propping herself against a mound of pillows. She didn't appreciate being robbed of her beauty sleep; on the other hand, it *was* gratifying to have a captive audience for her stories about the glamour of Paris.

"We did and saw *everything*," she told Jessica. "We shopped till we dropped on the Champs Élysées, saw the Mona Lisa at the Louvre, went to the opera and the theater, had coffee and people-watched on the Rive Gauche . . ." She wiggled her eyebrows.

"You mean guy-watched," said Jessica.

"Right," Lila confirmed with a grin. "And the city is just *crawling* with celebrities—really cool European celebrities, not boring Hollywood types. They practically *all* have royal titles."

Jessica's eyes sparkled. "It sounds wonderful."

"It was," Lila drawled. "Needless to say, I didn't want to come back."

"Oh, yes, you did. Your New Year's Eve ball is the day after tomorrow!"

"That's right, the ball." Lila patted her mouth, smothering a yawn. "I almost forgot about it."

"Well, *some* of us had nothing else to do over Christmas but look forward to this party," Jessica reminded her. "How many invitations did you end up sending out?"

"Oh, a hundred or so." Lila waved a hand. "I don't remember exactly."

"Did you buy a dress yet?"

"I picked up something in Paris, but I'm not sure if it's quite right," said Lila.

"Can I see it?" Jessica asked eagerly.

"Geez, Jess, I haven't even *unpacked* yet," Lila groaned. "I'll show it to you later, OK?"

"Sure. How about the music? You never told me which band you decided to hire."

"The big swing band," Lila replied. "It seemed like the most elegant and traditional for a formal New Year's Eve party."

"I can't remember," Jessica rattled on. "Are you serving dinner or just finger foods? I mean, if it's dinner, I don't want to fill up beforehand—"

Lila burst out laughing. "Enough questions already—get a grip, will you? It's just another party. You'd think it was the first one you'd ever been invited to!"

Jessica smiled, a strange, fervent glow in her eyes. "It's *not* just another party. It's going to be the biggest, best party you've ever given. It's going to be the most important, unforgettable night of our lives."

Lila couldn't help smiling, too. *I do throw the best parties in Sweet Valley—probably in the whole state of California!* "Well, when you put it that way . . . !"

"I'll be ready in half an hour, Jess," Lila called over her shoulder as she shuffled into the bathroom to take a shower. "Just make yourself at home, OK?"

"I'll do that," Margo called back.

As soon as she heard the water running, Margo stepped out into the hall. *Yes indeed,* she thought with a sly smile, *I sure could make myself at home here. Too bad the Wakefields' house isn't more like Fowler Crest!*

From what Margo knew of Lila, it would take her longer than half an hour to shower and get dressed for their expedition to the Pancake House and the mall. With Mr. and Mrs. Fowler still asleep in the master bedroom, it was a perfect opportunity to snoop around the rest of the mansion. Margo strolled down the plushly carpeted second-floor hallway, casing out each and every room, closets and bathrooms included. *What a spread,* she thought as she traced her fingers along the top of a gleaming cherry dressing table in a guest bedroom that looked as if it belonged in Versailles. Valuable paintings were scattered about the walls; the room was almost cluttered with Chinese vases, silver candlesticks, and crystal knickknacks; a priceless Oriental rug muffled the sound of her footsteps. *Maybe I'll get to sleep in this room someday. It'll be pretty cool to be friends with someone this rich!*

Yes, Margo decided as she opened a door on the hallway and discovered yet another walk-in linen closet, as soon as *she* became Elizabeth, she was going to start being *much* nicer to Lila. *Liz has never given Lila a fair shot,* Margo reflected. Reaching the end of the long hall, she turned around and started making her way back down the other side. *God knows why—Lila's a million times more fun than that drip, Enid!*

One more guest bedroom . . . Margo scanned it quickly, memorizing the locations of the windows and closets. She wasn't taking this tour solely for aesthetic reasons, after all; she had a very important motive for familiarizing herself with every inch of Lila Fowler's palatial home.

Margo walked down the wide staircase to the first floor, smiling in anticipation. *It's going to happen here,* she thought as she waltzed across the high-ceilinged foyer and into a living room the size of a ballroom. *At the New Year's Eve ball—what better way to kick off the new year?*

Investigating the kitchen next, Margo paused to examine an impressive array of German cutlery mounted in a case on the wall. Her palms itched at the sight of the gleaming stainless-steel blades. Any one of the knives would be a perfect murder weapon.

She bypassed the knives, her eyes still searching. Choosing a weapon was easy. What she needed to find now was the right place to *use* the weapon.

Margo thought of all the empty rooms upstairs. The house was big, but not so big that a scream would go unnoticed. And Elizabeth might very well scream when Margo took her life.

I need someplace private, Margo mused. *Someplace where I can dispose of the body so that it will never be found.* There could only be two Wakefield girls; the third had to disappear without a trace.

Wandering back into the enormous living room with its full-length French doors, Margo suddenly stopped in her tracks. Through the windows she could see the Fowlers' swimming pool . . . and the Fowlers' pool house. *It's perfect!* she exulted, grasping one of the long brocade curtains and pressing herself up against the glass. The pool house was set apart from the main house, and with continued bad weather in the forecast, no one was likely to venture outside on the night of the party. And just beyond the pool house, a stretch of mani-cured green lawn extended to the woods. *I'll sneak over at some point tonight or tomorrow night,* Margo planned, already smelling the sweet, wet scent of the earth. *I'll dig the grave in the woods. It will be ready and waiting.*

"Ready to go?"

Margo jumped at the sound of the voice behind her. Quickly composing her features into a bland, harmless smile, she turned to face Lila, who'd traded her nightgown for a red miniskirt and baggy black sweater. "Yup. Let's go," Margo replied.

They left the house, a now fully awake Lila chattering about the Parisian boutique where she'd purchased the sweater, but Margo was only half listening. As she stepped over the threshold, her mind was already on Friday night. *I'll walk into the mansion as myself . . . and walk out a few hours later as Elizabeth Wakefield!*

Chapter 15

Jessica hopped out of bed just long enough to pull on a pair of itchy old wool knee socks that she hadn't worn since junior high. Her teeth chattering, she leapt back under the covers. But even wrapped in a blanket, bedspread, and down comforter, she couldn't seem to get warm. She was cold right down to her bones—nothing seemed to help. *Maybe I'll never be warm again,* Jessica thought morosely. Maybe for the rest of her life she was going to be as cold as she'd been the night before on the pier with the rain soaking through her clothes—as cold as the ocean waves that washed over James's body as it lay on the merciless rocks below. . . . Jessica's own phone was unplugged, but now she could hear the extension in Elizabeth's room ringing. *Someone else calling to see how I'm holding up,* she guessed. *I bet it's Amy this time.* The news of James's death had been in the morning paper, and a few of her friends had already called to express their sympathy and concern. Jessica had asked Steven to field the calls; she just wasn't up to talking to anyone yet.

In the distance the phone stopped ringing; Jessica imagined Steven giving his little speech: "Yes, she's all right, but she's still asleep. Sure, I'll tell her. Thanks for calling."

Jessica pressed her forehead against her tucked-up knees, listening to the silence. Her room was so quiet and lonely—*Maybe it* would *make me feel better to talk to someone,* she reflected.

Hanging off her bed, she plugged her phone back into the jack and then picked up the receiver to dial Lila's number. She set it down again with a sigh. It was after lunch, but still too early to bother Lila—she'd be jet-lagged from her flight and would probably sleep most of the day. *And she won't have heard about James yet,* Jessica thought. *What would I say? "Welcome back from Paris, my boyfriend got murdered while you were away"?*

Shivering, Jessica drew the comforter more tightly around herself. No, she didn't want to have to pronounce those words out loud: James, dead. She didn't want to talk about what had happened; she didn't want to *think* about what had happened. But of course, she could think about nothing else.

I wish I could go to sleep and wake up in a year, Jessica thought, her eyes filling with tears. *I wish I could just sleep through all this pain.* She almost felt as if she could do it, too. She was exhausted because her sleep the night before had been broken by horrible nightmares—about the girl with the butcher knife and about James plunging through the railing to his death. Jessica simply didn't know which was worse: being awake with her heart breaking at the loss of James, or falling asleep only to be tormented by violent dreams.

Jessica jumped at the knock on her bedroom door. The door swung open, and Steven stuck his head into the room. "How're you doing?" he asked.

Jessica shrugged. "OK. What's up?"

"Billie, Liz, and I are going to a matinee. Get dressed and come with us," Steven urged. "I think it'll do us all good to get out of the house for a couple of hours."

The idea was definitely appealing. The house still felt creepy to Jessica after last night's dreams and screams—she didn't want to be left alone in it. But she didn't relish the prospect of sitting in the dark in some movie theater, either. She was too depressed to move. "No, thanks," she mumbled, managing a weak smile for Steven's benefit. "You guys go on. I'll be all right. Have—have Mom and Dad called yet?"

Steven shook his head. "Not yet. Don't worry, we won't be long," he promised.

Steven closed her bedroom door, and Jessica listened to his footsteps thump away down the hall. A few minutes later she heard a car engine roar off. They were gone and she was alone in the house . . . alone in the world.

I wish Mom and Dad would call, Jessica thought, a fat tear rolling down her cheek. She wanted to tell them about James; she wanted them to come home. *Why didn't they call last night?* she wondered. *Why aren't they at the hotel they said they'd be at?* Suddenly an irrational fear crept into Jessica's wounded heart. What if something bad had happened to her parents, too?

Two people she'd loved, Sam and James, had met with violent, untimely deaths. *What if I'm under some kind of curse?* Jessica thought, her eyes wide with dismay. *What if this is only the beginning?*

Slouched down in the driver's seat of her parked car, Margo watched as Steven, Elizabeth, and another girl drove off down the street. *That must be Steven's girlfriend, Billie,* she speculated. *She's cute. Wonder where they're off to?*

She waited a few minutes and then walked around to the side of the house, letting herself in through the unlatched basement window. *I might be pushing my luck,* she thought as she eased open the basement door and stepped quietly into the first-floor hallway. *Maybe those three were just running out for a few minutes.* But Margo didn't care about the risk. She couldn't stay away. As the day of her eternal transformation approached, she couldn't resist returning to the house again and again, even when she knew it wasn't necessarily smart.

I'll just sneak up to Elizabeth's—my room, Margo thought. *Jessica's probably asleep—I bet they gave her tranquilizers or something. I'll read Elizabeth's latest journal entries and then I'll leave.*

She glanced into the den as she passed on her way to the staircase. To her surprise she found herself staring right at Jessica, who was sitting on the couch wrapped in an afghan with a bag of microwave popcorn on her lap.

At the sudden sight of Margo, Jessica's eyes flew open and she jerked her arm, popcorn spilling everywhere. "Geez, Liz, you scared the living daylights out of me!" she gasped. "What are you *doing* here? I thought you went to the movies!"

"Uh, I . . . ," Margo stammered. For the first time in ages, she found herself at a loss for words in a tight situation. *Why would Elizabeth have changed her mind abruptly about going to the movies? Think. Think!* Margo commanded herself. "I . . . I have a really bad headache," she

199

mumbled. "I decided not to go."

Jessica bent to sweep up some of the spilled popcorn. "You still have the headache you had last night, huh?"

Last night? "Um . . . yeah," said Margo. "I should probably take something for it."

"What about the aspirin Steven went out to buy for you?" Jessica asked. "Didn't you try those?"

Steven . . . aspirin? The little pieces of missed information pricked Margo like needles. She broke out in a sweat, her head spinning. How could she have forgotten that? *You've got to remember everything, or you can't stay in control,* she reminded herself.

"Well, yeah, I did try them," Margo spluttered. "I just meant I should probably take some more. Look, I don't feel well enough to talk, OK?" she burst out.

Jessica gaped at Margo, her mouth in a dismayed frown. She seemed surprised and hurt . . . or was she suspicious? Margo's fingers curled into fists; her breath came fast and hard. She knew she was on the verge of giving herself away. *Just get out of here. Get out now!* Turning on her heel, she bolted from the room.

In the kitchen she fumbled a glass from the cupboard and filled it with water, draining it in one long gulp. The cool water sliding down her hot throat calmed her somewhat, but as she slammed the glass back down on the counter, she continued to pant, her eyes flashing. Curses bubbled up inside her; she pressed her lips together tightly to prevent them from spilling out. She wasn't sure who she was angrier at: Jessica for asking so many questions, or herself for bumbling like an idiot, for getting overeager and sloppy.

That look in her eyes—did she guess that I'm not Elizabeth? Margo wondered. It would be her ultimate test, after all: Could she fool the other twin?

Margo's eyes strayed to a paring knife someone had left lying on the counter. She grabbed it impulsively, immediately soothed and empowered by the feel of the handle in her hand. *I could kill Jessica right here and now,* Margo realized, an eager light rising up in her eyes. *We're alone in the house; it would be easy.* Jessica wasn't the twin Margo had intended to become, but when it came right down to it, what difference did it make? She'd studied them both; she'd impersonated them both.

Maybe I shouldn't wait for Elizabeth, for New Year's Eve, Margo thought greedily. *Maybe I should just go for it!*

Huddled under the afghan in the den, Jessica felt more depressed and lonely than ever. Reaching into the bag of microwave popcorn, she stuck a few salty kernels into her mouth. *Liz made it pretty clear that she'd rather die than pass the time with me,* Jessica reflected sadly. *She took care of me and comforted me last night, but that was just because she had to. She did her duty, and now things are back to the way they were before—she's avoiding me like the plague.*

She continued to munch the popcorn without really tasting it, her thoughts suddenly turning to the murderous psycho who was now locked up, thank heaven, in the county jail. Jessica remembered the strange things he'd shouted when Todd tackled him on the pier, about someone named Margo who looked just like her and Elizabeth; he'd accused the girl of murdering James, and a bunch of other people, too. Jessica sniffled, tossing the popcorn bag aside in order to grab a tissue from the box on the end table. *Poor James, randomly becoming the victim of a crazed maniac on the rampage,* she thought, blowing her nose. *It's just not fair. Why did it have to be* him? *Why?*

It was a good question. Jessica threw the balled-up tissue on the floor and reached for another one. James just happened to be on the pier when that nut came along. *And all because he was meeting me there,* Jessica thought miserably. *He wanted to see me—he had something to tell me.* She remembered how urgent he'd sounded on the phone, remembered her gut feeling that something was terribly wrong. How prophetic it had turned out to be! *What did he want to tell me?* Jessica wondered, heaving a deep sigh. *I guess I'll never know now.*

The doorbell rang, and Jessica waited for Elizabeth to get it. She heard a metallic clatter coming from the kitchen, as if Elizabeth had dropped something, but no footsteps. With another sigh Jessica got to her feet and shuffled into the hallway, dragging the afghan with her.

Maybe it's Amy or Lila, Jessica thought, suddenly hopeful. She peered through the glass. It was just Todd. Jessica pulled open the door. "Hi," she said dully.

Todd stepped into the hall, looking at her uncertainly. After a moment's hesitation he slung an arm around her shoulder and gave her a quick, brotherly squeeze. "How are you holding up, Jess?"

Suddenly, Jessica's throat constricted; tears threatened once more. Todd's concern for her was heartwarming, but also heartbreaking. *Elizabeth still has Todd, but I have no one*, Jessica thought, ducking her head to hide behind a curtain of uncombed hair. "I'm all right—thanks for asking. I think Liz is in the kitchen." Before Todd could spy her damp eyes, Jessica fled back to the den.

❖   ❖   ❖

Quickly, Margo bent to pick up the knife that she'd dropped when the doorbell rang. She shoved it into a drawer just as Todd entered the kitchen.

"I've been so worried about you!" Todd exclaimed, hurrying forward to wrap his arms around her in a warm embrace.

Margo rested her head against his chest, taking advantage of this quiet moment to try once more to get her thoughts in order. *Thank God he can't see my eyes!* she thought. She had a feeling they were still a little wild.

"I'm worried about Jess, too," Todd murmured into Margo's silky blond hair. "She looks like a zombie. Is she going to be able to deal with this? I mean, first Sam and now James—how much can the poor kid take before she cracks?"

"Oh, she'll survive," said Margo.

She realized her mistake when she felt Todd flinch. *Oops—that must've sounded callous.* "What I *meant* was, she'll probably mourn James for a long time," she added quickly. "She loved him. But she's tough. She's got a lot of inner strength to draw on."

"Hmm." Todd sounded thoughtful. "Actually, I wonder sometimes if she really *is* all that tough, if under the surface maybe she isn't more messed up by all this stuff than people realize."

There was a question in his voice, but Margo didn't have the faintest idea how to respond to it.

What was Todd getting at? Would the real Elizabeth know?

Time to change the subject and get out of here! Margo decided. She definitely didn't intend to touch this Jessica topic. It was too dangerous, and she couldn't afford the tiniest mistake, not this late in the game. *Keep it light,* she advised herself. *Play it safe.*

Pulling away from Todd, Margo looked up at him with a bright smile. "You know, I was still too stressed out to eat breakfast this morning, but now I'm starved. Pizza would hit the spot—what do you say?"

"Should we see if Jessica wants to come?" asked Todd as Margo took his hand and dragged him from the room.

"No," she said—too quickly, too adamantly. Todd frowned, apparently puzzled by her tone. "She . . . she told me she wants to be alone," Margo added in a softer voice, "and I think we should respect her wishes." She tugged on his hand, by this time positively desperate to hop in the BMW and leave. "C'mon, Todd. Let's go!"

As the front door swung shut behind them, Todd had time to glance over his shoulder and see Jessica standing halfway up the stairs. She stared after them, looking offended and pained.

Her lips moved; Todd heard her mutter something about a "miraculous recovery." *What's that supposed to mean?* he wondered. *Was she talking to Liz?* He looked inquiringly at his girlfriend.

"Have you rented your tuxedo for the New Year's Eve ball yet?" Elizabeth chattered, completely oblivious to Jessica. "I still haven't decided what I'm going to wear. . . ." *Slam.* The door was shut and bolted.

Todd trailed after Elizabeth as she walked briskly toward his car, still babbling about the upcoming party. *This is too weird,* he thought, remembering how overwrought Elizabeth had been the previous night, how worried about Jessica's physical and mental well-being. Now, less than twenty-four hours later and with Jessica still a total wreck, Elizabeth was ignoring her sister and acting as if the horrible murder they'd all witnessed had never even occurred.

As Elizabeth belted herself into the passenger seat of the BMW, Todd glanced surreptitiously at her profile. All of a sudden he felt a wave of uncertainty and mistrust. Something was off, but he couldn't quite say what. Immediately he was reminded of his date with Elizabeth a week or so ago, the night they went to the old movie at the Plaza Theater and he finally decided he wasn't with Elizabeth at all, that Jessica was pulling a twin switch for some mysterious reason. *If I didn't know better, I'd swear this isn't Elizabeth, either!* Todd thought. *But it can't be Jessica, because I just saw her.*

Suddenly Todd realized Elizabeth was gazing at him, an intent, expectant look in her blue-green eyes. "Ready to go?" she prompted. "Is anything the matter?"

Snap out of it, Wilkins, Todd ordered himself. *That psycho, with all his ranting and raving about a Wakefield twin look-alike, has your imagination running overtime.* He shook his head. "No, nothing's the matter," he said with false heartiness as he started the engine. "Let's head out."

Margo lurked in the Wakefields' side yard, hidden by the shadows of a misty, gray twilight, after Todd had dropped her off. As soon as his BMW was safely out of sight, she hurried to her own car, parked halfway down the block.

She drove back to the guest house, breaking the speed limit and drumming her fingernails distractedly on the steering wheel. She'd just spent a couple of hours with Todd—they'd had pizza at Guido's and then gone for a drive by the ocean, which was still stormy and rough. Todd hadn't wanted to park, though; he'd insisted that they keep driving, as if he were afraid she'd molest him if he stopped the car for five seconds.

He didn't even try to kiss me good night, Margo thought, her mouth twisting with bloodless amusement. *He probably thinks sweet, gentle Elizabeth is still traumatized about what happened to James and needs to be handled with kid gloves.* Oh, well; there would be plenty of time for passion and romance after Margo became Elizabeth. She just hoped Todd didn't become suspicious of her; it would be a shame to have to do away with such a hunk!

As she let herself into her room at the Palmers' guest house, Margo couldn't keep from grinning. She thought about Josh breaking into her room the previous night—he thought he was so smart! "I'd like to see him break *out* of where he is now," Margo said to herself with a giggle.

Tossing her handbag onto the rumpled bed, she sat down at the writing table to review her notes about Elizabeth. Her less-than-memorable date with Todd, even her awkward encounter with Jessica, hadn't diminished Margo's self-confidence. *Everything's happening just the way I wanted it to,* she reflected as she practiced scribbling Elizabeth's name on a blank sheet of paper. James was dead, and the only other person who knew about her, Josh, was safely out of the picture, in jail and booked for murder. Mr. and Mrs. Wakefield were out of town on a wild-goose chase. Margo had successfully fooled everyone with her impersonations of the twins: Todd, Lila, Mrs. Wakefield, Steven. Yes, so far her strategy was perfect . . . and soon all her hard work would come to its final fruition.

All that's left are little details, easy things, Margo thought blithely. *Figuring out what the twins are going to wear to the ball so I can duplicate Elizabeth's outfit . . . and, of course, the murder itself.* Margo smiled. But *that* would be a piece of cake!

Chapter 16

First thing Thursday morning, the Wakefields' cab stopped in front of the offices of Kotkin, Greiner, and Burns. Mr. and Mrs. Wakefield ran into the building, dodging the raindrops. It was another wet, blustery day. *And it suits my mood exactly*, Mrs. Wakefield thought as her heels clicked across the marble floor of the lobby. For Mr. Wakefield's sake she was pretending that she, too, believed everything would fall into place that morning—all the questions would be answered, all the mysteries solved. But in her heart of hearts she couldn't help expecting the worst.

The receptionist smiled at them when they entered. "Good morning, Mr. and Mrs. Wakefield. I told Mr. Vasquez, the head of legal, about your situation, and he'll be happy to talk with you. He's waiting for you in the first conference room down the hall on the right."

Mr. Wakefield raised his eyebrows at Mrs. Wakefield as if to say, "See? Now we're getting somewhere!" She smiled weakly.

Mr. Vasquez was looking through some papers, but he rose to his feet and extended his hand when the Wakefields appeared. "Good morning, Mr. and Mrs. Wakefield," he said with a genial smile. "I hope I can be of some help to you."

"We hope so, too," Mr. Wakefield declared. Taking a seat, he quickly presented his side of the story: the letter from Michelle de Voice inviting him to interview for a lucrative consulting position; the enclosed plane tickets; the limousine that didn't materialize; the hotel reservations that didn't exist. "Finally, yesterday morning I arrived for my meeting only to discover there was no meeting scheduled," he concluded. "Not only that, but your receptionist informed me that nobody named Michelle de Voice works here!"

Mr. Vasquez tapped his mechanical pencil on a legal pad. "Ms. Capriatta wasn't misleading you," he said. "No one named de Voice works for us in any capacity. And as soon as I heard about your visit, I spoke with each and every member of our legal staff, *and* each departmental manager. I'm truly sorry, Mr. Wakefield, because I know you've traveled a long way, but no one knew anything about any consulting job you might have been considered for. No one had even heard your name."

Both Mr. and Mrs. Wakefield sank back in their chairs, flabbergasted. "But—but the letter," Mr. Wakefield muttered. "And the plane tickets. I just don't understand. . . ."

"Do you have the letter with you?" asked Mr. Vasquez. "Could I take a look at it?"

Wordlessly, Mr. Wakefield removed the letter from his briefcase and handed it to the other man. Mr. Vasquez glanced at it and immediately shook his head. "It's a forgery, plain and simple," he declared. "This isn't our procedure—this isn't even our *letterhead*." He shook his head again. "I really don't know what to say. I have to conclude that the whole thing was some kind of bizarre, elaborate hoax."

The three stood up. "I'm very sorry for all your trouble," Mr. Vasquez reiterated. "Would you leave me your phone number so that I can call you if by chance I learn anything that might help us unravel this mystery?"

Mr. Wakefield removed a business card from his briefcase. "Thank you for your time, Mr. Vasquez."

As soon as they were safely sequestered in the elevator, Mr. Wakefield's temper exploded. "Why on earth would anyone pull such a stunt?" he exclaimed, his eyes flashing. "This is outrageous!"

"And *who* would do it?" said Mrs. Wakefield. "Do you have *any* idea who might be behind it, Ned?"

Mr. Wakefield shook his head. "Absolutely none. I can't even begin to guess. I've never heard of anything like this in my entire professional career!"

This time, as they stood in the lobby, there was no question about what they should do next. "Let's go home," Mrs. Wakefield urged her husband, more anxious than ever to return to Sweet Valley and her family.

"We'll be on the next plane," Mr. Wakefield vowed.

"Are you sure these weren't supposed to be delivered to Pasadena for the Rose Bowl parade?" Amy joked on Thursday afternoon. "I've never seen so many flowers in my life!"

She and Lila stood in the main entrance of Fowler Crest, nearly buried by a mountain of fresh-cut flowers that had just been delivered by Petal Pushers, a local florist. "Aren't they wonderful?" Lila gushed, lifting an armful of deep-red roses to her face. "I could just drown in them."

"That's very poetic, Li," Amy remarked, "but if you want them to last until the party tomorrow night, you'd better stop sniffing them and get them in some water."

"Right," said Lila, all business again. She gestured toward the dining room. "Theresa dug up forty or so crystal and china vases for us to put the flowers in," she informed Amy.

"Forty?" Amy exclaimed in disbelief.

Lila shrugged. "I guess that's the kind of stuff people give as wedding gifts. And since Mom and Dad married each other twice—!" Both girls laughed. "So all we have to do is tastefully and artistically arrange the flowers."

"I'm pretty tasteful and artistic, if I may say so myself," said Amy.

"Then we'll set out the candles and drape the streamers," Lila continued. "And finally, last but not least, you have to help me figure out how to rig a big bag from the ceiling for the balloons and confetti to fall out of at the stroke of midnight."

"No problem!"

Each girl grabbed a box of flowers and carried it into the dining room. Stem by stem Lila started arranging a bouquet in a hand-cut crystal Waterford vase. "Maybe I should put some music on," she said after a few minutes of silence. "Maybe that would get us more in the mood."

Amy sighed. "Maybe."

"I mean, I could've hired somebody to do all this junk, but I figured it would be more fun for you and me and Jessica to do it ourselves," Lila explained. "I had no *idea* that . . ." Her voice trailed off.

"Well, how could you?" said Amy.

"Having somebody murdered really puts a damper on things," Lila observed. "Poor Jessica! I still can't believe that happened, and right in front of her eyes. What I really can't believe, though, is that she came over here yesterday morning all bouncy and cheerful. I mean, she wanted to go *shopping*. And she didn't say a single word about James getting killed!"

Amy frowned. "She was probably still in a total state of shock and denial," she hypothesized. "I see it all the time volunteering on the Project Youth hotline—a lot of people react that way to trauma." Sympathetic tears sparkled in Amy's gray eyes. "The poor kid, I bet she doesn't know *what* she's doing or saying these days."

"I wonder if she'll even come to the ball," Lila mused. "I mean, now that the reality of James's death is starting to sink in and all that."

Amy lifted her shoulders. "Last time I spoke to her, she said she'd be there. She didn't feel like helping decorate, but she said she wants to be with her friends on New Year's Eve. I think we just have to humor her, go along with her, with whatever kind of mood she happens to be in."

Lila nodded agreement. Tipping her head to one side, she examined the bouquet she'd just completed. *Poor Jess—she's had some incredibly tough breaks!* she thought. It really boggled the mind. This simply had to be the end of Jessica's tragic bad luck, though. *I'll just see to it that my party is the start of happier times for her,* Lila determined. *It's almost the New Year, after all!*

"I can't believe they couldn't fit us on a flight until dinnertime," Mrs. Wakefield complained on Thursday evening. She was nearly at her wit's end after killing time all day at the airport. Now she hurried up to the Arrivals/Departures monitor to check on the status of their flight.

"Flight number twelve-seven-seven to Sweet Valley . . ." Her eyes widened. "Canceled," she gasped.

"They're all canceled, or delayed for hours," Mr. Wakefield observed. "It must be the fog."

An airline representative confirmed this theory. "The airport is completely fogged in," he told the Wakefields. "At the moment no planes are landing *or* taking off. I can reserve seats for you on the first flight out in the morning. With any luck, by then conditions will have improved."

Mr. Wakefield turned to his wife with a sigh of utter frustration. "It looks like we're spending another night in San Francisco, Alice, like it or not!"

While Mr. Wakefield waited for the new tickets to be printed, Mrs. Wakefield hurried off in search of a pay phone. She dialed her own home phone number and then held her breath, hoping the kids weren't out. "Hello?" said a girl's voice.

"Liz? Jessica?"

"It's Elizabeth. Hi, Mom!"

Mrs. Wakefield's knees buckled with relief. "I'm glad I caught you at home, sweetheart. Your dad and I have some very strange news."

"Mom, that's terrible!" Elizabeth exclaimed upon hearing the details of her parents' trip. "If there's no such person as Michelle de Voice, who do you suppose wrote the letter?"

"We have absolutely no idea," Mrs. Wakefield replied. "In the meantime we'd hoped to surprise you by arriving home early, but now we're stranded up here by bad weather. We'll be on the first flight south tomorrow, though, I promise. Is everything OK at home?"

"Of course, Mom," Elizabeth answered. "We're all doing fine. We miss you, though."

"I miss you, too," said Mrs. Wakefield. "Give my love to your brother and sister. See you tomorrow."

" 'Bye, Mom."

Mrs. Wakefield hung up the phone and stood for a moment, her forehead wrinkled pensively. Then someone cleared his throat behind her. "Oh, excuse me," she said, moving aside so the man could place his call.

She walked back to where Mr. Wakefield waited for her, still thinking about her brief conversation with Elizabeth. Why didn't she feel better, having been reassured by Elizabeth that everything was fine at home? *I guess I won't rest easy until I see for myself,* Mrs. Wakefield concluded, wondering how she was going to bear another sleepless night in a San Francisco hotel. *I won't rest easy until I can actually hold my children in my arms again.*

Steven looked up from the newspaper he was reading as his sister walked by the den on her way to the stairs. "Who was that on the phone?" he called after her, a trace of anxiety in his voice.

Elizabeth stepped into the den for a moment. "Just Penny," she replied, pushing up the cuffs of her oversize green sweater.

Steven tossed the newspaper aside with a sigh. "I wish Mom and Dad would check in with us! I just don't understand why they haven't called. If they're not at the hotel they said they'd be at, then where are they?"

"Don't be such a worried old grandmother," Elizabeth teased. "They decided to stay at a different hotel, that's all. Gosh, they hardly ever get a chance to be alone together, away from the three of us. Can you blame them if they want a little privacy for once?"

Steven smiled crookedly. "Well . . ."

"Obviously things are going well, or we would've

heard," Elizabeth said. "No news is good news, right?"

With a flip of her ponytail she breezed back out of the room, and Steven relaxed somewhat. *Liz is probably right,* he decided. *No news is good news. I'm just overreacting to all this stress. But, hey, we're muddling through, aren't we? I'm keeping an eye on Liz and Jess—I'm keeping them safe. We'll be OK till Mom and Dad get back.*

He retrieved the newspaper, flipping it open to the sports section. Obviously he should take his cue from good old down-to-earth, sensible Elizabeth. She seemed to be looking at the bright side.

Elizabeth stood by her bedroom door for a moment, listening. Nothing. The phone had rung a minute or two earlier, and someone else had grabbed it before she had a chance to—Steven, probably. *I guess it wasn't Mom and Dad,* she thought, disappointed. *He'd let me know right away if he'd heard from them.*

Wandering over to her closet, she slid open the door and began flipping idly through her dresses. What on earth was she going to wear to Lila's ball tomorrow night? She remembered asking herself the same question before the Jungle Prom. Ultimately, she'd bought a dress—a dress that ended up in tatters, covered with blood.

Elizabeth bit her lip. *Why am I even going to*

this party? she wondered, squeezing her eyes shut in hopes of chasing away the vision of the bloodstained blue party dress. *It's not like I'm in the mood to celebrate!* What was there to be happy about these days? Just two nights earlier she'd been on the scene when her sister's boyfriend was brutally murdered by a psychopath; plagued by mysterious dreams and gory nightmares, it had been weeks since she'd gotten a good night's sleep; she and Jessica were still—and probably always would be—estranged. *And the weather isn't exactly helping any!* Elizabeth thought, glancing out the window at the black, rainy night.

Elizabeth couldn't help smiling wryly. "Boy, you're a real barrel of laughs, Wakefield!" she muttered to herself. *All these thoughts of gloom and doom—I can't give in to them.* She fingered the sleeve of a dark-purple silk dress. *Maybe I'll actually have fun at Lila's party.* The very faintest ray of hope and optimism brightened Elizabeth's eyes. *Maybe we'll turn this corner—maybe the storm will clear and we'll all get a new start in the New Year.*

She was jolted from her reverie by a knock on her door. "Who is it?"

"It's me, Jessica," a voice replied softly.

Elizabeth heaved a tired sigh. Then again, maybe things would never get back to normal!

Jessica never would have bothered knocking in the old days, Elizabeth reminisced sadly. *She always just barged right in!* "Come in," she called, continuing to rummage through her closet.

Jessica sat down on the edge of Elizabeth's bed. There was a moment of strained silence. *At least she's up and dressed,* Elizabeth thought, noting her sister's oversize green sweater and black jeans. *I was starting to think she'd never get out of bed again.* Her eyes flickered to Jessica's face, wondering what she wanted. But for a minute Jessica just watched Elizabeth intently, without speaking.

"What are you doing?" Jessica asked at last.

"Looking for something to wear to Lila's tomorrow night," Elizabeth answered. She wrinkled her nose, discouraged. "I'm not having much luck. Maybe I just won't go!" she cried, slamming the closet door shut.

"But you *have* to go," Jessica insisted, to Elizabeth's surprise. "Tell you what; you can borrow one of my dresses. Anything you want from my closet—you pick."

Elizabeth raised her eyebrows at this uncharacteristically generous offer. Usually, Jessica was the one who got tired of her own clothes and begged to borrow something of Elizabeth's—or sneaked something out of Elizabeth's closet without bothering to ask first. *What is she up to now?* Elizabeth wondered, instantly searching for an ulterior motive. *What does she want from me in return?*

A split second later Elizabeth was bowled over by a wave of remorse. *I can't believe I'm so suspicious!* Poor Jessica was going through an absolutely terrible time. Maybe her motive was pure; maybe she just wanted what Elizabeth herself secretly wanted more than anything—to be able to trust each other, to be close again. How could Elizabeth refuse this offer of peace?

Hurriedly, Elizabeth crossed the room to Jessica's side, hoping her sister hadn't noticed her hesitation. "Thanks, Jess," she mumbled, giving her sister an awkward hug. "I'd love to borrow a dress. You go ahead and choose one for me—anything you don't feel like wearing yourself."

Margo wrapped her arms around Elizabeth, hugging her back. A smile played on her lips as she thought about the next time she would hold Elizabeth like this. *Tomorrow,* Margo anticipated, her eyes gleaming. *Tomorrow night we'll meet again, Elizabeth, in the embrace of death. Your death, my birth.*

Of course, it wouldn't actually be the end for "Elizabeth Wakefield." Margo patted Elizabeth's shoulder before pulling back from the hug, her hand lingering on the other girl's arm. *It'll only be the end for this pretty little body. Your identity, your soul, will live on inside me.*

"I'll do that, Liz," Margo said softly, turning to glide from the room. "See you."

Tomorrow, tomorrow . . . The delicious word danced in Margo's brain as she slipped unobserved from the house. She'd entered the home stretch! She'd had only one little setback. According to the phone call she'd just intercepted, Mr. and Mrs. Wakefield had finally figured out that the consulting interview in San Francisco was a hoax. If they flew out first thing Friday morning, they'd be home by lunchtime, a full day earlier than Margo had intended.

But it really doesn't matter at this point, she concluded as she dashed through the rain to her car. *I've thought of everything—absolutely everything!* The scheme was brilliantly conceived, and it would be enacted with equal brilliance. Mr. and Mrs. Wakefield would say good-bye to Elizabeth as she left for the ball, and they would greet her when she returned. *And they will never guess that I'm not the daughter they gave birth to,* thought Margo. *They'll never, ever guess.*

She smiled, her eyes fixed on the misty gray horizon. Yes, she could see the finish line. Nothing could stop her now.

223

Chapter 17

Josh Smith sat on the edge of his hard, narrow cot, staring dully at the small barred window of the holding cell at the county jail. He didn't have a calendar—he didn't even have a wristwatch anymore—but since he'd now spent three nights in jail, he knew it had to be Friday. *The last day of December—New Year's Eve,* he realized, bitterness sweeping through him. *But I sure don't have anything to celebrate!* When the clock struck midnight, he'd still be sitting exactly where he was right now. That is, unless they decided to cart him off to the state penitentiary in the meantime.

It's the end for me, Josh thought mournfully. The end of a terrible year, and it might as well have been the end of his life, too. For him New Year's Eve didn't carry the promise of a new beginning. He had nothing to look forward to but a long prison sentence and the tormenting knowledge that he'd failed miserably in his quest to avenge his baby brother's wrongful death.

How did I get myself into this mess? Josh almost laughed out loud; it really was ludicrous to think that *he'd* ended up behind bars while Margo continued to walk free. He didn't laugh, though; his situation was too serious. *Things do not look good,* he had to admit to himself as he gazed around the bare, cold cell. No one believed his account of what really happened on the pier the other night. The Wakefield twins and Todd Wilkins all stated incontrovertibly that Josh was the one who pushed James—they didn't see anybody else. Telling the police that he'd trailed Margo all the way to California from Cleveland only confirmed their opinion that he was nuts. And if they didn't believe Margo even existed, how could they be expected to take seriously Josh's warnings about danger for the Wakefield girls?

Meanwhile Josh was still trying to get in touch with his mother. He'd been calling her for days, but he never got an answer—apparently she'd gone out of town. He had no friend, no ally. He was trapped—and powerless.

All at once the last three anguished, sleepless nights seemed to catch up to Josh, and he dropped his head heavily into his hands. *She won,* he thought. *Margo won.* She'd gotten away with killing Georgie and the young man on the pier, and with who knew how many other heinous crimes, and now no one would be able to stop her. If Margo harmed Elizabeth Wakefield, if she took the other girl's place as Josh knew she intended to do, who would ever know? How would Josh ever be able to prove anything? Josh pictured his dead brother's face, and tears welled up in his eyes. "I'm sorry, Georgie," he sobbed. "I'm sorry I let you down."

For a minute Josh just sat crying quietly, remembering Georgie. Then the image of his brother's face slowly faded from his mind, and another vision took its place. Now he found himself picturing the two young girls who looked so much like Margo . . . so alike, and yet so different. The Wakefield twins, with their warm, innocent, *human* eyes, were nothing like Margo and her cold, soulless gaze.

Suddenly, Josh pulled back his shoulders and sat up straight. *No,* he thought, his heart pounding with a new sense of determination. *The battle's not over yet! As long as I have breath in my body, I'll keep after her. I'll stop her; I won't let her ruin any more lives.*

Filled with a renewed sense of purpose, Josh leapt to his feet. There was only one big problem. He gripped the iron bars of his cell, shaking them with all his might. *I've been arrested and charged with murder,* he reminded himself. *They've locked me up and thrown away the key.*

The key . . . There was nothing else for it, Josh realized after considering his very limited options. Margo had manipulated circumstances so that the full force of the law came down on Josh's innocent head; in order to extricate himself, he would have to break the law. It was time to beat Margo at her own game.

A plan came to him in a flash of inspiration. Josh lay back down on his cot and let out a loud groan. When the guard didn't respond right away, he groaned again even louder. "Help," he cried. "I'm really sick."

A moment later the guard materialized outside the cell. He peered curiously at Josh, who now lay doubled up on his cot, clutching his stomach and moaning. "What's the matter with you?" the guard demanded, sounding more annoyed than suspicious.

"My stomach," Josh whimpered. "There's this sharp pain—I think it's my appendix. I need a doctor."

"You need a doctor, all right," the guard agreed with a humorless chuckle. "A *head* doctor." But he unlocked the door to the cell and walked over to Josh. "You probably just have indigestion, fella— the food here's not so hot. How 'bout you roll over and let me take a—"

Before the guard could finish his sentence, Josh sprang up from the cot and drove his fist into the other man's jaw with all his might. Taken by surprise, the guard stumbled backward. Josh punched him again and the guard fell, hitting his head with a crack against the edge of the washbasin. His eyes rolling back in his head, the guard slid to the floor, unconscious.

Josh rubbed his knuckles, staring at the other man's limp body. *I did it*, he thought in disbelief. *I've been a docile prisoner, so the poor guy trusted me. I pulled it off!*

There wasn't time to stand around congratulating himself, though. Quickly, Josh yanked off the unconscious man's shirt, trousers, and shoes. Stripping off his own flimsy prisoner's garb, he dressed again in the guard's uniform. The shoes were too big, but Josh didn't plan to let that slow him down.

Pausing at the door to the cell, Josh glanced up and down the concrete corridor. There was no one in sight; his little scuffle with the guard had gone unnoticed. *Good, I'll get a head start*, he thought as he sprinted from the cell and into the nearest stairwell. *Five minutes is all I need. I just need to catch Margo before they catch me.*

Taking the coffeepot from the hot plate, Margo filled her mug to the brim. She sat back down on her unmade bed and lifted the steaming cup to her lips. This was her third cup that morning, but she was still bleary-eyed. *Too many long days and late nights,* she thought, slurping the coffee and not caring—not even noticing—that it scalded her tongue. *All that spying and studying and practicing.*

But now it was here at last, the day she'd been waiting for all her life, the day she'd been preparing for nonstop since she arrived in Sweet Valley: her very last day as Margo the abused, unloved foster child. Just over the horizon awaited a new dawn, a new year—a new life.

Draining the last drops of coffee from the mug, Margo looked dispassionately around the rented room that had been her home for the last few months. *I'm finally getting out of this pit,* she thought. *What a mess.* The walls were plastered with photos and newspaper articles and notes to herself about Elizabeth's habits and activities; clean and dirty clothes mingled in piles on the floor; a couple of knives lay next to her on the bed along with some little trinkets she'd stolen from the twins; there was rotting, stinking garbage everywhere—all dimly illuminated by the feeble glow of the one bare bulb dangling from the ceiling.

Suddenly, a dizzying wave of nausea rose up in Margo, and along with it a profound feeling of self-hatred and disgust. For a split second she seemed to see the darkness and filth of her external surroundings for what they really were: a reflection of her own inner self. *My God,* she thought, staring with wide, wild eyes. *Is this* me?

"No, this isn't me," she muttered hoarsely. Jumping to her feet, she hurled the coffee cup against the wall with all her might. It shattered into a million pieces. "This isn't me," she shouted again, her voice rising to a hysterical screech. "I deserve better than this!"

Blind with rage, Margo tore around the room, trashing everything she could get her furious hands on. She slashed the wallpaper into ribbons with a knife, then plunged the blade repeatedly into the mattress and pillows, sending feathers flying. Tossing the knife aside, she seized the wooden desk chair and bashed it into splinters against the writing table. She kicked out the legs of the table and turned next to the windows. She wanted to rip the curtains to shreds—she wanted to slam her fist through the glass and feel the blood trickling down her arm. . . .

But she'd run out of steam. Panting, Margo stood in the middle of the room, looking around at her ruinous handiwork. *When Mrs. Palmer sees this, she'll kick me out, maybe even call the police,* she thought, biting her lip.

Then she smiled to herself. *It doesn't matter,* she remembered. *I've spent my last night in this dump—I won't be coming back here! Margaret Wake—Margo—is about to disappear forever. She'll be gone, and starting tonight, I'll be sleeping in a warm, clean, cozy bed in a big, beautiful house. After tonight, I'll be Elizabeth.*

Yawning, Jessica sat up in bed and looked out the window. "Ugh, another rainy day," she mumbled to herself. "How gross." She considered rolling over and going back to sleep, but when she glanced at her clock radio, she saw that it was almost noon. *And it's New Year's Eve,* Jessica thought. *Maybe I should start trying to psych myself up for the ball.*

It was going to be hard, though, without James. Too hard. Jessica pressed her fingers against her eyelids, willing herself not to burst into tears. She had already cried too much. It was the reason she hadn't gone to James's funeral that morning. She'd known she wasn't strong enough—it would have pushed her over the edge. *And I don't think I'm up to this party, either,* she thought. *Oh, James, it's still too soon for partying.*

Just then Jessica heard her bedroom door creak open. She looked over, giving her tired, bloodshot eyes one last rub.

Elizabeth popped her head into the room. "Good, you're awake!" she said cheerfully.

"That's actually open to debate," Jessica said with a weary sigh. "What's up?"

"I just wanted to ask you a teeny, weeny favor," Elizabeth explained. "I really don't have anything to wear to the party tonight, and it's kind of late to buy anything—I don't want to spend the money, anyway. So I was wondering . . ." She flashed a sheepish, ingratiating smile. "Could I borrow one of your dresses?"

Jessica blinked at her sister's sweet, chatty tone. *Is this the same Liz who's been giving me the coldest of cold shoulders?* "Well, uh, sure," she said.

"Thanks a lot." Elizabeth strolled over to Jessica's closet. "Which one are you planning to wear?"

Jessica shrugged. "I'll probably end up staying home," she admitted forlornly. "Go ahead and take whichever one you want."

Elizabeth pivoted on her heel and fixed her sister with a fond, encouraging look. "You *have* to go to the ball, Jess," she urged. "I know it's difficult, with all that's happened. But it just wouldn't be a *party* without you there." She dropped her eyes almost shyly. "It wouldn't be worth ringing in the New Year."

Jessica's jaw dropped. *She's really worried about me!* she realized, now doubly surprised. *She cares.* Jessica's heart swelled with emotion; tears sprang to her eyes again. But these were happy tears—hopeful tears. *Maybe things are going to be different between us in the New Year.*

James is gone, but maybe I'm going to get Elizabeth back.

"OK," Jessica said, managing a smile. "I'll give it a shot."

"It'll be just the thing to cheer you up," Elizabeth promised. "So which dress should I leave for you?"

"You pick first," Jessica replied.

"All right." Elizabeth considered the selection and then pulled a short, strapless fuchsia dress from the closet. "How 'bout this one? The tags are still on it—would you mind if I was the first to wear it?"

Jessica raised her eyebrows. The dress was new, and so sexy and daring that she hadn't even gotten up the nerve to wear it yet herself. "Wow," she exclaimed. "That's not exactly your usual style, Liz! But, sure. Go ahead." She shook her head, bemused. "I guess you're planning to start off the New Year with a bang, huh?"

A secretive smile curved Elizabeth's lips. "A bang? You might say that, yes."

Because it was New Year's Eve, the stores in the Valley Mall were all closing early. Her heels tapping briskly in the nearly empty mall, Margo headed straight for Lisette's, the shop where Jessica had bought the fuchsia dress.

The clerk greeted her with a wide smile. "Ah—

you came back for one of those dresses," she said knowingly.

Margo gave the woman a suspicious look. *That's right,* she recalled. *She was working a couple of days ago, when I came in with Lila, pretending to be Jessica.* "That's right," Margo replied. "I decided to buy something new for my friend's New Year's ball after all."

"Better late than never!" the clerk declared.

This time Margo didn't bother responding. She really wasn't in the mood to make small talk with that stupid woman; she was on an important mission and the clock was ticking—she didn't have a second to waste.

Striding over to a rack of dazzling party dresses, Margo began thumbing through them rapidly. *They've just* got *to have another fuchsia dress like Jessica's,* she thought, pushing aside velvet and sequined dresses of all styles and colors. *Or rather like Elizabeth's, since she's the one who'll be wearing it tonight, though she doesn't know it yet.*

With a surge of triumph Margo spotted the dress she was looking for. Short, strapless, sexy, bright pink . . . She checked the tag, holding her breath. It was a size six. *This is my lucky day!* Margo gloated, grabbing the dress from the rack.

She hurried over to the counter, pulling out her wallet as she went. The saleswoman took the dress from her, stroking the silky fabric as she slid it off the hanger. "Hmm, I don't remember you trying this one on the other day," the clerk remarked idly as she rang up the sale.

"I changed my mind. Is there any law against that?" Margo snapped.

The woman lifted her overplucked eyebrows, looking offended. "No, there certainly isn't," she said, her tone polite but chilly.

In the recent past Margo would have said something sweet and placating to smooth the woman's ruffled feathers. Her primary concern had been to avoid arousing suspicion, even in encounters with the most insignificant strangers. Now, though, she really didn't care if her behavior struck people as odd or insulting. It was too late for anyone to cause trouble for her; too late for anyone to discover the truth.

Margo tapped her fingers impatiently as the clerk folded the dress with painstaking slowness and placed it in a shopping bag. Then the clerk began writing out a sales slip, also at a snail's pace. Before she could finish, the telephone rang.

"Good afternoon, Lisette's," the clerk said brightly. "Oh, it's you. Hi! How's business at your end of the mall?"

Margo felt the steam building up inside her; if she didn't get out of there soon, she was going to explode. She cleared her throat in an exaggerated fashion, but the clerk ignored her and continued chatting on the phone. "I'll meet you at my car in half an hour," she told the caller. "It's the metallic-blue Honda right out front. That's right, you've been in it before. Well, do you want to go back to the same place we went that night? I thought the food was pretty good. . . ."

It's personal—it's not even a business call! Margo fumed. Well, she wasn't going to wait around an instant longer. *You just lost your last chance this year to make a sale, lady.* Margo shoved her wallet back into her purse. *I hope they make you pay for this yourself!*

Grabbing the shopping bag, Margo bolted from the store without paying—and without a backward glance. By the time the clerk realized what had happened and shouted after her, Margo was already halfway to the parking lot.

Outside, she paused to suck in a lungful of cold, damp air. Then she strode across the lot, her face as dark as the storm clouds overhead. On the way to her own car, Margo spotted a metallic-blue Honda. The clerk's asinine telephone conversation echoed in her brain. As Margo came abreast of the Honda, she yanked a small knife from her purse. Bending, she punctured two of the tires with careful precision, relishing the whistling sound of the air leaking out. "Happy New Year, lady," she muttered with a grim smile.

✼   ✼   ✼

"This is cozy," Billie murmured, snuggling close to Steven on the couch in the Wakefields' family room. "So which movie do you want to watch first?"

They'd rented three to make sure they'd have enough entertainment to last until midnight. "I feel bad," Steven said, putting an arm around her. "This is going to be a pretty boring New Year's Eve for you."

"No way!" Billie protested, smiling playfully. "This party has *everything*. A pot of your dad's secret-recipe nuclear-meltdown chili, two flavors of ice cream to cool off our mouths afterward, popcorn, soda, movies . . ." She kissed Steven on the nose. ". . . *you*."

"Yeah, but you can have me any night of the week," he pointed out. "New Year's Eve only comes once a year. Are you sure you wouldn't rather go to that bash up at school? I'd understand."

"I'm absolutely sure," said Billie. "I want to be with you, and I agree that you should stick around here in case your parents call and, well, just in *case*."

"Yeah, we need to stay close to home. Mom and Dad are bound to call tonight." Steven shook his head. "Man, will they flip when they hear what's been going on the last few days! They're going to feel awful that they didn't know about James."

"How's Jessica holding up?"

Steven stroked Billie's hair thoughtfully. "It's hard to say. She's been pretty much staying holed up in her room. She didn't go to his funeral this morning—I guess it was just more than she could take."

"But she's going to Lila's tonight?"

Steven nodded. "For a little while, anyway. I wouldn't be surprised if she came home before midnight, though."

"Another reason we should stick around," Billie commented. "She might need someone to talk to."

"I'm here for her," Steven affirmed. "But I've got to tell you . . ." His eyes twinkling, he bent his head to kiss Billie. It felt so good to be near her; he was happy that they were finally getting some time alone. For a couple of hours he wanted to forget his worries and responsibilities—he wanted to lose himself in the sweetness of Billie's kisses. "I hope Jess doesn't come home early," he murmured. "I hope they both have a great time and stay out really, really late."

"I can't take it anymore," Alice Wakefield exclaimed late Friday afternoon. "I simply can't take it anymore!"

She and Mr. Wakefield had been waiting all day for the situation to change, but the San Francisco airport was still closed because of the weather.

Their early-morning flight to Sweet Valley had been delayed until late morning, and then afternoon; now there wasn't even an estimated departure time listed on the board. "At this rate our flight might not leave until *midnight*, if then," Mrs. Wakefield surmised. "There's just no way of knowing when this horrible fog will lift. We could wait forever! Ned, we've got to find another way to get home."

"You're right," Mr. Wakefield agreed. "Let's take a taxi to the train station and see if we can get a seat on Amtrak."

This is more like it, Mrs. Wakefield thought twenty minutes later as she and her husband dashed into the train station and elbowed their way up to the Amtrak ticket counter. *Trains don't care about fog. We're going to get home—we're finally going to get home!*

"When does the next train to Sweet Valley leave?" Mr. Wakefield inquired briskly. "We'd like to buy two tickets."

The ticket agent checked his monitor. "Number twenty-two for Sweet Valley leaves in . . . five minutes," he replied. "There are only two seats left— you're in luck!"

Mr. Wakefield gave his wife the thumbs-up sign, and she smiled faintly. Finally, something was going their way!

Mr. Wakefield handed the agent some cash,

and the agent printed out the tickets. "Track four," he informed them. "And you'd better step lively!"

Tickets in hand, Mr. and Mrs. Wakefield hurried toward track four. A few feet short of the platform, Mrs. Wakefield spotted a bank of pay phones. "Ned, I've got to stop for just a second," she announced breathlessly.

Mr. Wakefield pointed to the big clock on the wall. "Our train leaves in two minutes!"

But Mrs. Wakefield was already punching in her calling-card number. "I'll be fast," she promised. "I just want to tell the kids we're—"

She stopped speaking abruptly, her forehead wrinkling. "Is it busy?" Mr. Wakefield guessed. "No one home? It's New Year's Eve, remember. They may all be at Lila's already."

Mrs. Wakefield shook her head, mystified. She wasn't getting a busy signal—the phone wasn't even *ringing*. Instead, a recorded voice had just informed her, "We're sorry, but the number you have reached is not in service at this time."

Mrs. Wakefield hung up the phone. "I didn't get through at all," she told her husband, her eyes wide. "The line is dead."

All day long a new storm had threatened Sweet Valley. Now, as darkness fell, the skies suddenly opened up, and a cold, stinging rain began to pour down. Her wet hair streaming behind her, Margo ran through the soggy grass away from the Wakefields' house, a knife clutched tightly in her hand.

Only seconds before, she'd cut the telephone line—just one more way of isolating the family. *They can't call out and no one can call in,* Margo thought with satisfaction. *I have them exactly where I want them. They're mine, all mine!*

Rain streaming down her face, Margo smiled back at the house. Its brightly lit windows twinkled in the mist like loving, welcoming eyes. "Next time I return to you," Margo whispered ecstatically, "it will be as your cherished daughter, Elizabeth." Her plan had been set in motion. The countdown had begun!

Jumping into her car, Margo revved the engine and sped down the street. Lightning flickered on the horizon as she bent to turn on the radio. The storm made the transmission crackle, but through the static Margo managed to catch a few words. "Countywide alert . . . escaped killer . . ."

She turned up the volume quickly. "This is a special report," the announcer repeated. "Murder suspect Josh Smith has escaped from Sweet Valley county jail."

Josh—escaped! *He's out and he's coming after me!* Margo thought, her heart leaping into her throat. *He's going to try to stop me—he's going to try to come between me and Elizabeth!*

She pressed her foot down hard on the gas pedal. For a few minutes she drove at a reckless pace, careening around corners and blazing through stop signs without even tapping the brakes. Then, slowly, Margo relaxed again. Josh's escape from prison *did* make it even more urgent that she enact the identity switch without further delay. *But I'll pull it off because I know what I'm doing,* she thought, buoyed by confidence once more. *I'm a genius, whereas Josh Smith is an idiot. He's bound to slip up and be recaptured. I have nothing to worry about!*

She tuned back in to the radio broadcast. "Local residents are advised to be on the alert," the announcer continued. "The escaped murder suspect is mentally unbalanced, possibly armed, and highly dangerous."

Margo's lips twitched with amusement. Josh Smith, dangerous? *He couldn't hurt a fly,* she thought scornfully. *Still, I bet everybody in Sweet Valley locks their doors tight tonight. Too bad they don't know who the enemy* really *is!*

Chapter 18

Early Friday evening Elizabeth sat on her bed in her bathrobe, holding her journal on her lap. She'd already showered and washed her hair, but she still had an hour to play with before she needed to start getting dressed for the ball. That reminded her . . . Putting down her pen, she frowned in the direction of her closet. *I never did make up my mind what to wear!* she thought. *I'll have to take Jessica up on her offer to lend me something.*

Then, as her eyes wandered around the room, Elizabeth noticed the deep-pink dress draped across the back of her desk chair. She recognized it as a new one of Jessica's, one her sister hadn't even had a chance to wear yet.

Wow, looks like Jess picked that for me, Elizabeth realized. *But what on earth was she thinking?* Her lips curved in a bemused smile. *She's always getting after me to spice up my image—I guess this is a kick in that direction!* Elizabeth's smile deepened as she imagined how her friends and Todd would react when they saw her in the daring, strapless dress. *Well, it'll be fun to wear it,* she decided. *That nice bright fuchsia will lift my spirits.*

At that moment a loud clap of thunder shook the house, rumbling low and long like the growl of a lion. Elizabeth's smile faded and she shivered, tucking her legs under her bedspread. Retrieving her pen, she scribbled a few lines in her journal. *I just don't have a good feeling about tonight,* she wrote. *I can't help remembering the last time I went out to a big party, the night of the Jungle Prom.* Another shiver brought out goose bumps on her arms. She stared out the window at the rain, picturing the wet, slick streets, thinking about skidding off the road, losing control. She'd have to make sure Todd drove extra slowly and carefully.

Elizabeth's face stretched in a yawn, and she glanced at the clock on her bedside table. If it were any other party, she'd be incredibly tempted to skip it. But it was a big holiday, and everyone she knew would be at Lila's to celebrate the arrival of the New Year. *How am I going to last until midnight?* Elizabeth wondered with another yawn. *A catnap—that's what I need.* Crawling under the covers, she let her eyelids droop shut. Just for a few minutes . . .

Almost immediately, Elizabeth was sound asleep and dreaming. Once again she was going to the Jungle Prom, and again every detail was vivid and precise. Wearing her light-blue dress, Elizabeth stood looking at herself in the mirror, arranging her hair and putting on her jewelry; she smelled the fresh flowers in the corsage Todd gave her; she smiled for her father's camera and kissed her parents good-bye. Then they arrived at the gym and were swept up in the high-spirited revelry. She danced with Todd, and then she danced with Sam.

It felt very romantic dancing with Todd, but with Sam it was just nutty. He was a total ham, dipping her and spinning her and making her laugh so hard she couldn't catch her breath. "I'm dizzy!" Elizabeth finally gasped, smiling up at him. "And my throat is absolutely parched. Let's take a break, OK?"

They started back to their table together, still talking and laughing. But what was that she glimpsed out of the corner of her eye? Elizabeth turned her head, focusing. For a brief moment, through the crowd, she saw a puzzling vignette. Jessica was talking to a strange boy, one of the gang from Big Mesa. The boy held a cup, and now, as Elizabeth watched, he poured some of its contents into Jessica's cup. And Jessica hurried off, heading . . . somewhere. . . .

Elizabeth lost sight of her sister, and a moment later she and Sam reached their table. Picking up their punch cups, they drained them dry. *The punch,* Elizabeth thought, tasting it again in her dream. There was something funny about the punch. It burned her throat going down, and immediately after drinking it, her head began to whirl. Instead of refreshing her, it made her mouth feel as dry as cotton. When she and Sam started dancing again, they were giddy and silly and clumsy and loud—and *drunk*.

Another clap of thunder rattled the night, waking Elizabeth with a start. She sat bolt upright in bed, her hair tousled and her eyes wide, the images from the dream still spinning around in her head. The consensus had always been that her punch was spiked that night. That was how she and Sam managed to get drunk without even knowing it. What nobody could figure out was *who* spiked it, and *why*.

But my dream held the answer all the time, Elizabeth realized now. With the help of her subconscious memory, a connection had finally been made—something had finally clicked. *Oh my God,* Elizabeth thought, all color draining from her face. *The punch* was *spiked. And* Jessica *was the one who spiked it!*

"No. No, it can't be," Elizabeth murmured, pressing her hands against her eyes. But she couldn't block out the images. Everybody knew the Big Mesa kids came to the prom looking for trouble, many of them acting as if they'd been drinking. And there was Jessica, bold as brass, talking to the boy from Big Mesa and sharing whatever it was he had in his cup. She didn't drink the booze herself, though. She'd simply transferred it to Elizabeth's cup!

Suddenly, rage as hot as lava boiled up inside Elizabeth. She saw now with perfect clarity that Jessica had been the one to spike her punch, and she knew with equal certainty *why* Jessica had done it. Elizabeth remembered the mood of the night, of all the weeks leading up to the Jungle Prom—the mood of intense competition and bitter rivalry. *She did it just to sabotage my chance at the Prom Queen title!* Elizabeth realized. *She wanted to make me look bad so people would vote for her instead. She did it just so she could wear a silly paper crown on her head!*

What a cruel, selfish, reprehensible stunt! But it wasn't the worst thing Jessica had done to Elizabeth, not by a long shot. *She got me drunk and then she let me drive away.* Elizabeth's whole body started shaking, suddenly feeling as cold as ice. *And she never came forward to admit what she'd done, to take some of the blame for the accident. She stood*

247

by and let me go through the horror and humiliation of that trial—she let me suffer with the agony of thinking I was responsible for Sam's death, when all the time she was just as guilty. My God, how could she have done that to me, her own sister?

A dry, anguished sob broke from Elizabeth's throat. She thought about all the horrible things she'd had to endure since the prom and the fatal car accident: her sorrow and guilt over Sam's tragic death, the manslaughter trial and her fear that she'd be sent to a juvenile reformatory, the devastation of her family and the near destruction of her relationship with Todd. Her whole life had been disrupted, turned upside down. There'd been so much pain.

But all of that was nothing, Elizabeth thought, *compared to this.* All at once the incident of Todd's stolen letter seemed trivial. The scope of *this* betrayal was almost inconceivable. *My own sister, my own flesh and blood, did this to me.*

"No," Elizabeth whispered out loud. "No, she's not my sister anymore. She's a stranger, a monster."

Elizabeth didn't know whether to scream in rage or sob with endless sorrow. The sadness only made her anger burn hotter; the two emotions fed each other in a fire that Elizabeth knew had the power to consume her. As the rain lashed against the windows, she buried her face in her hands, too devastated even to cry.

"We're finally moving!" said Mrs. Wakefield, squeezing her husband's hand in excitement. The train surged forward, gaining speed as it left the city behind. "I was starting to think we'd have to spend the rest of our lives in San Francisco." Placing her face near the glass, she gazed out the window at the dark, murky night. "I just wish we could go *faster*."

Mr. Wakefield chuckled. "This is fast enough. We'll be there before you know it. Why don't you try napping? The trip will pass more quickly if you sleep through it."

Mrs. Wakefield sank back in her seat with a restless sigh. "If I thought I could, I would. But my mind's just too busy." She frowned anxiously. "I can't stop thinking about that dead phone line. What do you suppose it means?"

"It means the weather's as bad down south as it is up here in the Bay area," Mr. Wakefield replied. "A storm probably knocked out a power line, that's all."

"I just hate not being able to get in touch," Mrs. Wakefield persisted. "I hate not *knowing*."

"You shouldn't worry about the kids," Mr. Wakefield told her. "I'm sure they're just fine."

"But what if—" Mrs. Wakefield struggled to put her vague, shapeless fears into words. "What if something *happened*, something bad?"

"Like what? You're getting in a stew for no reason, Alice. The girls are fine," Mr. Wakefield repeated, "and if by chance anything *does* happen before we get home, Steven's there with them, and you know we can rely on him to be sensible and responsible. Right now the three of them are probably getting ready for Lila's big New Year's Eve party, as safe and happy as can be."

Happy? The twins hadn't been happy for a long time, Mrs. Wakefield reflected. As for safe . . . for some reason she simply couldn't believe that, either. *Well, there's no point talking about it anymore,* she decided, closing her eyes. *We'll be home when the train gets us there, and not a minute sooner.*

For a while Mrs. Wakefield pretended to sleep, her thoughts still racing around in frantic, tired circles. She realized she must actually have drifted off when all of a sudden she was jolted awake by a loud, metallic screeching. The train lurched to a grinding halt, throwing the Wakefields forward in their seats. Baggage burst from the overhead bins, and people who'd been standing in the aisle stumbled and fell. "What's going on?" Mrs. Wakefield cried, clutching her husband's arm. The whole car echoed with screams of fear and surprise. "What's wrong?"

"I don't know," he replied, twisting in his seat to look down the aisle. "It could be an equipment failure, or there might be something blocking the tracks—"

At that moment the lights in the car flickered and went out, plunging them all into inky blackness. Mrs. Wakefield let out a startled gasp. Her heart racing madly, she peered out the window, trying to determine what had caused the train to slam on its brakes.

She found herself staring out into empty space, black night punctuated only by an occasional finger of lightning. The train was perched on a winding, cliff-top track hundreds of feet above the Pacific; from her window Mrs. Wakefield could look straight down the cliff to the rocky beach far below. The sight made her instantly dizzy. *What if we derail?* she thought, panic rising in her throat as she imagined the train plunging from the tracks and falling . . . falling . . .

Turning away from the window, she pressed her face against Mr. Wakefield's shoulder. For a few minutes they all sat silently in the dark, tense with waiting and wondering. Then, to Mrs. Wakefield's immense relief, a conductor holding a flashlight appeared at the door to their car.

With his first words, however, her relief dissolved again into dread and anxiety. "We won't be able to continue through to Sweet Valley and Los Angeles tonight," he informed the dismayed passengers as he made his way down the aisle. "There's an electrical storm up ahead—it's too dangerous to proceed." As if to confirm his story, thunder boomed in the distance, and a dozen lightning bolts lit up the sky like a Fourth of July fireworks display. "We'll be pulling into the next station, five minutes down the track in Lonetree Heights, to wait it out," the conductor continued. "Could be a few hours—could be all night."

As the conductor stepped through to the next car, the lights blinked back on, and the train began to move forward again slowly. "A few hours? All *night*?" Mrs. Wakefield repeated, staring at her husband with utter disbelief. No doubt about it, this had been an ill-fated trip from the beginning—and it looked as if their bad luck wasn't over yet.

Standing in front of the bathroom mirror, Todd adjusted the bow tie of his rented tuxedo. His reflection in the mirror was somber and unsmiling, and the dark suit seemed to accentuate his mood. *Lighten up, buddy,* he told himself, cracking an artificial grin as he ran a comb through his hair. *After all, you're going to a party, not a funeral!*

The smile didn't last, though. Heading back down the hall to his bedroom, Todd recalled the last time he got dressed up to take Elizabeth somewhere. *The Jungle Prom—what a disaster.* Before they even got to the dance, the night was tainted by the bitter rivalry between Elizabeth and Jessica over the Prom Queen title. Then, just as Todd noticed Elizabeth and Sam carrying on, the prom exploded into violence as a crowd of Big Mesa High troublemakers started an all-out brawl. And then . . . the Jeep wreck.

Todd pushed the memory from his brain; he didn't want to relive the moment when he and Jessica, chasing after Elizabeth and Sam in Todd's car, pulled up at the site of the crash. The flashing lights, the sirens, the shattered glass, the blood . . . Yanking open a dresser drawer, Todd searched through the tangle of white gym socks for a couple of dark dress socks. What a night. What a nightmare.

It's behind us, though. Time heals all wounds, right? He considered this maxim as he pulled on the socks and tied his shoes. True, but even as old wounds started to heal, it seemed as if new ones opened up. Elizabeth had weathered the traumatic experience of the trial; she'd come to terms with her guilt and her grief, and the two of them had repaired their injured relationship. But death and disaster had struck again, and all of them, Jessica especially, were still reeling from the emotional blows. *How much can we take before things really fly to pieces?* Todd wondered. *Will life in Sweet Valley ever get back to normal?*

Standing up, he crossed to the wall shelves

where his stereo system was set up and flicked on the radio. An upbeat rock tune began to pulse through the speakers, and immediately he felt a little better. *Enough of this gloom and doom—let's make this a fun night,* he prepped himself. *It's New Year's Eve—time to put the past behind us and move forward.*

Just then the song on the radio was cut off in mid-guitar solo. A deep newsman's voice announced a special report. *A storm warning—flash floods or traffic accidents or something,* Todd guessed as he hunted for his wallet in the pockets of various pants and jackets. Thunderclouds had been lurking off the coast all day, and by the sound of the static on the radio, they'd finally struck.

But the announcer's message had nothing to do with the weather. "Murder suspect Josh Smith has escaped from the county jail," the newsman declared just as Todd found his wallet in his backpack. "Local and state police have established roadblocks on all major throughways, and an intensive search is in progress in Sweet Valley and surrounding counties. The suspect, who overpowered a guard and escaped on foot, may be armed and is considered highly dangerous."

Josh Smith—the man who murdered James! Todd realized, the shock of the news sending a jolt of adrenaline coursing through his veins. Josh Smith, the deranged maniac Todd himself helped apprehend, had escaped from jail and was at large that very moment!

Todd stood frozen, his heart racing. He pictured the killer's wild eyes and heard again his strange, frightening words. *He talked about Elizabeth,* Todd recalled, *about someone being after Elizabeth.* Were the words a warning . . . or a threat? *My God, what if he's after her himself?*

His eyes flew to the phone on his desk. Instead of reaching for it, however, Todd stuck his wallet in his trouser pocket and strode into the hall, heading for the stairs and the door. There was no point wasting time with a phone call when he could be by Elizabeth's side in five minutes. *Or less,* he thought, revving the engine of the BMW and peeling out of the driveway.

Still wearing only her bathrobe, Elizabeth sat on the edge of her bed staring at the clock on the nightstand. *Todd will be here any minute,* she realized. *I should get up—get dressed.*

But her body felt heavy, as if invisible weights had settled on both her shoulders, preventing her from rising to her feet, and two invisible hands seemed to be pressing on either side of her skull, making her head throb. She'd been paralyzed since the moment she'd understood Jessica's role in the drunk-driving crash. The mental trauma was almost like a physical injury; Elizabeth hurt all over just thinking about it.

And she couldn't *stop* thinking about it; her head whirled with fragments of memory all coming together in a kaleidoscope of new and horrible realizations. She reflected on how strangely her sister had been acting for the last few weeks, and all the occasions on which Jessica seemed to be trying to tell her something. *I thought her conscience was just bothering her because of stealing the stupid letter,* Elizabeth thought bitterly. *If she has a conscience at all, that is! I don't think she does, though. I think she's some kind of monster—a selfish, amoral monster. How could she have treated me this way?*

Taking a deep breath, Elizabeth made a Herculean effort and stood up. Slipping out of her robe, she put on underwear and stockings and then stepped into Jessica's fuchsia dress. She didn't want to wear it now, but there was nothing else in her closet that was appropriate. And it *was* a gorgeous dress, and it *did* fit like a charm.

Reaching behind her to pull up the zipper, Elizabeth walked over to her dresser. Standing in front of the mirror, she began mechanically brushing her hair into her favorite style. Suddenly she noticed that her hands were shaking violently; she could barely maintain her grip on the hairbrush. Staring at herself in the mirror, Elizabeth watched her face crumple. "But, Jessica," she whispered, "since the day we were born, you've always meant more to me than anyone else in the whole world. How could you? How *could* you?"

Tears gushed from Elizabeth's eyes. Dropping the brush, she buried her face in her hands, crying as if she would never stop.

Jessica zipped up her dress and then padded in stockinged feet to examine the effect in the bathroom mirror. *Hmm, not bad,* she decided, pivoting to check it out from the back. When Amy had called that afternoon, Jessica had confessed that she had nothing to wear to Lila's ball. Ten minutes later Amy showed up with a sequined cobalt-blue dress that Jessica had always been crazy about. "Wear it," Amy had commanded. "*Keep* it. It's a better color on you, anyway."

Jessica twirled again, giving the gown's ruffled taffeta hem a flirty flip. The sequins, the bare spaghetti straps—the look was both sexy and elegant, Jessica's favorite combination. *I could stop traffic in this dress,* she thought glumly, settling back flat on her feet and pouting at the mirror. *But who cares? What's the point?*

As she stepped back into her bedroom, Jessica thought she heard a voice—a whisper. She froze, listening intently. Had it come from Elizabeth's room? She turned to the window, peering out at the dark, rainy night. Or did it come from outside?

Jessica shivered, goose bumps rising on her bare arms. *I'm imagining things,* she decided. *There wasn't any voice.* But even as she shook her head, dismissing the possibility of ghosts and spiritual messages, she felt sure of something deep in her heart. *I shouldn't go out tonight. I should stay right here. It's safer.*

Safer than what? she asked herself an instant later. She laughed out loud. "What am I going to do, snuggle down on the couch with Steven and Billie? They'd really appreciate that!" She flounced over to her dresser to look for some jewelry that would complement the blue dress. *No,* she concluded, *there's no way I'm staying in this house tonight.* The thought of spending New Year's Eve alone in her room with the memory of all that she'd lost was absolutely unbearable.

Jessica considered a pair of rhinestone teardrop earrings, and then a chunky gold necklace, but neither seemed quite right for the dress. Then inspiration struck. *I know what would be perfect,* she thought, pawing through a cluttered drawer stuffed with various fashion accessories. *Those little silver bow earrings with the fake sapphires.*

Her hand touched something she didn't expect to find in the drawer—a small book of some sort. She lifted it out, her eyes widening when she recognized the miniyearbook that had been distributed as a souvenir at the Jungle Prom. *I didn't realize I kept one of these,* Jessica thought, turning it over in her hands. *I didn't want a souvenir—I didn't want to remember that night.*

She opened the book, reading the first page. The names of people who'd helped put the yearbook together were listed, and at the top of them all was Elizabeth Wakefield. Jessica's hands tightened on the book. *That's right—this was Liz's pet project,* she remembered. *Just one of the zillion things she did to help plan the prom and show her school spirit.*

With an effort Jessica thought back to that time, before Sam's death. She remembered how she and Elizabeth had come up with the Jungle Prom theme together and, after presenting the idea to the student body, had been named cochairs of the Prom Committee. *That was when I got lazy,* Jessica admitted to herself. She hadn't really wanted to be bothered with any of the nitty-gritty details of organizing a school dance; she'd opted to campaign for Prom Queen by leading special cheers at pep rallies and distributing Jungle Prom / Save the Rain Forest buttons. Whereas Elizabeth . . .

Flipping through the glossy pages of the miniyearbook, Jessica bit her lip. *Liz deserved to be Prom Queen. If only I hadn't been so greedy and selfish. If I'd just accepted the fact that she was* the best candidate and let her win instead of trying to ruin her chances, Sam would still be alive today. And James would, too, because there never would have been a Sam Woodruff Memorial Rally—so we never would have met, and James wouldn't have been waiting for me on the pier that night. None of this would have happened.

Jessica knew it was deadly to allow her thoughts to take this course; guilt and sorrow welled up in her like a rising tide, threatening to suck her down into depths from which she would never return. *There's no going back*, she reminded herself. *I can't live my life over. I can't change what I did in the past. But what I do in the future* . . . Slowly, it dawned on her. *I'm in charge of that. It's still ahead of me; I can choose how I want to act, what I want to do and say, who I want to be. The future is mine.*

It was New Year's Eve, the last day of the year, an end—but also a beginning. Jessica looked at herself in the mirror. Her eyes were shadowed and sad, but also determined. Straightening her shoulders, she made a silent vow to herself. *I'm going to do it, and this time I won't chicken out. I'll tell Elizabeth what really happened that night. Maybe if we make peace with the past, we can be part of each other's futures.*

Quickly, before she had time to lose her nerve, Jessica stepped out into the hall and approached Elizabeth's door. Just as she lifted her hand to knock, however, she heard the sound of another knock on the front door downstairs. *Todd's here to get Liz,* she realized, her shoulders sagging with disappointment. Another chance missed.

Jessica ducked back into her room before Elizabeth could catch her lurking in the hall. Leaving her door open a crack, she watched her sister go down to meet Todd. *The night is only just beginning,* Jessica consoled herself. *I missed an opportunity, but it won't be my last opportunity. I'll just have to find another one at Lila's.*

Returning to her dresser to put on the earrings, Jessica dared to smile at herself in the mirror. The smile was a little shaky, but it was also hopeful. There wasn't a shade of uncertainty in it; this time she'd really made up her mind once and for all. She would confess to Elizabeth before the clock struck midnight, no matter what she had to do to get Elizabeth alone, and no matter what the outcome.

Maybe Liz will understand, Jessica thought. *Maybe she'll forgive me.* Her smile faltered momentarily. *Or maybe she'll hate me for the rest of our lives.*

She swallowed her dread and turned away from the mirror, marching purposefully to the door. It was a risk she had to take. She had to start the new year on an honest footing with her sister.

Margo stood in front of the cracked mirror in her rented room, gazing raptly at her own reflection. She was wearing the strapless fuchsia dress she'd bought that afternoon at Lisette's; her glossy blond hair was swept up on one side and secured with a single rhinestone-studded barrette; her soft, golden skin and blue-green eyes were highlighted with just a hint of natural-looking makeup. *I look beautiful,* she thought, her lips parting in a self-satisfied smile. *I look pure and good and kind. I look loved, desired, envied. I look exactly like Elizabeth Wakefield.*

She reached for something bright and glittery that was lying on top of the dresser. Slowly, she fastened the gold lavaliere necklace around her slender throat. It was the final touch; the transformation was complete.

As she stared at the girl in the mirror, Margo's whole life seemed to flicker before her eyes. She watched the person she used to be. The abandoned baby, helpless and hungry; the small, scared foster child dodging the angry blows and cruel words; the young girl hiding in closets and corners, hoping to evade the unwanted, abusive attentions of her older foster brothers; the teenager finally becoming wise in the ways of the world, learning to fight back, to turn the tables, to repay neglect and abuse with weapons of her own: theft, arson, murder.

For a long time Margo had been trying not to think about where she'd come from, what she'd had to do, to reach this place and time. But now she reveled in the gory, glorious memories. *They tried to erase me,* she thought, dabbing some pale-pink gloss on her lips. *They tried to crush me under their heels like an insect. But instead of curling up and dying, I got bigger and stronger and smarter and braver.* She'd taken all the pain the world had dealt her and turned it into raw power. The suffering had been worthwhile. Now she was going to reap what she had sown since she'd come to Sweet Valley; she was going to seize her fate.

Turning away from the mirror, Margo took one last look around the room. Some of the furniture was damaged, and the wallpaper was torn in places, but otherwise the room was now clean and empty. She'd thrown away the garbage and all her personal belongings; she'd destroyed every scrap of evidence of her spying on the Wakefields, all traces of her former identity. She didn't need the notes and photographs anymore. She'd committed the information she'd gathered to memory; she was ready to plunge into the role. *The role of a lifetime,* she thought. *A role for a lifetime. I am Elizabeth Wakefield.*

Her eyes came to rest on the nightstand next to the bed. Two items stood on the table: a little beaded evening purse and a clock. Margo looked at the clock as she picked up the purse. "Time to go to the party," she said with a soft, evil smile.

Chapter 19

"This isn't much of a car," Ned Wakefield remarked as he steered the old Ford sedan out of the Rent-a-Wreck parking lot. He accelerated slowly down the main street of Lonetree Heights, grimacing when the engine backfired. "If it gets us all the way to Sweet Valley, I'll be pretty surprised."

"We were lucky to find it," Mrs. Wakefield reminded him. "The last car in the only rental place in town."

Mr. Wakefield braked at a stop sign and then made a left turn onto the coast highway, which they planned to take until they found a place to cut over to the wider, faster inland freeway. "I still think our best bet would've been to stay put on the train," he said.

"And sit there going nowhere all night long?"

Mrs. Wakefield shook her head emphatically. "This was the right thing to do. The car is—" She tried to think of something positive to say about the battered old vehicle. "It's very, um, sturdy. It will get us there." *It* has *to get us there,* she added quietly to herself.

For half an hour they plowed through the lashing rain and gusting winds in tense silence. Mr. Wakefield's jaw remained tightly clenched; Mrs. Wakefield could tell it was taking all his powers of concentration to stay on the road. They both breathed a sigh of relief when they made it over the coastal mountains to the inland highway, but clearly it was still too soon to feel themselves home free. The weather showed no signs of improving; if anything, as the night wore on, the rain seemed to be getting heavier and the winds wilder.

Although the speed limit on the freeway was fifty-five miles per hour, the sedan crawled along at barely forty. Mr. Wakefield leaned forward in the driver's seat, squinting past the windshield wipers at the deluge. "I'm not sure how smart this is," he pronounced at last. "I know you're eager to get home, but don't you think we should just pull over somewhere and check into a motel? This drive would be a lot easier, and a lot less dangerous, by daylight."

Mrs. Wakefield had been nervously folding and unfolding the road map that came with the rental car. Now she stared down at the crumpled paper, searching for their present location. "We're making progress," she insisted. "We'll reach Sweet Valley before midnight."

Mr. Wakefield slapped his hand against the steering wheel. "Does that really matter, Alice? Is it worth risking both our lives just so we can get home in time to put on party hats and toast the New Year?"

"That's not it," she said, pressing a tight crease in the map. She couldn't deny to herself, though, that there was something compelling about the midnight hour, tonight of all nights. . . . It was part of her inexplicable mother's intuition: There was trouble at home, and it was essential that she get there before the clock struck twelve. "You're a good driver, Ned. You're doing just fine. We have to keep going. I simply won't spend another night apart from the kids."

Mr. Wakefield glanced at her, his dark eyes questioning. She looked back at him, her own eyes naked with pleading. "I wish I could explain it," she whispered, "but I can't. I just know we have to keep going. They need us."

At last Mr. Wakefield nodded agreement, his gaze fixed once more on the dark, rain-slick highway. "OK, Alice. We'll go for it. I'll get you home by midnight."

❖   ❖   ❖

Elizabeth descended the staircase and crossed the hall to the front door, her heels clicking. Unbolting the door, she pulled it open, giving Todd a wide smile of welcome to disguise the fact that she was still tremendously upset about her dream. "Great tux!" she greeted him as he stepped in quickly to get out of the rain. "You look fantastic."

She waited for him to return the compliment, to bend and give her a hello kiss. Instead, he kept his distance, staring at her with a startled, uncertain expression on his face. "Todd?" she said questioningly.

"Jessica?" Todd ventured.

Elizabeth's stomach contracted in a painful knot. *It must be the dress*, she thought. An understandable mistake . . . or wishful thinking on Todd's part? "No, it's me," she said with a tight little laugh. "This is Jessica's dress, though. I know it's not my usual style, but I figured, it's New Year's Eve—why not go a little wild?"

Todd hesitated a moment longer, looking intently at her. His eyes bored into hers as if he were trying to read her very soul. Elizabeth stood up to the scrutiny, staring back at him with a wondering expression. *Don't you* know *me?* she wanted to ask.

All at once Todd tossed his dripping umbrella on the floor and reached out for her, wrapping her up in a big bear hug. "It *is* you," he murmured gratefully, brushing her cheek with his lips.

Elizabeth laughed again. "Of course it is! Who else would it be?"

She started to pull back from the embrace, but Todd pulled her close again, holding her even more tightly. "I'm not going to let you go, Liz," he whispered. "Not tonight—not ever."

Elizabeth looked up at him, her eyes suddenly misty with tears. What had happened between her and Jessica was terrible, but she was still incredibly lucky—she still had Todd. "No," she said softly. "Don't ever let me go."

For a moment they stood in the front hall, their mouths melting together in a passionate and yet incredibly tender kiss. "Let's skip Lila's," Todd suggested, his voice husky. "Let's just stay here."

Elizabeth smiled. "Steven and Billie already have dibs on the couch in the den," she told him. "Besides, everyone's expecting us. C'mon, let's say good-bye."

Peeking into the family room, Elizabeth and Todd waved good-bye to Steven and Billie. Then they stepped outside, into the wild and stormy night.

"What a night!" Elizabeth cried as the wind seized their umbrella, whipping it inside out.

For a split second she felt tempted to take Todd up on his half-joking suggestion and retreat back into the warm security of the house. There was something frightening about the trees tossing madly in the storm, about the howl of the wind, and the relentlessness of the rain. She glanced over her shoulder, imagining she saw a shadowy figure dart behind the shrubbery. *Maybe it would be nice to spend a quiet New Year's Eve at home, like Steven and Billie,* she thought. *Todd and I could curl up together somewhere, and I could tell him about my dream. He could help me understand it, help me decide what to do about Jessica.*

Todd wrestled with the umbrella, inverting it back to its proper shape. Then he held it over Elizabeth's head. "OK, if we're going to go, let's go."

Elizabeth peered up at him, suddenly wondering about his somber and preoccupied expression. *He's worrying about something, too,* she suspected. "Is anything on your mind?" she asked.

Todd opened his mouth and then snapped it shut again. If he'd been on the verge of confiding something, he'd changed his mind. "Nothing in particular," he said. "I was just thinking about how beautiful you are, and how much I love you."

Standing under the precarious shelter of the umbrella, they exchanged another warm, sweet kiss. Then Todd wrapped his arm tightly around Elizabeth's waist, and they walked cautiously down the slippery walk toward his car.

It'll be OK. Everything will be OK, Elizabeth decided, relaxing as Todd pressed her close to his side. He was so tall and strong; she knew she could count on him to protect her against any trouble, real or imaginary. *It's just rain—it's just wind,* she told herself. *I'm safe with Todd.*

Josh crouched in the bushes outside the Wakefields' house, peering at Todd Wilkins and the Wakefield girl through glossy, dripping leaves. He was soaked to the skin by the driving rain, but he didn't feel the cold; his sense of urgency and danger kept him warm.

He'd spent a long, terrifying day hiding in the toolshed of a large private residence a few miles from the county jail. As soon as it was dark, he'd made his way through alleys and back streets, hiding in the shadows of trees and cars, until he'd reached Margo's boardinghouse only to find room number 12 abandoned.

He was light-headed with hunger, not having eaten since his prison breakfast; still, it wasn't difficult for Josh to decide what to do next. From the Palmers' guest house, he'd hoofed it across town to Calico Drive.

I don't know where Margo is, and I don't know exactly what she plans to do, Josh thought now, watching as the girl—he guessed it was Elizabeth—slipped on the wet path and Todd clutched her arm to prevent her from losing her balance. *But I do know her plan hinges on the*

Wakefield twins. If I follow them, sooner or later, they'll lead me to her.

Josh darted from the shrubbery, taking shelter behind the wide, hairy trunk of a palm tree. *Sooner or later they'll lead me to her.* His lips curved in a grim, determined smile. And then, Margo was bound to give the game away; assuming he was out of the picture, she'd be cocky, overconfident. The minute she made any kind of move toward one of the twins, he'd be there to intercept her and put a stop to her murderous exploits once and for all. He *had* to stop her, now more than ever; his own freedom—and very likely Elizabeth Wakefield's life—depended on it.

Todd and Elizabeth reached the BMW. After settling Elizabeth in the passenger seat, Todd walked around the front of the car and hopped in on the driver's side. The engine started with a muffled roar; the car rolled backward out of the driveway.

As soon as the BMW was pointing away from him, Josh ran forward to the next palm tree. He gave Elizabeth and Todd half a block's head start and then started after them on the sidewalk at a steady jog. *Lucky the roads are so bad,* he thought, sucking in deep lungfuls of wet, cold, bracing air. Todd was setting a cautious pace; Josh should be able to keep the BMW in sight and trail Todd and Elizabeth all the way to their New

Year's Eve destination . . . and to Margo.

" 'Bye, Steven, Billie," Jessica called, waving from the door. "I promise I'll drive safely."

"Have a good time," Steven replied.

Billie looked up from the video she and Steven were watching. "So long, Jess," she called brightly. "See you later tonight."

"Yup, sure," Jessica mumbled as she turned to cross the hall to the kitchen. "I probably won't be late."

Boy, this is a real riot, she thought grumpily as she coasted the Jeep out of the garage and down the driveway. *Driving by myself to a New Year's Eve ball on a rainy night in a borrowed dress. Talk about pathetic.*

Reaching for the dial, she turned the radio on full blast. There was no one to talk to—she might as well belt out a few tunes. "Yes!" she exclaimed as her favorite new Jamie Peters single came on. She tapped out the beat on the steering wheel, singing along. "If I catch you talkin' to her, yeah, talkin' to her—if I catch you walkin' with her, yeah, walkin' with her—"

The music stopped abruptly. *Hmm, the rain must be messing things up,* Jessica guessed.

Just as she was about to fiddle with the dial, a male voice boomed loudly from the car speakers. "Once again we interrupt this broadcast to report

273

that suspected killer Josh Smith has escaped from Sweet Valley county jail."

With a gasp of shock Jessica slammed on the brakes. She pulled the Jeep over to the side of the deserted road and sat for a moment gripping the wheel tightly. *He escaped,* she thought, her blood turning icy with terror. *Ohmigod, he's loose!*

Instantly, this rainy night seemed to transform itself into another rainy night. Jessica was back on the pier, a scream splitting her body in two as she watched James tumble to his death on the rocks below. She grew dizzy again, remembering how Josh Smith had shouted madly, denying that he'd killed James and blaming it on some imaginary girl who supposedly looked just like Jessica and Elizabeth.

He saw us—he'd remember us, Jessica thought, glancing fearfully into the black, stormy night. Suddenly, she realized what a target she offered hanging out there on the side of the road—a girl alone in a car, a total sitting duck. The Jeep lurched forward as she stepped hard on the gas.

Jessica sped toward Lila's neighborhood. A cat darting across the road, the shadows of storm-tossed trees, an old man in a raincoat walking a tiny poodle—everything made her heart pound with fear. *He's out there somewhere,* Jessica thought, her teeth chattering. *He saw us—we caught him and turned him in. What if he wants revenge? What if he comes after us?*

Suddenly, the needle of fear probed deeper into Jessica's heart, and an overpowering premonition grabbed hold of her emotions. Josh Smith was on the prowl, and that meant danger for someone—she felt absolutely sure of it. Danger for . . . A familiar, well-loved face flashed before Jessica's eyes. For *Elizabeth*?

With an effort Jessica forced herself to focus on the road before her. All at once she realized she was approaching the curve where Elizabeth and Sam had crashed the night of the Jungle Prom. Jessica began to shiver uncontrollably; it was all she could do to keep her hands firm on the steering wheel. Sam—James—death—danger—

The events of the past few months were so awful, they almost didn't seem real. *And is it over yet?* Jessica wondered. James's killer had escaped from jail—Josh Smith was at large, perhaps stalking his next victim at this very moment. *Supposedly, bad luck comes in threes,* Jessica reflected, her palms starting to sweat. *First Sam died, and then James.* She caught a glimpse of her own pale, terrified face in the rearview mirror. Who would be next?

Chapter 20

Lila snapped her fingers as she strolled through the crowd in the living room of Fowler Crest. *What a party!* she thought, mentally patting herself on the back. No doubt about it, it was the most fun, most elegant, coolest, hippest party she'd ever thrown. *Bet we make the social page of tomorrow's L.A. Times,* she gloated as the ten-piece band swung into another jazzy dance tune.

"Isn't this a blast?" she shouted to Bruce and Pamela over the sound of the music. "Great dress, Pamela."

Pamela looked terrific in a strapless plum velvet sheath that seemed molded to her slender figure. Bruce, meanwhile, could have stepped out of the plate-glass window of a Rodeo Drive formal-wear boutique. His double-breasted tuxedo hung from his athletic frame as if it had been custom-made. *Which it probably was,* Lila speculated. She had to hand it to him—Bruce really knew how to dress.

"I'm just wild about *your* dress, Lila," Pamela raved. "It's breathtaking."

Lila gave the skirt of her flouncy black chiffon dress a little flip. "Just a little something from Paris," she said lightly. "Glad you approve."

Bruce slung an arm around Lila's shoulders and planted a loud smack on her cheek. "You're a babe, Fowler," he drawled. "Definitely the hostess with the mostess, the belle of the ball, the standard by which all other fair females must be judged."

"Keep talking, Mr. Smooth." Lila winked at Pamela. "I love it!"

"Seriously, though," said Bruce. "This is a fabulous party. I couldn't have done better myself."

Lila laughed. "High praise. Well, have fun, you guys. I'm going to circulate."

Slipping back into the crowd, Lila made a beeline for Amy and Barry, who were standing by the buffet table on the other side of the room. Her mood lifted higher and higher as she observed what a great time all her guests were having. Fowler Crest was jam-packed with people dancing, eating, talking, and laughing, their formal dresses and suits mingling in a sparkling rainbow of color. All of a sudden the flowers, party hats, balloons, and streamers Lila hadn't been able to get very excited about when she and Amy decorated the place seemed just right. *I thought no one would be in the mood for a party, but I was wrong,* she mused. *Maybe this was just what the whole town needed— to let go and have fun again.* Maybe her New Year's Eve ball would literally bounce them all right into a great New Year.

She'd nearly reached Amy and Barry when her eye was caught by one of the couples on the dance floor. Todd Wilkins was cutting a rug with—Lila narrowed her eyes. She'd assumed the girl in his arms would be Elizabeth, but suddenly she was unsure. She recognized the fuchsia dress, and it was definitely *not* part of Elizabeth's wardrobe; in fact, Lila had been with Jessica when she bought the dress at Lisette's. *What's Todd doing dancing with Jessica when he's supposed to be back together with Elizabeth?* Lila wondered. *What's Jessica doing?*

Changing course, Lila headed over to investigate. *I hope Jess isn't flipping out like she did after Sam died and making another pass at Todd,* Lila worried. *Things are such a mess between her and Liz as it is. But why would Todd encourage Jess to—*

At the edge of the dance floor Lila stopped dead in her tracks, her eyes glued to the face of the girl who was dancing with Todd. *Wait a minute, that's not Jessica,* she realized. The soft, gentle smile, the hairstyle, the way she moved . . . it might be Jessica's dress, but Elizabeth was wearing it.

Lila blinked at the couple for a moment longer. She still couldn't quite believe her eyes, because her eyes insisted on seeing double. It was the strangest sensation, like an optical illusion. *I've known Jess and Liz forever—since when do I have trouble telling them apart?* Lila wondered, shaking her head as she turned away.

"I love this kind of music," Elizabeth said to Todd as the band swung into another jazzy dance tune. "It makes me feel like a character in *The Great Gatsby* or something."

Todd twirled her around and then pulled her body up against his. "I like it, too."

Instead of releasing her for another twirl, he continued to hold her close. Elizabeth laughed, her cheeks turning pink. "Todd, this isn't a slow song!"

"I don't care." His eyes burned into hers. "I'm not letting you go, remember?"

Smiling, Elizabeth clasped her arms around his waist and rested her head on his chest. As they swayed gently to the music, holding one another tightly, Todd's eyes kept moving. He spotted Lila talking with Barry and Amy; Winston and Maria were dancing, as were Ken and Terri, DeeDee and Bill, and Penny and Neil. Andrea Slade, Nicholas

Morrow, Jean West, Scott Trost, Annie and Tony, April and Michael, Sandy and Manuel . . . Todd checked out the scene in every direction, his gaze passing over the familiar faces, searching for a stranger among them.

His vigilance was probably uncalled for; what were the odds that Josh Smith would show up at Fowler Crest? *He'd be crazy to—he'd just get caught,* Todd thought. Then he remembered: Josh Smith *was* crazy. There was no predicting what a nut case like that would do.

Maybe the police recaptured him already. With all the troopers they have out looking, he could be back behind bars by now. It was a comforting thought. Still, Todd's gaze continued to rove, and his arms remained tightly wrapped around Elizabeth. Everyone was cutting loose and enjoying around yet about the prison break, or else people had heard but weren't worrying about it.

Todd couldn't relax, though. He didn't intend to let down his guard for a single second—and he didn't intend to let Elizabeth out of his sight. As long as that homicidal maniac was running around, he planned to stick to Elizabeth like the Secret Service stuck to the President.

Two more cars pulled into the long driveway of Fowler Crest. The headlights flicked off and the engines died; a couple stepped out of each car.

Josh watched as the young people greeted each other, the girls admiring one another's dresses and the boys joking about their tuxes, yanking on their bow ties and making faces as if they were choking. Finally, they went inside and the coast was clear.

Josh darted from a cluster of palm trees and crossed an open stretch of lawn. Reaching the side of the house, he plunged into the shelter of a large rhododendron bush. For a moment he crouched on his hands and knees, struggling to catch his breath. Cold and hunger were beginning to take their toll; he was winded and shivering. Curiosity revived him, however. Slowly, he rose to his feet in order to peer through the tall picture window at the scene within.

It's like a movie, Josh thought, leaning closer to the glass to hear the muffled sounds of revelry. The elegant mansion was packed with people in festive attire; the bandleader, wearing a white dinner jacket and black bow tie, snapped his fingers and tapped his foot while a man with a shiny saxophone played a solo. While some kids danced, others stood in small groups chatting happily. And eating. Josh's mouth watered at the sight of a long table draped with a snow-white cloth and laden with platters of food. He hugged himself, shivering in his thin, rain-soaked clothes. *If I could only get a bite of something,* he thought wistfully. *I need the fuel; I need the strength.*

Just then he spotted a familiar figure: the tall, dark-haired boy who'd tackled him on the pier, the one whose car he'd followed tonight, Todd Wilkins. The boy was dancing with a pretty blond girl in a deep-pink dress—his girlfriend, Elizabeth Wakefield. Josh's heart began to pound, hot blood pumping fast through his veins as he realized how close he was to the final confrontation. Elizabeth . . . *or was it Margo?*

Josh lifted his hands as if to touch the window, as if to touch the girl. *I'm watching you, Margo,* he said silently. *I'm watching your every move.*

Just then he heard the sound of high heels on the flagstone walk behind him, and he dived down into the bushes for cover.

Her heels tapping, Jessica walked briskly along the walk toward Lila's front door, one arm bent over her head to protect her hair from the drizzle since she'd forgotten to bring an umbrella. Suddenly, right next to her, she heard something rustle in the rhododendrons. Jessica jumped, clapping a hand to her mouth to prevent the escape of a startled squeak. *It's just a squirrel or a bird, silly,* she told herself. Even so, she picked up her pace, glancing apprehensively over her shoulder as she hurried on. She was still shaken from the news report about the escaped killer. She could think of only one thing; one thing only impelled her forward. *Elizabeth. I have to make sure she's OK.*

The heavy front door of Fowler Crest swung open as Jessica approached. She stepped into the party, her expression a little wild, her eyes searching frantically.

Spotting Elizabeth's bright-fuchsia dress almost immediately, Jessica's knees buckled with relief. *There she is by the buffet table, talking to Enid,* Jessica thought, inhaling deeply to stop her heart from racing. *She's all right. She's fine. Of course that psycho didn't get her—geez, what was I freaking out about?*

She stepped forward into the crush of bodies. "Hi, Jeanie," she called, waving. "Hey, Robin, I love your dress!"

The tension melted from Jessica's body as she became part of the lively crowd. It was a horrible, ominous, rainy night, but they were all safe and warm and dry inside Lila's big house. *The danger, if there is any, is out there,* Jessica decided. *No harm can come to us in here.*

The song they'd been dancing to ended, and Elizabeth and Todd drew apart reluctantly. "Thanks," Elizabeth said softly. "That was fun."

"Let's not stop," Todd urged, reaching for her again. "Let's dance all night."

"I wouldn't mind sitting down for a few minutes," Elizabeth told him, smiling. "I'm wearing heels, not track shoes. In fact, what if we—"

She considered drawing Todd aside to talk to him about her latest Jungle Prom dream. As she looked for a place to sit down, she spotted Enid standing near the buffet table on the other side of the room. "Enid's here—I'm just going to pop over and say hello," Elizabeth told Todd. "Be right back, OK?"

"Wait, Liz, I'll come with—"

But Elizabeth was already weaving her way through the swirl of dancers, leaving Todd behind. "Hi, how are you?" asked Elizabeth as she stepped up to Enid's side and put out a hand to touch the sleeve of her friend's dark-green velvet dress. "Enid, this is *beautiful*—it matches the color of your eyes exactly."

"Hi again yourself," Enid replied with a bemused smile. "And thanks again for the compliment!"

Elizabeth tipped her head to one side, puzzled. *Again?* "What do you mean—"

At that moment she caught sight of someone over Enid's shoulder. Jessica had just arrived at the party and was greeting her friends.

As if sensing Elizabeth's gaze, Jessica raised her eyes and looked right at her sister. Their eyes locked for a split second, and Elizabeth saw a hesitant smile flicker across Jessica's face. To Elizabeth's dismay Jessica turned and started heading in her direction.

Elizabeth's heart began to race; a sea of tumultuous emotions welled up inside her. *I can't act civil and normal toward Jessica,* she thought, desperately looking around for a place to hide. *I can't pretend I'm still ignorant about what she did to me the night of the prom.* At the same time, Elizabeth knew she wasn't ready to confront Jessica with what she'd learned from her dream; not yet, and certainly not at Lila's New Year's Eve ball with zillions of people around!

Out of the corner of her eye Elizabeth could see Jessica getting closer. *I can't deal with her. I've got to get out of here.* "I—" Racking her brain for an excuse to beat a hasty retreat, she came up with a classic. "I'm going upstairs to the bathroom," she announced abruptly, shoving past Enid. "See you later."

Startled, Enid stepped out of the way. "Sure," she said, looking baffled as Elizabeth sprinted off toward the staircase.

Jessica stopped in her tracks. Elizabeth had whirled around and was now elbowing her way through the party guests, heading for the hall. *Is she leaving?* Jessica wondered. She watched as Elizabeth hurried up the main staircase that led to the second and third floors of Fowler Crest, taking the steps two at a time.

She's just going to the powder room, Jessica

concluded. *But she sure ran off in a hurry.* She bit her lip. *Was it because she saw me?* It was starting to look as if making this confession would be harder than she thought. If Elizabeth couldn't stand even to be in the same crowded room with her . . .

I can't wimp out, though. I made a resolution, Jessica reminded herself. It was going to be tough, but it would only get more difficult the longer she put it off.

She lingered a moment longer, figuring she'd give Elizabeth a chance to start back downstairs before she waylaid her. Just then Lila strolled up and gave her a quick hug. "Hey, Jess. I'm so glad you came!"

"Me, too," Jessica fibbed. "This is probably the fanciest, best New Year's Eve party in the history of Sweet Valley."

"That was my goal, anyway," said Lila. She patted Jessica's arm sympathetically. "I see you lent Liz your newest dress and you got stuck wearing one of Amy's hand-me-downs."

"It's not so shabby," Jessica protested. "Amy's only worn it once or twice."

"I didn't say it was *shabby*," Lila assured her. "But I personally think it's more fun on a night like this to wear something you bought just for the occasion. Don't worry, you look gorgeous." She patted Jessica's arm again. "But it *is* too bad you didn't settle on any of the dresses you tried on when we went shopping the other day."

"Hmm?" Jessica murmured, her eyes wandering back to the staircase. "What are you *talking* about?"

"That purple dress was really cute," Lila explained. "And you might notice that nobody's wearing purple tonight, which means you would've stood out in the crowd. But I also liked the black one with the . . ."

Lila continued to blab on about some shopping trip that Jessica was pretty sure must have taken place in Lila's mind, since the two of them hadn't gone to the mall together in ages. Jessica, meanwhile, tuned out her friend's chatter. Eyes on the staircase, she mulled over various strategies for stealing a moment alone with Elizabeth. *I have to get this crushing weight off my shoulders,* she thought. *I have to confess to Elizabeth before the clock strikes midnight.*

For a second Todd lost sight of Elizabeth in the sea of revelers. Then he glimpsed her talking to Enid and started after her. By the time he reached Enid, however, Elizabeth was gone.

"She went upstairs," Enid told him. "She'll be back in a minute or two."

Enid seemed about to say something else, but Todd didn't feel like making small talk. Continuing out into the entryway, he gazed up the wide, curving staircase. The second-floor hallway was shadowy and deserted.

I'll just wait outside the powder room, he decided, taking the stairs two at a time. Elizabeth was going to think he was crazy, but he just didn't want to chance it. He'd vowed to keep her in sight every minute; it was the only way to make absolutely certain no harm came to her.

Todd was fairly familiar with Lila's house from previous parties, so he knew that there were two bathrooms on the second-floor hallway, one near the stairs and the other six or seven doors down. The door to the first was ajar and the light was out—no Elizabeth there. And to his surprise and consternation, the other powder room was also vacant.

Where can she have gone? Todd wondered, an irrational feeling of panic sweeping over him. Striding to the far end of the hall, he started opening doors one after the other. Guest bedrooms, master suite, sitting rooms—all dark and apparently empty. Opening another door, Todd peered into the shadows, his eyes making a quick search. Again, nothing. He slammed the door and hurried on to the next. *I'm going nuts,* he thought, breathing fast. *She can't have just disappeared into thin air. She must be here somewhere!*

Grasping the knob, he yanked open another

door, prepared for disappointment. But instead of being dark, the guest bedroom he burst into was bathed in the warm glow of a small lamp. And standing in front of the dressing table, fluffing her hair in the mirror, was Elizabeth.

"Here you are!" Todd exclaimed with relief. Hurrying up behind Elizabeth, he wrapped his arms around her waist. "What are you doing, hiding like this?"

Elizabeth met his eyes in the mirror. "I'm not hiding—just freshening up a little." She smiled, her dimple flashing. "I was hoping you'd come looking for me."

Bending his head, Todd nuzzled the back of Elizabeth's neck. "I told you I wouldn't let you out of my sight tonight—or out of my arms. . . ."

Elizabeth leaned back against him, closing her eyes and sighing deeply. "Well, that's just fine with me."

As Todd kissed her neck again, his lips touched cool gold. "I didn't notice before that you were wearing your necklace," he said. "You found it!"

"That's right." Turning to face him, Elizabeth ran her hands up his arms, massaging his shoulders with her fingers. "I've found *everything* that rightfully belongs to me."

She slid her hands to his neck, pulling him toward her for a kiss. Eagerly, Todd brought his mouth down to hers. Their lips brushed in a tantalizing fashion . . . and then Todd stiffened, his arms still locked around Elizabeth.

Her eyes were half-closed, her lips parted in a tiny smile of anticipation. What was it about that smile? It was lovely and inviting, but also eerie, almost sinister. It was the smile of a stranger. *Something isn't right,* Todd thought. *Some*one *isn't right.*

With a jolt of recognition he realized this was the same unnerving feeling he'd experienced a few days before Christmas, when he went to the movies with Elizabeth . . . or rather, with Jessica pretending for some mysterious reason to be Elizabeth. Paralyzed with uncertainty, Todd stared into the face of the girl he held in his arms. Was this Jessica again, trying to dupe him? *No, it can't be,* he thought. *Jessica's wearing blue—I just saw her downstairs. This is Liz, in the pink dress. Of course it's Liz.*

Dismissing his doubts, he bent his head to kiss her. Again, as their lips met, he froze. A wave of repulsion shook his body; every nerve seemed to cry out, "No!" *This is crazy,* Todd thought. *What's with you, Wilkins?* Crazy or not, though, he couldn't control his feelings. And all he wanted at that moment was to get out of the room—to get away from Elizabeth. "Let's go back downstairs to the party," he suggested lightly. "We're missing all the fun."

"Forget the party, Todd," Elizabeth murmured,

smiling slyly. Todd had taken a step backward, trying to hold her at arm's length, but she pulled him close again. "We can have our own party right here. Doesn't *that* sound like *more* fun?"

The words and the tone hit Todd like a bucket of ice-cold water. Instantly he knew he wasn't with Elizabeth. Elizabeth would never say something like that, unless her body had been taken over by aliens. And even Jessica . . . *Even Jessica wouldn't go this far,* Todd realized, his eyes widening. *So that means . . .*

Todd stared at the blue-green eyes, the smooth golden skin, the girl's hair, her lips, her throat, her shoulders. *All the features are right, but—* He remembered Josh Smith at the police station, ranting and raving that someone else pushed James—Margo, a girl who looked just like the twins.

He wasn't lying, Todd realized, the blood draining from his face and his knees buckling. There was someone else on the pier that dark, rainy night; someone else *did* murder James. Someone who looked so much like Elizabeth that she could impersonate her—that she could even fool Elizabeth's own boyfriend.

The girl was watching Todd closely, her expression suddenly wary. Todd grasped her arms, his eyes boring into hers. *They're the right color,* he observed, *but everything else about them is wrong.* The girl's eyes were somehow empty, soulless. They held no emotion, no warmth, no humanity. They were like the eyes of a china doll . . . or of a mad person. Of a killer.

There was no longer any room for doubt. "You—you're not Elizabeth," Todd sputtered, horror nearly robbing him of the power of speech. "And if you're not Jessica either, who—"

The beautiful mouth he'd come so close to kissing twisted into a hideous grimace. The girl writhed in his arms like a snake, struggling to escape. Todd's fingers tightened, digging into the bare flesh of her arms. "Who are you?" he cried, shaking her hard.

Snarling like a wildcat, the girl wrenched from his grasp, astonishing Todd with her strength. Reaching behind her, she fumbled on the dressing table, grabbing something. Before Todd could raise a hand to shield himself, she swung her arm, aiming straight for his skull.

Chapter 21

Margo stood panting, Todd's unconscious body sprawled at her feet and a brass statuette still clutched in her hand. "The idiot," she muttered, wiping the sweat from her upper lip. "The big, stupid idiot." Didn't he know a good thing when he saw it? Didn't he realize he'd have a lot more fun with her than he ever had with Elizabeth?

Margo stared down at Todd, watching his chest rise and fall. He was out like a light, but he wasn't dead—far from it. Her fingers itched, and she reached for the statuette again. *I'll hit him once more,* she thought. *And this time I'll crush his skull—kill him. I* have *to kill him—he knows about me.*

She stroked the smooth, cold brass, considering. Now that the heat of the moment was passing, she could look at the matter objectively. *No,* she decided at last, *it's not really necessary.* Killing Todd would ruin the purity and simplicity of her plan. There would be only one perfect death that night—Elizabeth's.

But he'll wake up and tell people what happened in here. He'll tell them I'm not Elizabeth. Margo chewed her lip, her brow furrowed. Then her face cleared and she smiled. Yes, he'd tell them that, but so what? Why on earth would anyone believe him? It was such a wild, improbable, *impossible* story! They'd think he was nuts, a raving lunatic. *Yes, poor Todd went insane. That's what I'll tell people, and it won't be too tough for them to see it for themselves.*

As Margo stepped carefully around Todd's prostrate body, she heaved a sigh of regret. He really was incredibly handsome. *But Elizabeth—I— won't have any trouble finding a new boyfriend,* she thought, smiling with anticipation at the prospect of auditioning prospective new suitors. *One who's not quite so stuffy!*

Margo licked her lips. She really couldn't wait. *Not tonight, though,* she reminded herself as she slipped from the room, switching off the light and locking the door behind her so no one would stumble upon Todd while he was sleeping it off. There was no time for flirting tonight. She still had very important work to do; there were still three Wakefield girls wandering around where there should only be two.

Elizabeth sat on the edge of the tub in Lila's bathroom, her chin in her hands. She wondered if Jessica had followed her upstairs, if Jessica was checking the powder rooms, if it would occur to her that Elizabeth might be hiding in the bathroom in Lila's bedroom. *Not that I'm hiding, exactly*, Elizabeth rationalized. *I just needed some peace and quiet, a place where I could hear myself think.*

The bathroom was certainly quiet; not a single sound penetrated from the party below. But Elizabeth's state of mind remained far from tranquil; though her body was motionless, she still felt as if she were strapped into some kind of terrifying amusement-park ride, spinning out of control.

Getting to her feet, she stood in front of the mirror. *Gosh, I look like I just saw a ghost! I've really got to pull myself together.* She fumbled in her purse for some lip gloss and spent a minute touching up her makeup. Then she brushed her hair with measured strokes, trying to inhale and exhale in a slow, even rhythm. Watching herself in the mirror, she saw her expression begin to grow calmer; gradually, she started to look more like herself, like someone capable of handling anything that came her way—even this crisis with Jessica.

Jessica, Elizabeth thought, staring deep into her

own eyes. As she thought about her sister, a strange thing happened. Just for a moment the face in the mirror seemed to change ever so slightly. Just for a moment Elizabeth found herself looking at *Jessica's* face in the mirror rather than at her own reflection.

Jessica's eyes were almost unbelievably sad, tortured by grief and remorse; her trembling lips were on the verge of spilling forth words of apology. For the first time since the Jeep accident, Elizabeth felt as if she were seeing her sister clearly, and all at once she recognized just how awful this had been for Jessica, too. In her imagination Elizabeth traveled back in time and stood squarely in Jessica's shoes on that fateful night, and all the days that followed. The pain of it was heart wrenching. What an agonizing burden for Jessica to bear, knowing that Sam had died in part because of her own thoughtless prank!

Spiking the punch was a mean, stupid thing to do, but I went overboard with the whole Prom Queen rivalry, too, Elizabeth reflected. *And when she did it, she couldn't have known where it would lead. She couldn't have anticipated how the night would end. She was just being typical, thoughtless Jessica.*

A knock on the bathroom door jolted Elizabeth from her reverie. "Just—just a moment, Lila," she called. "I'll be right out."

"Liz, it's me, Jessica," a voice said softly. "I really need to talk to you. In private."

Elizabeth felt cornered. There was only one reason Jessica could want to talk to her so badly, only one thing she could need so desperately to get off her chest. Sooner or later they had to confront the monstrous obstacle that stood between them. But right now? *I'm not ready for this conversation,* Elizabeth thought. *Please, Jess, just go away.*

But Jessica was still there, on the other side of the door. "Please, Liz," she pressed. "It's really important. I'll wait for you out at the pool house, OK?"

Elizabeth took a deep breath. *We might as well get this over with.* "Let's just talk here," she said. Her suggestion was met by silence. "Jessica?"

Elizabeth opened the door. Lila's bedroom was dark and empty. Crossing to the outer door, Elizabeth peered into the hallway. There was no one there.

"We're so close," Mrs. Wakefield moaned, pulling her raincoat more tightly around her. "I can't believe this happened just a stone's throw from home!"

"I've almost got it fixed," Mr. Wakefield grunted. "A few more bolts . . ."

Standing in the rain by the side of the highway, Mrs. Wakefield watched her husband wrestle the

297

flat tire off the rental car. Fortunately, there had been a jack and a spare tire in the trunk, but even with the necessary tools it was going to take half an hour to deal with the flat. *It's unbelievable, simply unbelievable,* she reflected. Everything that could go wrong on this trip *had* gone wrong. She was starting to think they would never make it home.

Mrs. Wakefield glanced at her watch. Fifteen minutes until midnight . . . and only a few miles from Sweet Valley. *I'd probably get there quicker if I walked!* She bit her lip, gazing down the hillside at the distant, twinkling lights of Sweet Valley. She'd been so eager to get home tonight, before the arrival of the New Year; the feeling was so urgent, so compelling. *Why?* Mrs. Wakefield asked herself for the hundredth time. *How could it matter?*

She didn't know; she only knew that, for some inexplicable reason, it *did* matter, and now it looked as if they wouldn't be able to pull it off. Mr. Wakefield was working as fast as he could; obviously he had no desire to spend any longer than he had to changing a flat tire in the pouring rain. But time stopped for no one. The minutes continued to race by.

Mrs. Wakefield continued to stare toward Sweet Valley, wishing that she could see in the twinkling lights of the distant town some sign that her children were safe and well. But the lights seemed cold rather than reassuring; they didn't tell her anything. Mrs. Wakefield shut her eyes, her lips moving in a silent prayer.

I know she came up here, Jessica thought, hurrying down the second-floor hallway of Fowler Crest. *So where is she?*

Jessica checked each room on the floor one by one, searching for Elizabeth. The door to the powder room nearest the staircase was locked, but when it opened after a few minutes, its occupant turned out to be Sally Larson, not Elizabeth. The guest bedrooms and sitting rooms, Lila's parents' suite, the far powder room—all turned out to be dark and empty.

Jessica pushed open the door to Lila's room. Immediately, she saw a sliver of light; the bathroom door was ajar. Someone was in there!

Of course, anyone who knows about this bathroom would come in here instead of using the ones in the hall, Jessica reasoned. *It's a lot more private.* "Liz?" she called. "Is that you?"

There was no answer. Her feet soundless in the thick carpet, Jessica crossed the room and gave the bathroom door a gentle push. It swung inward, revealing . . . nothing.

Jessica stepped into the bathroom, a frown creasing her forehead. For a moment she'd felt so sure she'd found Elizabeth. She almost *sensed* her sister's presence in the room. *I'm getting vibes, all right,* Jessica thought. *The question is, are they good vibes or bad vibes?*

She turned to leave. As her gaze strayed along the countertop, it was arrested by a tiny pot of lip gloss standing somewhat separate from the clutter of other beauty products. Jessica picked up the lip gloss, examining it. It was a pale-rose shade, almost translucent—a color she knew Elizabeth liked. *And Lila never wears this stuff,* she thought. *She likes lipstick, the redder the better.*

If Elizabeth had been in the bathroom, though, where had she disappeared to? Returning to the hallway, Jessica checked the last few guest rooms. Two were empty and one was locked. Jessica crouched to see if any light was coming under the door of the locked room, but it looked as dark as all the others; she rapped lightly on the door and was answered with complete and utter silence. *It's empty, too,* she concluded. *They're all empty.*

Standing alone in the deserted hallway, Jessica fought down an irrational feeling of panic. To anyone else the atmosphere on the second floor would have seemed peaceful and quiet, but to Jessica it was charged with mystery and danger. Vibrations seemed to pulse through the air; a dreadful certainty seized her heart, choking off the pulse of blood. *Liz is in trouble.*

Frantically, Jessica made her way back down

the hall, double-checking all the rooms. A clock in a small sitting room caught her eye. Eleven fifty— just ten minutes until midnight. Jessica remembered her vow to bare her soul to Elizabeth before the New Year. More than ever she longed to be with her sister at that moment—not just for her own sake now, but for Elizabeth's, too. *I have to find her,* Jessica determined. *I have to protect her.* From what? Or from whom? Was she just upset about the news that Josh Smith had escaped from jail—was she overreacting? Jessica didn't know the source of her fear; she only knew that some mysterious impulse urged her on like a whip stinging at her heels. She had to keep on looking.

"Let's put the movie on pause," Billie suggested, sitting up on the couch so she could reach the remote control. She hit the stop button for the VCR and the movie disappeared, a local TV news program taking its place. "I mean, who are we kidding? We're not watching it!"

Steven lowered her back against the pile of throw pillows. "Speak for yourself," he teased as he pressed kisses all the way up her throat to her chin. "I haven't taken my eyes off the screen for a second."

Billie wrapped her arms around his waist and their lips met in another leisurely, delicious kiss. "Umm," Steven murmured. "I guess you're right.

Who needs movies? Real-life love scenes are a lot more fun!"

"We've got to be careful not to steam up the windows *too* much, though," Billie said with a throaty laugh. "What'll your sisters think?"

Steven really didn't care. He couldn't focus on anything except how good it felt being there with Billie. "I wish we could stay right here forever," he told her, brushing a strand of hair back from her forehead. "I don't think I'd ever get tired of kissing you."

She smiled, playing with the buttons on his polo shirt. "You'd better not, buddy!"

Their mouths melted together in another kiss as hot as a forest fire. Steven closed his eyes, giving himself up to the magic. When Billie suddenly pushed him away, he blinked at her in surprise. "What's the matter?"

"Ssh," Billie hissed, pointing at the TV. "Listen to this!"

Steven sat up in time to see the solemn face of a newscaster give way to a black-and-white photo of a man. "My God," Steven breathed when he realized what the story was about. "That's the guy who killed James. Don't tell me he—"

"He escaped from jail," Billie confirmed, her eyes wide as saucers. "This morning, it sounds like. And they still haven't caught him!"

The reporter gave an update on the search for

the escaped murderer, and then the program switched to a weather report. Steven continued to stare at the screen, his mouth suddenly dry as dust. "He's on the loose," he whispered. The vague worried feeling that had haunted him all night despite the distraction of Billie's company now blossomed into full flower. "He's loose and he knows my sisters and Todd, because they were the ones who caught him. What if he goes after them?"

"He wouldn't," said Billie, but without much conviction. "He'd want to hightail it out of here, don't you think? It wouldn't make sense to stick around Sweet Valley when there are a million cops looking for him."

"This guy doesn't *have* sense," Steven reminded her. "He's a psycho, a lunatic!" He reached for the phone, placing the receiver against his ear, his other hand poised to dial. "I'm going to get Lila's number and call Fowler Crest," he told Billie. "I'll feel a hundred percent better if I can just touch base with Liz and Jess."

Even as he punched out the numbers for directory assistance, though, Steven realized something was wrong. Instead of the dial tone, he heard silence.

He tried hanging up and then picking up the phone again. He jiggled the buttons, listening hopefully. "Nothing," he finally announced. "The line's dead."

"Dead?"

"Dead," Steven repeated.

"I didn't realize the weather was that bad," Billie commented, wrinkling her forehead. "Maybe we should— Steven, where are you going?"

Steven had jumped up off the couch. Sticking his feet into his loafers, he hurried to the hall closet to grab a jacket. Billie ran after him. "Where are you going?" she asked again.

"Fowler Crest," Steven replied. "I'll be back in a flash. I just have to make sure—" Steven didn't know exactly what he was afraid of. "I just have to make sure they're *safe*."

Outside lightning flickered, and a crack of thunder splintered the night. Billie gripped Steven's arm just as he was about to bolt from the house. "Wait for me," she begged. "It's too creepy—I don't want to stay alone here. I'm coming with you!"

Jessica rarely had reason to venture to the third floor of Fowler Crest—she didn't know what lay behind half of the closed doors on the shadowy hallway. *Elizabeth can't be up here,* she thought as she eased open a door and fumbled on the wall for a light switch. *Then again, she has to be somewhere.* And she definitely wasn't at the party; after searching the second floor, Jessica had gone back downstairs, where she'd discovered that not only

Elizabeth, but Todd, also, seemed to be missing.

She found the switch and flicked it on, holding her breath. The room, an unfinished studio of some sort, was dusty and empty. Running down the hall, Jessica tried the next room, and the next. A bedroom, a bathroom, a huge walk-in storage closet—all were vacant, looking as if no one had entered them in ages.

At the end of the hall, Jessica stopped and stood panting as if she'd just finished an especially energetic cheerleading routine. *She's disappeared into thin air. What if—what if he got her?*

Jessica pictured Josh Smith on the pier—only this time his murderous hands were grasping for Elizabeth. *I've got to sound the alarm,* Jessica decided. *I'll tell everybody Liz and Todd are missing and . . .* And what? She imagined her friends' response. They'd just laugh and elbow each other. Liz and Todd left the party early, huh? Wink, wink. "They'll just tell me I'm worrying about nothing," Jessica said out loud to herself. "*Am* I worrying about nothing?"

She tried to step outside of the situation for a moment, to see it objectively. Yes, it *was* possible nothing was amiss. Elizabeth ran upstairs, Todd went after her, and for whatever reason, the two of them decided not to hang around for the big New Year's Eve countdown. No big deal.

The scenario made sense, but it didn't put

Jessica's mind at ease. Her heart continued to pound like a drum solo; a cold sweat beaded her forehead. She had a hunch, so strong it was almost like a telegraphic message: Something's wrong, something's wrong. *It's my twin's intuition,* Jessica recognized. *For months Liz and I have barely been on speaking terms, but we're still connected. I've always known—I'll always know—when she needs me, and she needs me now.*

The question remained, though: Where *was* she? Jessica pressed her forehead against the diamond-shaped window at the end of the hall that looked down over the back lawn and swimming pool. *Where should I look next?* she wondered. *Who should I go to for help?*

Just then a lightning bolt sliced through the distant sky, briefly illuminating the scene below. Jessica glimpsed a flash of pale hair near the dark pool house, the glimmer of a deep-pink dress. Just as quickly as it had appeared, the ghostly figure disappeared from sight. But Jessica had seen enough. *Someone's out there,* she thought, turning to sprint toward the staircase. *Elizabeth!*

Josh crept around the side of Fowler Crest, keeping close to the house and the shelter provided by the shoulder-high shrubbery. *This isn't going to work,* he realized, raising his head to peek into a living-room window. The glass panes were beginning to fog up, and even if he had been able to get a clear view, the party was so crowded now that it would be impossible to keep tabs on Todd Wilkins and the Wakefield twins simply by running from window to window.

I can't go inside, though. In his ill-fitting, sopping-wet prison guard's uniform, and with his pale, gaunt face and desperate eyes, Josh knew he looked exactly like what he was: an escaped convict. *They must be looking all over for me—the kids would just call the police, and I'd be back behind bars in no time.*

He couldn't risk it. Then again, he couldn't risk *not* going inside, either. For all he knew, at this very moment Margo herself was a guest at the party, impersonating one of the twins and preparing to commit another evil crime. It could happen tonight, in Fowler Crest, while he stood outside in the rain, powerless to intervene.

I'll look for a back door, Josh decided, crawling through the bushes. *I'll hide in a closet or something. I've got to find her—I've got to stop her.*

Reaching the corner of the enormous house, he stood up for a moment, stretching his body to get out the kinks. Raindrops ran down his face and into his eyes, causing him to blink. But what was that? Even with his vision blurred, he was able to see the figure of a girl floating across the grass on the far side of the lawn. *The pink dress,* Josh realized, squinting. *And the blond hair.* It was the girl he'd seen through the window earlier, dancing with Todd Wilkins. Elizabeth Wakefield! *Or could it be Margo?*

The girl disappeared into a small building—a pool house, Josh guessed. Before he could make a move to follow her, however, another figure appeared, hurrying through the rain. *Another* slim girl with fair hair and a deep-pink dress.

Josh blinked, wondering if the rain in his eyes or his own fatigue and desperation were causing him to see double. *No,* he thought, *I saw what I saw.* Two identical girls in identical dresses. One of them had to be Margo! But which one? Who was who?

Josh hesitated for a moment, puzzling over the odd sight. Then he realized it didn't matter which girl was Margo and which was Elizabeth. The two girls had left the party, heading for a dark, deserted outbuilding . . . the perfect setting for foul play. One of them had to be Margo, and she was about to act!

Which meant it was time for *him* to take action as well. Josh dashed forward, slipping and sliding on the wet grass. He had to reach the pool house before . . .

Elizabeth hurried the last few yards to the pool house, shivering in the cold drizzle. *What a strange place for Jessica to pick!* she thought, glancing back over her shoulder at the bright lights of Fowler Crest. In that whole, huge house hadn't there been one spot she could've chosen that wouldn't have involved tramping across the muddy lawn in the rain?

The door to the pool house was ajar, but no light was on inside. Elizabeth hesitated, wondering if she'd made a mistake. *Why would she wait in the dark? Maybe I heard her wrong.* She stepped forward, giving the door a tentative push. "Jessica?" she called, her voice small and uncertain. "Are you in here?"

Elizabeth thought she heard something—a footstep, a whispered word. She entered the pool house just as a girl stepped out of the shadows. Elizabeth caught her breath, for an instant thinking that she was looking into a mirror.

The girl took another step; she was real, not a reflected image. *But—but the dress,* Elizabeth thought, surprised. The dress wasn't cobalt-blue like Jessica's; it was fuchsia, strapless—the same dress Elizabeth herself was wearing! *Someone else at the party bought the same dress, that's all,* Elizabeth thought, raising her eyes to the girl's face in the hope that she'd find herself looking at a stranger. But, no—the face was her own; every feature was identical. And around the girl's throat a gold necklace glimmered. *My lavaliere,* Elizabeth thought with surprise.

309

She stood staring at the girl, her eyes wide with shock. She'd been expecting Jessica, but this wasn't Jessica. Something was terribly wrong. The blood drained from Elizabeth's face, leaving her pale as a ghost. "You—you're not Jessica," she whispered.

"No." The girl's lips curved in a smile, and a tiny dimple creased her cheek. But the smile didn't reach her blue-green eyes—they remained as cold and hard as stones. "No," she repeated softly. "I'm not Jessica. I'm Elizabeth."

Chapter 22

The stoplight turned from red to green, and Steven gunned the engine of his VW, accelerating across the intersection like a race-car driver. Billie braced herself, her foot pressed down on an imaginary brake. "Take it easy," she advised Steven. "The road is pretty slippery, and these tires are kind of old and bare."

Steven moderated his speed for a block or two, but soon he found himself stepping hard on the gas again. The feeling of urgency was irresistible; he had to get to Fowler Crest as soon as possible.

He whipped around a corner, tires squealing. Billie gasped. "We're almost there," Steven said, glancing at her apologetically. "Don't worry, Billie. I know these roads like the back of my hand—I wouldn't drive this fast if I didn't think it was safe."

They entered a straight stretch of road and Steven increased his speed. Faster, faster . . . Country Club Drive was coming up on the right, and Steven flicked on his turn signal. Approaching the turn, he tapped the brakes briefly. It wasn't enough. As he swung onto Lila's street, the car fishtailed on the wet blacktop. Steven yanked the steering wheel hard in the direction of the spin, but it didn't do any good. The car skidded around in a full circle, 360 degrees, the wet night whirling madly through their windows.

They came to rest straddling the curb, the engine stalling out. For a long moment Steven sat as stiff as a statue, clenching the steering wheel with white-knuckled fingers.

Billie had covered her face with her hands. "Can I look?" she squeaked. "Are we alive?"

Steven exhaled in a huge sigh of relief, his shoulders slumping. "We're OK. Geez, that was scary. I'm really sorry, Billie." Reaching for her, he gave her a reassuring hug. "I *was* driving much too fast, given the road conditions. But—"

"But what?"

Turning the key in the ignition, Steven restarted the engine. "But we have to keep going," he said. As he steered the car back onto the street, bumping down from the curb, he glanced at the clock on the dashboard. Now that he was over the fright of almost crashing, the feeling of urgency returned full force. "We've got to get to Fowler Crest. It'll be midnight in a few minutes, and kids may start taking off soon after that. I just can't risk not connecting with Liz and Jess." He stepped on the gas, driving at a slower pace than before but probably still a little too fast for Billie's taste. "I have to make sure they're all right!"

Mr. Wakefield threw the jack and other tools into the trunk of the rental car and strode briskly to the driver's-side door.

Mrs. Wakefield was already in the passenger seat, her shoulder belt fastened. "Tell you what," she said to her husband as he started the engine and pulled off the gravel shoulder back onto the road. "Let's not go straight home—let's stop at Fowler Crest first."

Mr. Wakefield accelerated to cruising speed. "Fowler Crest? You mean the New Year's Eve ball?"

Mrs. Wakefield nodded. "That's where the girls will be, and I—" She stopped, struggling to find words for what she was feeling.

"It'll be a madhouse there," Mr. Wakefield predicted. "It's almost midnight and the kids will be going wild." He smiled wryly. "Jess and Liz will die of embarrassment if their parents barge into the party to check up on them."

"I don't care," Mrs. Wakefield said stubbornly. "I want to see them."

"Alice, the girls are fine. They're at Lila's having fun. Can't we wait until they get home to talk to them? Last I heard, Steven said he and Billie would be spending New Year's Eve at the house—he'll be able to fill us in on any news."

"That's just it," Mrs. Wakefield whispered. She put a hand on her husband's arm, her eyes pleading. "I can't wait, Ned. I know you think I'm foolish—I know you think it's crazy. But I have to see them—I have to hold them in my arms. Please."

The Sweet Valley exit was approaching. As Mr. Wakefield turned off the highway, he glanced at his wife. "If you feel that strongly about it, of course we can swing by Fowler Crest first."

Mrs. Wakefield sank back in her seat, her eyes fixed on the passing landscape. *We're almost there,* she thought. *Just a few more miles.*

Elizabeth stepped backward, her wide, terrified eyes glued to the girl in the fuchsia dress—the girl who was now wielding an enormous butcher knife. *A door—there must be another door,* Elizabeth thought desperately, fumbling behind her with her hands. Instead of a door, though, she found herself pressing against the smooth, unbroken surface of a wall. She was trapped; there was no way out.

The other girl approached with slow, measured

steps, her right arm raised. Lightning flickered outside and the deadly blade glittered, white and cold. *This can't be happening,* Elizabeth thought, her heart beating so hard and fast it created a roaring in her ears. *It must be a dream—it can't be real. . . .*

A dream. Of course! All at once Elizabeth realized why this horrible moment seemed so familiar, so inevitable somehow. She remembered the dream that had haunted her since the Jungle Prom—the dream about the girl who looked like Jessica, but turned out to have dark hair—and a butcher knife. *This is my dream, come to life,* Elizabeth thought, her head spinning. *I'm finally finding out how it ends. Oh my God, I'm going to die.*

The girl took another step toward Elizabeth. She was close enough now—close enough to kill. But she made no move to sink the blade into Elizabeth's body. Elizabeth flattened herself against the wall, her fingernails digging into the wood, and stared at the other girl, mesmerized.

She was looking at her own face, at Jessica's face, and yet she wasn't. This face was different under the surface. *It's her eyes,* Elizabeth thought. *The eyes are supposed to be the windows of the soul.* She gazed into the girl's eyes and shuddered at what she saw. Evil . . . pure evil.

"Who are you?" Elizabeth whispered.

The girl smiled. "You heard me," she said softly. "I'm Elizabeth. I used to be Margo, but now it's my turn to be Elizabeth. Which means it's time for you to go."

Elizabeth glanced desperately toward the window, hoping against hope that someone had seen her enter the pool house and was about to come to her rescue. But the window revealed nothing but black sky and rain. *They're all inside, waiting for the New Year's countdown. Todd, Enid, Jessica— they won't have noticed yet that I'm missing. I could yell and no one would hear me.*

Facing Margo again, Elizabeth licked her lips. *I have to talk to her; I have to stall her. It's my only chance. . . . .* "Time for what?" she asked, her voice cracking from the strain of suppressing a scream. "What do you mean, it's your turn?"

"My turn to live the kind of life I deserve," Margo explained calmly. She lowered the hand that held the knife and ran her fingers along the edge of the blade, her expression pensive. "My turn to have a real family, and friends, and a future."

All at once Margo's face darkened; Elizabeth cowered, her eyes on the knife. "You don't even know how lucky you are," Margo snarled. "You don't know what it's like to be abandoned, unloved, passed from one foster family to another, yelled at, starved, beaten. I've had nothing." Her voice rose

316

to a shout. "Nothing! I've been treated like garbage for sixteen years." Once again Margo's face underwent a sudden, startling transformation. A heartless smile replaced the angry scowl. "I'll make the most of your life, Elizabeth," Margo said sweetly. "I promise. Oh, I'll love every minute of it."

"*My* life? What do you mean, my . . ." Elizabeth's voice trailed off. Her eyes widened; all at once she grasped the true import of Margo's words. It was no accident that this girl who looked just like her was dressed like her, too—no accident that she spoke with Elizabeth's voice and mannerisms. *She's not just going to kill me—she's going to kill me and take over my identity,* Elizabeth realized, dizzy with horror.

"You can't do this," she whispered.

"Oh, yes, I can," Margo replied, her manner supremely confident. "I've planned it all very carefully—nothing can go wrong now." She smiled almost tenderly. "It doesn't take long to die, Elizabeth, and I have a place waiting for you—a resting place, a restful place. It will be over before you know it. And best of all, no one will ever find out. What happens in here tonight will be our little secret."

Margo might as well have been talking about the weather; her blandly conversational tone sent chills up Elizabeth's spine. "But they *will* find out," Elizabeth protested, forcing herself not to faint with terror, to remain alert and ready to spring for the door should Margo let down her guard for a single second. "You won't get away with it. You can't just *become* me—you can't fool my parents, my sister and brother, my boyfriend. They'll know the difference. It will never work!"

Margo tipped back her head and laughed uproariously. "You think so? Well, Elizabeth, let me put your mind at ease. I've studied for this part. I've been watching you and your family for weeks. I've been in your school, your house, your bedroom—I've worn your clothes and read your diary. I have it all down pat."

"It was *you*," Elizabeth gasped, remembering the afternoon when she'd discovered that her desk drawers had been rifled through. She'd accused Jessica—what else was she to think? In a million years how could she ever have imagined *this*? *All those times I felt like someone was watching me, I wasn't just being nervous and paranoid. Someone was watching!*

Elizabeth slumped back against the wall, her last reserves of strength deserting her. Margo grinned, clearly relishing Elizabeth's reaction to her tale. "James helped me, did you know that?" she boasted.

"James?" Elizabeth gasped in disbelief. "James helped *you*?"

"I hired him to feed me information about

318

Jessica. But then he fell in love with her, the stupid bum. He was ready to rat on me—he wanted to play knight in shining armor and ride to your and Jessica's rescue. Needless to say, I put an end to that fantasy."

Elizabeth stared at Margo, the realization dawning slowly. "That—that guy, Josh Smith, the one who went to jail," Elizabeth stammered. "On the pier that night, he kept yelling about some girl who looked like me and Jessica. He said she was the one who pushed James—he said he didn't do it. We just thought he was crazy. But it was true! We didn't see you, but you were there. You killed James!"

Margo smiled. "Yes, I killed James. I was there," she confirmed. "I've been everywhere, Elizabeth. I've already fooled them, you know. All of them. Your mother—"

"No," Elizabeth cried.

"We've talked—she's hugged me and accepted me as her daughter," said Margo. "And I've fooled your brother and your twin sister and . . ." She paused, dragging out the torture. "And that tall, handsome basketball player you love so much. Todd Wilkins."

Elizabeth placed her hands over her face. "No," she sobbed.

"Yes." Margo smiled triumphantly. "Your family, your friends, and even Todd. I've been with Todd.

I've touched him and kissed him, and he didn't know I wasn't you."

Elizabeth shuddered, her body convulsing, crumpling. "No," she whispered again.

"He didn't know, and he'll never know," Margo continued. "No one will ever know you're gone. So get ready, Elizabeth." Margo's voice dropped to a whisper. She took another step, looming over Elizabeth, the big glittering knife raised high. "Say good-bye."

Chapter 23

Jessica pushed and shoved her way through the mob of party guests, her anxious eyes fixed on the French doors that led out to the veranda and the lawn. "Hey, Jess, where's your party hat?" Winston asked, blowing a noisemaker in her face.

Jessica elbowed past him, only to be stopped by Amy. "Where are you off to in such a rush?" Amy shouted over the hubbub of excited voices. "Grab some confetti—it's only a minute until midnight!"

Shaking her arm loose from Amy's grasp, Jessica hurried off without a reply. By the time she reached the doors, she was breathless, but she didn't pause. Yanking open one glass-paned door, she stepped out into the wet, windy night.

Did I really see someone out here? Jessica wondered, raising a hand to protect her face from the drizzle. She gazed across the lawn toward the swimming pool. The pool house looked dark, forsaken. . . .

No, I saw what I saw, Jessica decided, setting off across the lawn at a quick trot. *She probably went outside for some fresh air and then had to duck into the pool house to get out of the rain. I saw her. I definitely saw her.*

"Darn," Jessica exclaimed as her heel sank deep into the soggy grass and her foot pulled right out of the shoe. Balancing on one leg, she retrieved the shoe and stuck it back on, resuming her course. It was slow going, though. Mud splattered her ankles, and she nearly lost her shoes again with every squishy step; the soaking-wet taffeta of her skirt wrapped around her thighs, hobbling her.

Behind her Jessica heard a sudden, loud shout. "Ten!" She glanced over her shoulder at the house. The French door she'd come through was swinging open; beyond it she could see everyone at the party facing in the same direction, watching the big clock on the wall. *Ten seconds till midnight,* Jessica realized, hurrying on toward the pool house. The countdown had begun.

Slowly and painfully, Todd pushed himself up to a sitting position. He put a hand to his head, wincing. *Wow, someone really tried to knock my block off,* he thought, exploring the bump on his

322

forehead with tentative fingers. *What happened? Where am I?*

With an effort he focused his eyes, taking in the shadowy features of the strange room. Getting to his feet, he stumbled toward the wall and flicked on a light switch. *Lila's—I'm upstairs at Lila's,* Todd remembered. *I came looking for Liz and instead I found . . .*

Instantly, all the horrible details of the scene that had taken place in that room just a short while before rushed back over Todd. *The girl,* he thought. The name came to him, the one Josh Smith had shouted out on the pier and then again at the police station before he was dragged off to his cell. *Margo. She hit me with something and took off. Where? What was she going to do next?* Todd licked his lips, tasting the blood that had trickled down his cheek. *How long have I been unconscious? My God, what if—?*

Todd tried to run toward the door, but he was still light-headed from the blow, and his feet behaved as if they weren't properly attached to his body. Tripping, he fell sideways against the dressing table. His head throbbed; he felt himself slipping back into darkness. *No,* Todd commanded himself, gritting his teeth. *I have to find Margo. I have to find Elizabeth!*

Recovering his balance, he launched himself forward again. Bursting into the hallway, he hurried toward the stairs. Margo . . . Elizabeth . . . their faces swam in his head, merging and then separating. *She probably killed James and she almost killed me,* Todd thought as he stumbled down the staircase, clutching the banister. *She's been impersonating Liz—that's who she'll go after next.* Terrifying pictures flashed before Todd's eyes: Margo with her hands around Elizabeth's throat; Margo with a knife at Elizabeth's heart. Panting, Todd pushed himself to move faster. He had to find Elizabeth before Margo did.

Even louder than the ringing in Todd's ears was the noise of the New Year's Eve party. Everyone was shouting in unison, their eyes on the clock and the big bag of balloons and confetti that was about to drop from the ceiling. Todd plunged into the crush, desperately searching for Elizabeth. "Liz!" he cried hoarsely. He spotted Ken and grabbed his arm. "Matthews, have you seen Liz?"

Todd's question was drowned out by the hubbub of the countdown. Ken just grinned and waved. "Eight!" the revelers roared enthusiastically.

Elizabeth crouched against the wall of the pool house, her face turned away from Margo and the knife. She knew the ruthless blade would slice into her flesh at any moment, but she didn't want to watch it as it happened.

In the distance she could hear the faint sounds

of the New Year's Eve party. *They're counting down the seconds until the New Year,* Elizabeth thought, a wave of helpless longing washing over her. *And I'm counting down the seconds until the end.* All her friends—Jessica, Todd—were busy celebrating. They wouldn't miss her. No one would hear her if she screamed for help; no one would hear her cry out in agony when Margo stabbed her to death.

"Seven!" yelled the crowd at the party. Elizabeth squeezed her eyes shut, every nerve in her body jangling from the strain of waiting. *There's no way out. . . .*

A kaleidoscope of images, of sounds and scents and colors, were whirling through Elizabeth's brain. Memories of childhood and of her high-school years, books she'd read, poems she'd written, songs she'd sung, faces, places—all the seasons of her life flashed before her. *My life,* Elizabeth thought, tears squeezing from her tightly shut eyes. *My sweet, happy life.* She could see Todd, as clearly as if he stood before her, and her beloved parents and Steven and Jessica, her very own dear twin sister.

"Six!"

As trapped and helpless as she was, Elizabeth suddenly realized that there was still one thing she had the power to do before she died—one thing she *had* to do in order to leave the world with a measure of peace in her soul. "I forgive you, Jess," Elizabeth whispered, the tears wetting her face like rain. "I love you."

In the distance the guests at Lila's New Year's Eve ball shouted, "Five!"

Margo stood over Elizabeth's cowering form, the big knife raised. It was nearly midnight; at long last the fateful moment had arrived. She was about to become Elizabeth Wakefield, once and for all. *Do it,* Margo commanded herself, her fingers tightening on the knife handle. *Right into her heart. Do it!*

But for some reason Margo couldn't move. She was frozen, arrested by a strange, unexpected uncertainty. *How can I when—?* She blinked, her purpose suddenly seeming fuzzy and confused. *Isn't this like—?*

The other murders had been easy. Her little foster sister, Georgie Smith, the old woman at the bus station, the hit-and-run victim, James . . . Margo hadn't needed to think twice when she struck the match, when she held Georgie's head under the water, when she pulled the scarf tight around the old woman's birdlike neck, when she stepped on the gas pedal, when she gave James the fatal push. She'd never imagined it would be this hard to kill Elizabeth Wakefield; this was supposed to be just another piece of business. *But it's not.* Margo's resolve faltered. *This is almost like killing myself.*

Margo stared at Elizabeth's pale, tearstained face. *Yes, that's the whole point*, she reminded herself. *I'm her, which means she's me. I'm just killing off the old Margo—I'm killing my past. Her death is my rebirth. Do it!*

Still, Margo hesitated. She heard the shouting at Fowler Crest getting louder, more frenzied. "Two!" the kids bellowed.

Maybe I can make it back to the party in time for a midnight kiss, Margo thought, joy and power surging through her body like an electrical current, galvanizing her.

"One!"

Her eyes on Elizabeth's bent neck, Margo slashed downward with the heavy blade.

Her high heels long since abandoned in the mud, Jessica ran the last few steps in her stockinged feet. She burst into the pool house just as the countdown reached its climax. The sight that met her eyes stopped her dead in her tracks.

Two identical girls were standing in the corner—one huddling with her head bent and eyes closed, the other standing tall and wielding an enormous knife, about to strike. Both had glimmering flaxen-blond hair; both wore fuchsia party dresses. *Elizabeth—and the girl from my dream. This is just like my dream!*

Both girls looked like Jessica's twin sister, but Jessica knew that only one of them could be. And she didn't need her twin's intuition to figure out that Elizabeth was the one in danger, the one at whom the murderous weapon was aimed—the one only milliseconds away from losing her life.

Jessica didn't hesitate. The scream exploded from her throat. *"No!"* Bounding across the room, she threw herself in front of the slashing blade.

Running into the Fowlers' mansion at the stroke of midnight, Steven and Billie were greeted by pandemonium. Balloons filled the air; confetti showered down; girls and boys were clapping and shouting, blowing noisemakers, grabbing each other for New Year's hugs and kisses.

Steven caught sight of someone he knew. "Maria!" he hollered. "I'm looking for my sisters. Where are they? Have you seen them?"

Maria Santelli put a hand to her ear, indicating that she couldn't hear him over the din. Then she smiled and threw a handful of confetti at him. Steven saw her lips move. "Happy New Year!"

Whirling, he shouldered his way through the mass of bodies, searching for Todd and the twins. Dana Larson was one of the people he practically trampled over. "Dana," he cried, grabbing her arm to steady her after nearly knocking her off her feet. "Dana, have you seen Liz or Jess?"

Dana tipped her head to one side. "What did you say, Steven?" she shouted.

Steven filled his lungs, yelling as loud as he could. "I said, have you seen—"

At that moment a piercing scream made itself heard over the sounds of celebration. Steven's heart leapt into his throat, choking off his words. *Jess,* he thought. *Liz!*

But the scream had come from Enid. With Billie close at his heels, Steven rushed across the room to where Enid stood staring out one of the big picture windows.

She was pointing, her other hand clapped over her mouth and her eyes wide with terror. "There's someone out there," she cried. "By the pool house. His picture was in the paper. . . . Steven, it's that guy who murdered James!"

Steven bolted toward the door, this time not caring if he knocked people down on his way. Exploding out of the house, he sprinted across the wet grass toward a dim figure on the far side of the lawn. As he drew nearer, Steven recognized the other man. Just as Enid said, it was Josh Smith, the escaped killer!

Steven's instincts had been right. *He's come to get the twins,* he thought, his arms and legs pumping faster. Another long stride, and he was almost upon Smith, whose attempt to flee was hampered by a severe limp, as if he'd sprained an ankle. Both arms extended, Steven dived through the air. His fingers dug into Josh Smith's shoulders; he tackled the other man hard to the ground, slamming his face into the mud.

Smith tried to wriggle out of Steven's grasp, but Steven pinned him, preparing to smash a rock-hard fist into his mouth. "Where are my sisters?" Steven demanded. "What have you done with them?"

A white-hot pain like a bolt of lightning seared through Jessica's body as the butcher knife sliced into her upper arm. Instinctively, she swung the wounded arm, knocking the knife from the would-be murderer's hand.

The girl was thrown off balance; her shriek of rage reverberated throughout the pool house. "You!" she spat at Jessica. "Stay out of this! Do you want to make me kill you, too?"

The girl dived for the knife, but so did Elizabeth, shocked back to life and hope by Jessica's entrance. Jessica hurled herself into the fray, her fingers grasping for the glittering knife. Life and death hinged on possession of the weapon. *If she gets it, we're dead,* Jessica realized. *Liz and I, we're both dead.*

Grunting, the three girls wrestled madly for control of the knife. Someone's fingernails raked down Jessica's injured arm; she cried out in pain.

Then she felt it with her fingertips: the smooth, cold handle of the knife!

With a shout of triumph, Jessica closed her hand around the knife and jumped to her feet. "Stand back!" she ordered. "Let her go, or *I'll* kill *you!*"

Jessica raised the knife . . . and saw that she was faced with an impossible dilemma. The two girls drew apart and faced her. Both were desperate and panting; each girl's blond hair was tangled, her skin streaked with blood from Jessica's wound. They were identical.

Who is who? Jessica turned toward the girl on the left, ready to strike. Was she the evil look-alike . . . or was she Elizabeth? Jessica's arm trembled; a wave of panic washed over her. *Oh, God, I can't tell.*

She glanced rapidly from face to face, desperately searching for a clue. "Liz?" she croaked.

"I'm Liz," whispered the girl on the right, her eyes pleading.

"No, *I'm* Liz," said the other girl, the one Jessica had been about to stab.

The words were the same—the voice was the same. Jessica looked from one to the other, her head spinning. Her life, and Elizabeth's, depended on taking action, but she couldn't. She couldn't be sure.

As Jessica hesitated, the girl on the left suddenly sprang forward. Her face contorting into a

331

bloodthirsty snarl, the girl swiped at Jessica's arm. Her fingers slippery with blood, Jessica lost her grip on the knife, allowing the other girl to seize it.

Instantly, their roles were reversed. The girl raised the knife, ready to strike. *Here it comes,* Jessica thought. *I wasted my chance. She's going to kill us.*

Even as her limbs went numb with fear, however, one last ray of hope and courage flickered in Jessica's heart. Nothing would quench it but death itself. *No,* Jessica vowed. *She can kill me, but she's not going to get to Elizabeth. Not as long as I've got breath in my body.*

As the blade flashed through the air, Jessica threw herself on top of her sister, shielding Elizabeth's body with her own.

Chapter 24

Mustering all his strength, Josh flung his body upward, throwing Steven to the side. He didn't completely escape Steven's grasp, however; they continued to roll over and over on the wet grass, Josh struggling to get free while Steven attempted to pin him again.

"Let me go!" Josh grunted, all his muscles straining frantically in the direction of the pool house. Rain and sweat dripped into his eyes, blinding him. "She'll kill them if you don't let me go!"

"What are you talking about? If I let you go, *you'll* kill them," Steven declared through clenched teeth. "No chance, you sicko." He flipped Josh, pinning him on his back. Twisting his head, Steven shouted over his shoulder. "Billie! Call the police! And *hurry*!"

It's probably already too late. The deadly realization filled Josh's mouth with bitterness. As he'd dashed across the muddy lawn, he'd slipped, spraining an ankle. At this very moment his weakness and slowness were probably enabling Margo to kill again. Had he traveled all those thousands of miles in search of revenge only to fail at last, to fall just a few yards short of his goal?

"I'm not the one you want," Josh cried. "It's Margo—your sisters . . ."

Steven's grip didn't relax in the least. Josh sucked in his breath, filling his lungs to capacity. Just as he prepared to make one final effort to break free, assistance came from an unexpected quarter. Running across the lawn at full speed, Todd Wilkins flung himself on Steven and yanked him off Josh. "He's not the killer!" Todd shouted. "It's a girl—a girl who looks just like Liz and Jess!"

His breath coming in ragged gasps, Steven sat back on his heels, staring at Todd in confusion. *"What?"*

It was the break Josh had been praying for. He didn't know how Todd had found out about Margo; all that mattered was that now they could join forces against their *real* enemy. Springing to his feet, Josh limped toward the pool house as fast as he could. "Come on!" he yelled. "Back me up!"

Reaching the pool house, Josh flung himself against the door, using his shoulder as a battering ram. As he crashed into the dark room, a bolt of lightning illuminated the scene. On the far side of the room, the Wakefield twins huddled at Margo's feet. Josh watched in horror as Margo lifted her right arm. A knife blade flashed in the lightning. Margo slashed downward, right at the neck of one of the twins!

With speed and strength born of desperation, Josh flew across the room, his eyes on the knife. It seemed to move in slow motion, one deadly inch at a time, even though he knew in reality it was plunging swiftly toward its mark . . . it was nearly there. . . .

A split second before the knife could sink into Jessica's flesh, Josh slammed against Margo, knocking her off her feet. The knife sailed from her hand, clattering harmlessly to the floor. Arms flung wide, Margo crashed backward through the large window overlooking the swimming pool.

Falling to his hands and knees, Josh saw Margo's eyes blaze with fury and her mouth open wide in a bloodcurdling shriek of pain and terror. Shards of glass flew through the air like raindrops. There was a sickening thud and the scream was cut off abruptly. Josh found himself alone with the sounds of the rain on the roof and the Wakefield sisters crying quietly.

Slowly, Josh rose to his feet and walked over to the shattered window. Looking down at the patio, he saw Margo lying motionless on her back. A large, triangular fragment of glass protruded from her throat; blood pulsed from the wound, mingling with the rain on the pavement. Her mouth was still stretched wide in a soundless scream and her eyes were open, but the horrible face was lifeless. Margo was dead.

Elizabeth swam up through murky, heavy waters of semiconsciousness, struggling to reach the surface, to fill her lungs with air. A familiar, well-loved voice came to her as if from a great distance. *Jessica*, Elizabeth realized joyfully. It *was* Jessica's voice she heard, not that evil, monstrous girl's. To Elizabeth it sounded like beautiful music.

"Liz?" Jessica grasped Elizabeth's shoulders, shaking her. "Liz, are you all right?"

Elizabeth blinked, her darkened vision slowly clearing. "Jess? Is it really you?"

"Oh, Liz." Jessica flung her arms around Elizabeth, hugging her tightly. "Liz, you're alive. We're both alive."

The two sisters held each other, rocking back and forth, tears streaming down their faces. "I can't believe how close I came to losing you," Jessica said, sobbing. "What would I have done without you?"

"You saved my life," Elizabeth whispered. "My last thought was of you, Jess, and then you came—

like an answer to my prayer. I knew you would. I love you, Jess."

Jessica's tears flowed faster. "Oh, Liz." Her voice cracked. "You can't love me. If you only knew—" Her words broke off; she buried her face against her sister's shoulder and sobbed.

Elizabeth's arms tightened around Jessica. She thought of the mistakes Jessica had made and the lies she'd told . . . and then she contemplated Margo's horrible, murderous plot. *I was just face-to-face with true malice, with pure evil,* Elizabeth recognized. *That girl was a monster. Jessica, though, she's only human. Like me, like all of us.*

"I *do* know, Jessica," Elizabeth said softly. "But it's OK." She smiled through her tears, overcome with thankfulness that she'd lived to say these words to her sister. "I forgive you."

Jessica and Elizabeth walked out of the pool house, their arms clasped about each other's waists and a blanket draped over their shoulders. Lights flashed in the wet, gray dawn; three police cars were parked on the lawn of Fowler Crest, and at long last the ambulance was ready to take Margo's body away.

Bright-orange tape marked the crime scene. Jessica glanced at the spot on the pavement where Margo's corpse had lain, and shuddered. "I don't know if I'll ever understand it," she murmured.

337

"She came all the way from Ohio to California to find you—to kill you, to *be* you?"

"That's Josh's story, and the police seem to believe him now," Elizabeth said. "I guess their next step is to get together with the authorities back in Josh's hometown. But it'll probably be a while before they piece together the whole puzzle of that girl's life—if that's even possible."

Jessica shook her head. "She was crazy."

"She was worse than crazy," Elizabeth concluded.

Jessica looked to the east. Beyond Fowler Crest the sky was turning pink; as the sun started to rise, she could see that the clouds were finally dispersing. "The storm is over," she observed. "Finally."

The party had long since broken up, but a small cluster of people still stood in the yard talking to the police: Mr. and Mrs. Wakefield, who had just arrived, Steven and Billie, Todd, Enid, Lila, Mr. and Mrs. Fowler. The twins walked slowly toward the group as their mother, tears streaming down her face, started toward them.

"Now that it's over, I can't believe any of this really happened," Jessica said to Elizabeth. She thought back over the events of the recent past, the long road of horrible incidents that had brought them to this climactic moment: the Jungle Prom, the Jeep crash and Sam's death, the trial,

James, Margo . . . Another fit of trembling shook her body. "It doesn't seem real—it's as though it were all a terrible dream."

Elizabeth squeezed Jessica reassuringly. "It did happen, but it's over now. It's all over." Elizabeth gestured toward the golden globe of the sun, just bursting over the horizon and bathing the world in fresh, pure light. "See? It's a new morning, Jess. It's a new year."

And as she said the words, the twins' mother reached them and pulled them both tightly against her. "My girls," she said, smiling through her tears, "my beautiful twin girls."